THE MEMORY OF YOU

SAMANTHA TONGE

Boldwood

First published in Great Britain in 2023 by Boldwood Books Ltd.

Copyright © Samantha Tonge, 2023

Cover Design by Alice Moore Design

Cover Photography: Shutterstock

The moral right of Samantha Tonge to be identified as the author of this work has been asserted in accordance with the Copyright, Designs and Patents Act 1988.

This book is a work of fiction and, except in the case of historical fact, any resemblance to actual persons, living or dead, is purely coincidental.

Every effort has been made to obtain the necessary permissions with reference to copyright material, both illustrative and quoted. We apologise for any omissions in this respect and will be pleased to make the appropriate acknowledgements in any future edition.

A CIP catalogue record for this book is available from the British Library.

Paperback ISBN 978-1-80415-428-1

Large Print ISBN 978-1-80415-427-4

Hardback ISBN 978-1-80415-426-7

Ebook ISBN 978-1-80415-429-8

Kindle ISBN 978-1-80415-430-4

Audio CD ISBN 978-1-80415-421-2

MP3 CD ISBN 978-1-80415-422-9

Digital audio download ISBN 978-1-80415-425-0

Boldwood Books Ltd
23 Bowerdean Street
London SW6 3TN
www.boldwoodbooks.com

For three lovely people – Sue Blackburn, Beverley Ann Hopper and Jan Wooller. Thanks so much for all the support. It means a lot.

Alex put in her wireless earphones and pressed play on a rap album her most recent not-boyfriend had recommended. She took the lift down to reception and nodded at the doorman in his top hat and frock coat, unaware that tonight would be her last sleep in the glass tower apartment.

Late May sunshine air-kissed her face as a nearby quarrel of sparrows fought over a chunk of focaccia from Bernardo's next door. Perhaps she'd pop in later for a celebratory nightcap. In time to the rap, she strutted past a wall of floral street art and left Great Northern Square. The Gothic John Rylands Library loomed into view, dominating Deansgate's skyline. Alex's phone vibrated; she took it out of her blazer pocket and turned down the music. Standing to one side of the pavement, next to a street cleaner and his luminous yellow trolley, she read the short text.

'Everything all right, flower?' asked the cleaner, as he cast her an appreciative glance.

Her handbag fell to the ground, and the contents skidded near to a street drain. He collected up the scattered belongings.

Eyes still on the screen, she snatched back her bag and walked off, bristling as other pedestrians stared.

'My pleasure, no need to thank me,' the street cleaner hollered.

Heat filled Alex's face. It had been good of him to help her.

At the top of broad and bustling Market Street she reached Piccadilly Gardens. The text must have been a joke. Yes, that was it. On automatic, she followed commuters marching up to the station one behind the other, like a queue of inmates heading for yard time. A taxi's horn told her off as she crossed another road without looking. Her feet loped over an arched metal bridge and down the other side. The Manchester Canal appeared, along with a flock of paddling ducks that overtook moored narrowboats in triangle formation. Alex passed a rainbow-painted oblong planter, drawn on further by fairy lights tied between trees and lampposts. Customers spilled out of a bookshop with sale posters and multi-coloured banners outside.

At five o'clock sharp, she stopped outside the bar, dance music pulsating inside. Clouds of fruity vape smoke wafted over from outside tables. She took out her earphones and went in, but ever punctual Miranda wasn't there. Alex gripped the back of a chair. The text had been serious. Her agent really wasn't turning up.

Having bumped into a young man wearing a studded neck collar and a tartan kilt, she then headed straight for the bar. As she rifled in her handbag, a woman with pale skin, wearing a baggy taupe sweatshirt and jogging trousers, came in. Alex's search became frantic. A pin in her hair came loose and strands tumbled down one side of her head as she rummaged in her bag.

'Let me pay for your drink,' said the other woman, gently.

'I've lost my purse,' snapped Alex and she shook her head. There were more important things than buying wine, or the cash or bank card. She cared about finding the old photo of her mum – not that anyone else needed to know that.

The woman stepped back and her chin trembled. 'I was only trying to help.'

'My terrier's got better manners than you,' said the man in the kilt. He glared at Alex. 'Kindness doesn't cost anything.'

Alex froze. As the back of his head disappeared into the mêlée of customers, her face contorted. Miranda's text message, the cleaner's shouts, being rude to this poor woman... But she wouldn't cry, Alex was stronger than that. She rubbed her cheeks with the back of her hand and went to apologise. However, the woman's fists curled into balls and a very small sob escaped from her chest. Shoulder to shoulder, the two women stood, eyes and noses streaming. Alex focused on the tiled floor, willing it to open up and swallow them.

'Are you okay?' Alex muttered.

'I will be.' The woman sniffed. 'It doesn't take much to set me off these days.'

'Nothing to see here, folks,' the bar manager called to a group of captivated drinkers. She tightened the neon bobble around her greying dreadlocks, shook her head, poured two large glasses of wine and pushed them across the counter. 'On the house.'

The other woman paused, but Alex spontaneously picked up both drinks and the bar manager's offer of a bag of crisps as well. They found a table in the corner and after Alex brushed it down with her hand, they sat on a black velvet couch in the shape of a pair of lips. The woman passed Alex a tissue, collapsed against the couch's back and blew her own nose loudly. Alex dabbed her eyes and thought back to one frosty morning, not long before her fortieth birthday, when she'd resisted crying in public. Black absorbed heat, perhaps it also absorbed feelings, because standing next to the coffin, in her designer charcoal dress, Alex hadn't felt a thing – not until she'd got home from the funeral, closed the door, and changed into her pyjamas.

'I'm Hope.'

'Alex.'

'You should ring your bank. Cancel your cards.'

'Would you mind looking up Santander's contact number, while I sort out my face?' Alex pushed her phone over, then took out her compact and powdered her cheeks.

'I've had six phone calls from my daughter, Leah, over the weekend and four texts so far today,' Hope mumbled, after Alex ended the call to her bank.

Alex scrolled down her phone.

'The last one talked about us eating wasp crackers.'

'I got a text too,' said Alex, 'it... You mean *wasabi*.'

'No. For the last three months she's been on at me to go travelling with her before her final year at university. She's saved for a couple of years, working in the student bar, and wants to go. For almost five weeks, leaving tomorrow and coming back on the 1 July. I went along with it in the beginning, got the jabs, bought myself a huge backpack, agreed that we'd get a flight from Manchester and meet at the airport – she's in Birmingham. But as the trip has neared, I've blocked it out – I can't face the lack of day-to-day planning, I'm used to my routines. As for the tropical weather, and insects I might be expected to eat...' Hope's talking gathered speed. 'And I've got a job I can't just leave. A life. Well sort of. It's not the best.' Her voice wavered. 'I'm in a rut, no doubt about it.'

Alex studied Hope's tired face, the round cheeks, the laughter lines, the unapologetic blemishes and shadows. A face that didn't lie.

'I just finished my shift and started walking, found myself

here in the Village.' Hope took a large mouthful of wine. 'Sorry, rambling, but it's such a relief to let it all out and—'

'*My* text was regarding a business meeting that got cancelled,' said Alex. 'Miranda, my agent, was due to travel up from London.' She paused and took a sip of her drink. She'd developed a habit over the last few years of butting in, as if her news was more important than anyone else's. Recently she'd become aware of this and was trying to stop herself.

'Agent? You do look familiar. What shows have you been...'

Tears forgotten, Alex sat more upright and pulled a signed photo out of her bag. She'd made sure the writing was illegible like the autographs of big stars. She thrust it upon Hope. 'You're welcome.' A couple at a nearby table giggled. Alex picked up the laminated bar menu, telling herself they weren't laughing at her. 'Miranda's new girlfriend grew up in the north-west and told her the bars here were the highlight of Manchester – misguided advice, the food in Spinningfields is far superior.' She tossed the menu aside. 'The meeting here was cancelled hours ago but Miranda's email must have bounced back and I didn't get it. She just texted because I hadn't replied.' Alex picked up a single crisp and chewed it slowly. 'Apparently my work has lost its passion,' she said in a smaller voice. 'She may as well have called me a has-been.'

Hope's eyes crinkled in a kindly manner. 'If it's any consolation, this last year or two, I've asked myself how I've ended up in my mid-forties in a one-bed flat above a café. Our kid insists I go abroad with her, that it'll do me good.' She glanced down at her top and loose bottoms. 'Thing is, I can't be bothered with anything much these days. It's all too much effort. Certainly a trip like this. There's no point me harking back to the more courageous woman I used to be. The cost of living and energy crisis have stolen her away.'

'Miranda suggested I take a break as well, from my career. But my job...' Alex placed her palm on her chest for emphasis. 'I'm an existentialist. This calling is who I am.' Alex knew it sounded pretentious but felt this was true. She thought, therefore she wrote. It meant everything to her.

'I was gutted when I lost my last job because it put a roof over my head and food on the table. The bills piled up. I ended up homeless and had to sleep on my daughter's sofa, in her student house, for a while.'

'Tell me about it,' said Alex with a dismissive wave. 'I've had tough times too, what with the rejection emails and petty reviews.'

Hope's brow furrowed like someone who'd listened to a joke but hadn't got the punchline.

Alex picked up another crisp but threw it back. 'You're not supposed to lose success after years of hard work.'

'You're not supposed to have reached my age without finding much success at all.'

They sat on the couch, each lost in their own thoughts. An outburst of quacks flew through an open window. Alex's mum had loved birds and passed on many snippets about birdlife, like how ducks could close down half their brain and sleep with one eye open, to keep themselves safe from predators. Alex wished she could close down half her brain, the part that saw everything in black and white, that told her if she wasn't Number One she'd 100 per cent failed; that if she didn't strive to keep herself young, the future would be bleaker than a dystopian novel. The thud of a tray caught her attention. The bar manager turned her head from Alex to Hope and pursed her lips.

'Let me give you both a word of advice,' she said. 'It's...' A clatter came from the bar. The bar manager tutted and hurried away.

Alex shook her head. 'I'm sick of people like her, like Miranda, acting as if they know best about my life.' Alex was forty-three, at the peak of her second career... well, she had been, until recently. That bar manager wouldn't know anything about losing face on the public stage.

Hope's phone pinged. She picked it up and cautiously opened a text. Without asking permission, Alex took the phone and read the message out loud. '"Mum, please ring me. All your text said yesterday was *see you on Tuesday*. We're supposed to have discussed how much currency to take with us. What's going on? Last minute nerves? Well, I've checked us both in online. You wouldn't want your daughter travelling across an unfamiliar continent all alone now, would you?"'

'That's emotional blackmail,' protested Hope.

'Nicely done,' said Alex approvingly.

'I've never travelled, unless you include all-inclusive holidays to resorts where everyone speaks English and eats eggs and bacon. What about my boss, Tom? I've not even told him about this holiday; I've kidded myself it's not going to happen. He'd find it hard to replace me that quickly. Not that I'd want him to; I'd need that job when I returned.' Hope took back her phone and read the text again. 'But if I don't go, my daughter will never speak to me again and I'll feel like I've let her down. I should have spoken to her as soon as doubts appeared. You don't fancy working in a café on my behalf until the beginning of July, do you?' she asked Alex, in a wry tone. 'I live in, that means as much coffee and cake as you want and no commute to work.'

Alex cocked her head. Right at this minute Hope's life sounded perfect, with an uncomplicated job, a child who clearly loved her, flights booked to somewhere sunny. But then people tended to think an author's life was enviable, with parties and high rankings. Often it was. Sometimes it wasn't.

'Only joking,' added Hope quickly. 'As if I'm flying to the other side of the world, as if someone like you would consider—'

'I might surprise you... Tell me about some of the things in your life that make you happy.'

'Well that's easy. Apart from my wonderful daughter, books. And more books.'

Alex leant forwards.

'Mum taught me to read before I started school,' Hope continued. 'Stories have been my best friends throughout the most difficult times. Comedies when I'm down, thrillers when my own life makes no sense, uplifting fiction when I want to feel as if there could be a bright future ahead. Fredrik Backman, Marian Keyes, Matt Haig, Sophie Kinsella, and many lesser known authors, writers of young adult fiction too.'

'A good book can turn a bad day around,' agreed Alex. 'Especially *Fifty Shades*.'

Hope grinned and the two women chatted more, comparing favourite novels.

'My colleagues in the café make me happy too. They are pretty special.'

'Wish I could say the same.' Alex pulled a face and Hope laughed. 'To be fair, my editor was encouraging; it's scary putting a debut out there but she gave me reassurance, even if all the changes she wanted making were challenging.' The criticism had been hard to take after a difficult couple of years. Alex shrugged. 'I imagine you must be special too, to fit in with those colleagues. Your daughter clearly thinks you are, to want to travel with her mum.'

Alex's phone pinged again. An email from her mortgage provider. Her heart raced. She'd been ignoring their messages lately.

'Oh, you've really cheered me up. Thank you, petal,' said Hope.

A warmth swept through Alex's chest that she hadn't experienced for a long time. Mum used to call her petal. What with that and their mutual obsession with books, it was almost as if fate had brought her and Hope together.

'It's extreme, granted... but let's say we don't dismiss your suggestion outright. Hypothetically, what would either of us have to lose?' asked Alex.

Hope eyed Alex up and down. 'Tom pays fair wages but nothing like you'd be used to.'

'Any earnings are welcome as I haven't got a new book coming out and loyal fans will have already bought my backlist.' Alex tried to sound upbeat, but her royalty payments kept getting smaller and smaller and were a far cry from the amounts that, at the beginning of her career, had made her mortgage very affordable.

If she lost her home, Alex had nothing.

'You're an *author*? Wow. You should have said.'

'Alex Butler, pleased to meet you,' Alex said and she sat a little bit taller. She was still a best-selling writer of escapist, high-gloss, racy romance after all.

'Right, of course, I recognise you now,' said Hope, and her hand caught her own drink. She jumped up to avoid wine spilling down her trousers. Cheeks flushed, Hope sat down again, dabbing the table with a napkin. 'I loved reading... *Glamour Puss*, wasn't that your debut? It was ace, really gripping.'

Alex warmed to Hope even more. 'Thank you. I was so excited to sign a three-book contract with my publisher. I assumed today's meeting was to discuss the next contract. Miranda only found out today that they don't like the three chapters I submitted for the next story and...' Alex didn't do negatives, not about her career, not in front of other people. Her social platforms were about maintaining a flourishing image. But then this was real life; she wouldn't lose followers or likes by talking in this room and she might not ever see this Hope again. '...they don't see their future with me. They're letting me go, say they're sure my *wonderful work* will find a new home.' She gave a sigh. 'My new project tips into cli-fi, that is—'

'Climate change fiction,' said Hope.

'Yes,' said Alex, surprised Hope knew about it. 'I set my story at a fracking company, bringing in a sub-plot of corruption and backhanders.'

'Your debut's Tabitha Stallion was such a brilliant character,' said Hope. 'Go-getting, no-nonsense. I wanted to be her.'

A wave of nostalgia swept over Alex and she shivered at the memory of when her first book came out three years ago. It had been a great way to celebrate her fortieth birthday. It had topped the charts, as did the next book that also won an award. She'd cut out all the reviews in magazines and newspapers and kept them in a special folder. Once, she'd taken them to the crematorium and read them out to her mum's ashes, which she'd scattered in the gardens there. But then the third novel had bombed...

'Everything went downhill when I got a review from the Eternal Springs blog.'

Hope gave her a quizzical look.

'It's one of the most successful book blogs out there, has thousands of followers who all rush there to get the lowdown on any new release. It had given my first two books great ratings but out of nowhere slammed the third, called it saccharin without the heart of my earlier novels. I'm convinced that swayed my readership.'

Hope smiled at the barman as he brought her a new glass of

wine. Immediately she knocked half back. 'Surely one blog can't wield that much power?'

'You think?'

'Negative words from a blogger might sting, but you want to try being on the end of a loan shark's rant. I was desperate a couple of years ago, trying to hold on to my own home.'

A loan shark did sound frightening and Alex's heart pounded again, at the thought of her own money troubles. She shot Hope a sympathetic glance. 'A fridge full of champagne is no use if you've nothing to celebrate. Miranda warned me a while back my publisher may not want to re-sign me, that the cost of living crisis is affecting publishers too, with falls in sales and rises in production costs. That's when she suggested a career break to find my mojo again, but I didn't believe her warning; my editor has always been so enthusiastic.' Alex took a moment. 'Miranda said if I'm set on carrying on writing, I need to reignite my passion. She wants at least the first three chapters of the cli-fi story rewritten and sparkling by 1 July, the day she gets back from Tuscany. It's the submission window deadline for what she's calling my last chance. There's a new publisher that has been inundated with queries from authors and is about to close its submissions window temporarily. Miranda is friends with the commissioning editor who, she reckons, would take a look, as a favour, even though I haven't written the whole thing yet. Otherwise it's going to be months of waiting until the manuscript is written, before anyone else will read it and, financially, that's not feasible. If I miss this opportunity...' Alex ran one finger horizontally across her neck. 'Perhaps it's fate. You and I would have the same end date – you getting back from a worldwide trip, me finding my va-va-voom again, here in Manchester, away from my apartment in a different living space, to get my creativity back on track.' Alex needed a change, a new mindset.

'Except yours isn't an end date, it's a deadline.'

Alex threw her phone on the table, took off her blazer and leant back on the couch. 'I've met publisher demands for the last three years, and at the start I felt part of a team, all of us equals and...' Her voice broke but didn't mend itself properly and the next words came out scratchy. 'I never used to doubt myself. Now, I wake up in the middle of the night and dissect the next day's writing, the plot twists, characters' quirks, changing my mind countless times, voices in my head throwing around quotes from snarky bloggers on Amazon and Goodreads. I've even had a couple of nights of panic sweats. I can't carry on like this.' There. She'd said it.

'Three o'clock in the morning, that's always the time for me,' said Hope. 'I'll dissect arguments I had with Leah's dad or old classmates in the nineties. I'll go over my day in the café, worried I've upset a customer or member of staff. I don't recognise the woman I've become.' Hope ran a finger over a stain on her sweatshirt. 'That's modern living for you. I've never asked for much. Brought Leah up on my own, ran my own business at the same time. We didn't have much but it was enough and made me feel good about myself. That feels like a lifetime ago now. I've lots to be grateful for, I know, but it's become increasingly difficult to stay positive.'

Alex related. She could hardly bear admitting it to herself, but she might need the new source of income, however low, that this café could provide, because if the new book didn't sell well, or didn't even get signed... Her savings had gone. Her bills were rising. Getting on the property ladder, by herself, wasn't the dream she'd imagined when she signed her publishing deal. Every morning Alex would consult the mirror, just about recognise the old her peering out from behind the Botox she'd started to have, despite being only forty-three, thinking it would make her feel better. But deep in the night, when your soul was the mirror, she couldn't find that independent daughter whose mum used to call her so capable, couldn't find that person who'd grasped a new life after her divorce and didn't fear the future.

'Sorry I was rude to you, earlier. I haven't much control over what comes out of my mouth these days.'

'Same,' said Hope.

'Were you serious about me having your job while you're away and moving into your flat? It's wild but, well...' She smiled. 'Mum did always tease me for not having a single spontaneous bone in my body.'

'What? Of course not, it's tiny. Don't get me wrong, I've made my flat cosy and the front side looks over a bustling square; it's quite comfortable, but also you living there would mean I *had* to go travelling and there's no way I'm—'

It sounded like just what Alex needed and the opposite of her flashy tower apartment. Alex had celebrated until the early hours the day she'd signed the mortgage agreement. However, since her career had stumbled and her earnings had dropped, the place had felt more and more like a trap.

'I need to get away from my four walls, from my office, the computer screen,' Alex said, not mentioning how five weeks without using electricity there, and perhaps scoring free meals in someone else's home, would help her scrape together enough to make a mortgage payment. She'd defaulted on the last two, counting on the advance from the new contract that had fallen through. Alex felt as if she was going to be sick just thinking about the financial difficulties she was facing. Five weeks living rent-free in Hope's flat was a lifeline, time to get her head straight.

A way-out idea? Yes. But what was the alternative? Sitting in her apartment each day, lacking inspiration, watching the days pass until the July deadline arrived without Alex having created the sparkling chapters Miranda wanted. And from a practical point of view, one of the main characters in her cli-fi story was working undercover in the fracking company's fancy staff coffee shop as a barista. Working in Hope's café would give her an authentic insight into the job.

'What a refreshing change, along with the simplicity of serving drinks and snacks, away from complicated publishing types,' she said in a voice braver than she felt. 'I need this, Hope – and you haven't got time to delay, your flight takes off tomorrow, your daughter is expecting you.'

'True.' Hope wrung her hands. 'I know you're right, and I need a little push. Just wish I had more time to think about it.'

'So? Are we on?'

'I'm not sure... I'll need to speak to my boss... and the place where I work, there's something you don't know...'

'Let's meet in Selfridges' coffee shop tomorrow morning with our bags packed. You can still change your mind. We can talk it through again. But if you're happy then it will simply be a matter of you handing over your keys and getting to the airport. Come on Hope, we can do this!' Alex looked more serious. 'It's a big thing, letting someone into your home. I know that. And I promise to look after it. It would be foolish to do otherwise, what with me being a public figure...'

Hope didn't say anything.

'What?' prodded Alex, gently.

'The idea scares me, Alex, it really does,' she whispered. 'Trusting my life to a stranger? Going off around the world? What if I fall ill? Can't keep the pace? I'm frightened of everything these days, like travelling in rush hour or going out for drinks to crowded pubs, normal everyday things. I lie in bed at night worrying I didn't turn off the hob or answer every notification on Facebook. I stress about climate change, world wars, that annoying ringing in my ears. I'm not me any more. The carefree Hope has gone, that determined woman who brought up her daughter after telling her cheating, abusive partner to eff off.'

Unused to being in the company of someone so open, who admitted their life wasn't shiny and successful, Alex took a deep breath. 'I... get it.' She'd never confided in anyone before about how, a few years ago, it was as if a kidnapper had arrived and stolen the more resilient Alex. Perhaps Hope had also suffered a bereavement, because when you lost someone close, you lost part of yourself too. Casual relationships helped because no one got close enough to see the damage and anger that she could pretend didn't trouble her. The slick Alex Butler brand gave her an identity to be proud of and, on a good day when she didn't feel like screaming, the grounded image readers and lovers admired almost felt real. 'But how can a five-week holiday make things worse? Whereas if you don't take it, your daughter will probably ghost you – and if I don't get out of my apartment and find inspiration, all I've worked for will be for nothing.' Her voice caught; she hoped no one had heard it.

Hope tilted her head. 'You honestly believe living at my place will help your career, don't you?'

'Does that sound ridiculous?'

'No. Perhaps it could. After all, where I work *is* pretty unique...'

'Okay. Great that we agree. Thanks, Hope. Thanks for persuading me this is a viable plan.'

'Wait, I only—'

'Don't be so modest. All credit to *you*.'

2

Alex strolled through Selfridges and past tables of designer handbags – Prada, Gucci, Chanel, names that were friends. Alongside her large pull case, she stood on the escalator and the San Carlo Gran Café came into view, on the lower ground floor. She stepped off at the bottom and relaxed as she soaked up the familiar high-end atmosphere. An especially heady scent of perfume filled her nostrils, a recent favourite. Luxury cosmetic stands and racks of deluxe sunglasses lined the way as she headed towards the coffee shop, with its grey and white marble tables and mint-green front. A server stood behind the counter, in a smart blue apron over his white shirt and black trousers, rows of champagne bottles behind him looking down on customers.

Last night she'd slept through for the first time in ages. No characters came calling. She'd dozed off within minutes, comforted by the knowledge that the next day wouldn't begin with an empty page to fill, her body planted at her uninspiring desk. Instead, she had several weeks to take her time, in a different setting, and rewrite the opening to her novel so that it left the new publisher begging.

In case burglars struck during her absence, this morning she'd locked away valuables in her apartment, like her late mum's engagement ring, passport, the Dior lipstick collection. Her hand had brushed against the glass awards she'd won during the time when Miranda would hold their meetings in The Ivy. Alex used to believe you were only as good as your characterisation and how much readers invested in your latest story. Bless. A clinical list of sales figures counted for much more. She'd picked up one of the awards and read her engraved name before leaving it and the others in their usual prominent position, on the ornamental mantelpiece. A whirlwind of a career, that's what Miranda had called it; she'd never known an author to rise so quickly. Perhaps that's why the fall had fast-forwarded.

As she checked the chair for crumbs and sat down, her phone pinged. The smell of warmed, sugary pastries felt as reassuring as a hug. An email had arrived, from Miranda. Alex closed her inbox without reading it. On the table opposite, a man with short grey hair shot her a smile. Alex didn't respond. Simon had been twenty-eight when they'd met – five years older than Alex – and already doing well at his software engineering career. Since he'd left she'd only dated younger men, more interested in no-ties sex than pillow talk. Ignoring the man – he was definitely over fifty – she scrolled through her Instagram feed. She should buy that new lip plumping cream. Her stomach rumbled. Quarter past ten. Fifteen minutes overdue; surely this Hope wouldn't bow out?

'Last-minute emergency, couldn't find my bum bag.' A large backpack clung onto Hope like a scared child not sure of the journey ahead. She pulled it off and collapsed into a chair. The other customers went back to their drinks. Alex called over the server. He returned with another espresso and a latte for Hope.

'I'm glad you came.'

'Nearly didn't. My boss Tom wasn't happy. But I told him you were confident that you could manage.'

'Of course I can.' Alex stared as Hope emptied three sugar sachets into her coffee.

'He said you'll be on a one-week trial and if you're not up to scratch he'll have to take on a new person. But if that happens, I could lose my income. Lose my home.' Her voice wavered. 'I'm still not sure I should do this.'

'You said yourself you were in a rut. When will you ever have another opportunity like this, to be adventurous? And alongside your daughter.'

Hope stared for a moment and then exhaled. 'I know, that's what I've been telling myself all night. Just... don't mess up.' She gave Alex a hard look.

So, this Hope did have a backbone. 'Don't worry. How difficult can it be? Slicing cake, carrying drinks on trays...'

'You should still know that—'

Alex held up her hand. What was it with so many other people, once they turned forty, needing to know the minutiae of what lay in the future? Taking on the life of a stranger reminded her of how she used to love the empty pages of a first draft, full of adventure and promise. She'd hurried out of the glass tower this morning as if Harvey Nicks had a sale.

'If you must tell me something, talk about this Tom.' Alex unzipped her green leather jacket and sipped her coffee. 'What's he like?'

'Good with customers. He likes reading, too, and gaming. His scones are second to none.'

'You'll have to do better than that, what with me being a romantic author. Use your imagination. What might a woman find attractive about him?'

'I suppose he's got amazing brown eyes like... chocolate.'

Her editor used to hate clichés and would probably have run red ink through Hope's sentence.

Hope checked her phone and sighed. 'I asked Leah to send me the itinerary but suspect she hasn't planned further than taking off from Manchester.'

'Where's your sense of spontaneity? All I care about is that you've washed the sheets in your flat and left me a little space in the wardrobe.' Alex knocked back her coffee. 'Text me your address.' Alex's phone pinged and she opened the message, jumping straight to the name of the street. The Northern Quarter? She hadn't imagined Hope working in such a trendy area. Alex tried to picture the café, perhaps a little quirky, frequented by arty types, and the owner, this Tom, wearing a vintage print shirt and chino shorts, with thick chestnut hair tied up in a man-bun.

'See you at the beginning of July.' Alex's chair scraped back, she got to her feet and grabbed her case's handle as if it was going to open a door to the perfect oasis. However, Hope remained in her seat. Alex sat down again. 'Problem?'

'You will water my plants, won't you?' she asked in a small voice. 'I'm entrusting my home to you, Alex. It may not have gold-plated fittings or a butler on call, but it's the one place in the world where I... I...'

'Can be you?' Hope was fortunate. Increasingly, Alex's apartment had become less comfortable, with its nut-white walls, oak herringbone flooring, and every room's decor being a classic, unhomely mix of white, teal and ivory. Its contrived, mood-lifting feng shui meant a lack of cosy, cluttered nooks she could curl up into. Even her study was streamlined and orderly.

Realising how much Hope was handing over, Alex fingered a gold chain around her neck, released its clasp and took off the glittering four-leafed clover pendant.

'Take this. It's my lucky charm.'

'Wow. Diamonds.' Hope held it in the air. 'I can't possibly... What if I lose it? It must mean so much to you.'

'Call it insurance. You get to keep it if a single one of your plants dies. Although I warn you now, I haven't got the greenest fingers, but I'll do my best.'

Hope's face lit up and she put it on straight away. Ryan had given Alex this last Christmas, told her she was the biggest bit of luck he'd ever had. She'd called things off in the New Year, having developed feelings for him, and that wouldn't do. If she let anyone through the cracks they might not like what they saw; there'd be no denying her vulnerability and then she'd shatter completely. Wearing the charm, every day, had been a reminder to hold it together, to find her old pizzazz, but there wasn't as much point now. It hadn't worked. She was out of contract and almost out of time.

Alex stood up again, held out her hand and pulled Hope to her feet. She gazed into those honest eyes and could tell they completely trusted that the lucky charm would work.

'You're happy to do this, Hope?'

'Not sure happy is the right word but... yes.' Hope lifted her chin. 'Let's go.'

'I... I'll try not to let you down, make sure you have a job to come back to. Okay?' Alex muttered. She wrapped her arms around the shapeless hoodie and held on to Hope a second longer than intended, surprised to realise she meant what she'd said. Alex went to go, but Hope took hold of her arm.

'Don't give up on your writing, Alex,' she mumbled. 'Channel Tabitha Stallion. You can accomplish anything.'

Tabitha Stallion had been created out of hate for her ex-husband, a strong woman who intimidated male characters. Alex had hoped that process would be cathartic, and eventually the hurt did pass. Alex nodded at Hope, overwhelmed by a sudden urge to cry. She squeezed Hope's arm and left hurriedly.

Rain threatened as Alex walked up Market Street, past buskers and open-air preachers. At the height of her success, bowled over by the popularity of her debut, with the crowded bookshop signings and large numbers of pre-orders for the next book, Alex had got carried away and considered moving to London, fantasising that the next step would be red carpet premieres of screenplays adapted from her stories. However, as her initial success faded, Alex valued Manchester, a place that had no expectations. It didn't care about your appearance, how you spoke, who you dated, or whether you wore designer or fake... On the days where she wore sunglasses to hide herself from the world, it made no difference; either way, this city wouldn't notice. Her fondness for Manchester's take-me-or-leave-me attitude, and the daily evidence it offered that everyone's life got messy, made her question, in recent months, why she wrote high-octane stories about the rich and famous, set in glamorous, clinical cities.

Alex had visited the Northern Quarter many times over the years, for coffees in her teens, drinks in her twenties with friends who had faded away after she got married. She hadn't been there much at all in her thirties; her ex-husband preferred branded restaurants. Then with what happened to Mum, followed by the whirlwind of becoming an author, Alex probably hadn't walked through the area for at least ten years, preferring to take dates to fancy restaurants and cocktail bars, or whisk them down to London for the night, first class all the way. She came to Lever Street and turned left. Walking along, she passed a bookshop, minus the usual urge to slip in and move her books to the front. Instead, she forged ahead and arrived in Stevenson Square. Down the middle, people chatted and laughed, sitting on rows of wooden tables with benches, belonging to the bars and pubs either side. From a distance it could have been a street party. She stood to admire a wall of street art. Hope had explained that the café was the first building on the left, when you reached the square.

With typical Mancunian irreverence, rain spat onto the ground as she made her way over. It was a three-storey building, with shabby brickwork, yet the outside was painted in bright primary colours, with a green windowsill and a blue door. Unlike the other places serving drink and food, there were no tables outside. It stood next to a shop selling candles and crystals. She was about to read the café's name when her phone buzzed. A text from Hope: 'You need to know that this café is...' Alex rolled her eyes and, without reading the rest of the text, put her phone away. She squinted through the window. In the near left-hand-side corner stood a tall tropical plant. If Alex hurried in, she could hide her case by the wall, under the glossy green leaves. The best way to get the sum of this place would be to go undercover.

She pushed open the door; customers carried on talking, apart from someone who blew a loud, wet raspberry in Alex's direction.

3

With customers and staff deep in conversation, Alex took in her surroundings, unable to spot the culprit. A coffee machine gurgled as she surveyed the room's circular tables. Covered in plastic yellow cloth, they resembled a troupe of twirling full-skirted ballroom dancers. Bold murals brightened the walls, like the one of Manchester's town hall set against a cloudless sky, with a red telephone box in the foreground. Smaller ones were of a bowl of fruit, a pile of muffins, and a rural scene with cows and sheep, set in the Peak District perhaps. On the right-hand wall, the juke box played 'You Make Me Feel So Young' by Frank Sinatra. Above it, in large print, was a list of instructions on how to select a track. Ahead of Alex was a counter with a glass front, keeping germs away from cakes that looked robust enough to protect themselves.

A story's setting could feel like one of the characters if it had a strong sense of uniqueness, but nothing in this building caught Alex's attention apart from the bright colours. The till was to the left, with a charity collection tin by its side. At the back, to the right of a coffee machine, was a silver hatch, behind which was the kitchen. To the right of that was a corridor leading to the kitchen and a flight of stairs, above which was a sign marked 'Private'. They must lead to Hope's flat. The only feature that stood out as different was the back wall of the café, in front of the stairs. Photos of the staff with customers covered it, yet none of them were famous. How boring.

Time turned back thirty-two years to Alex's first day at high school, sitting in the canteen not knowing anyone. Alex often forgot how she was lucky as an author, working from home without having to accommodate the instructions or needs of any other person. Oh she had her editor, agent, marketing team, but at a distance. On a daily basis she didn't have to be near their coughs or sneezes, force a laugh at their unfunny jokes, or tolerate them interrupting a brainstorming daydream. As for being told what to do... Miranda was firm and honest to a fault but Alex respected that; it made a change from her publisher's always-look-on-the-bright-side bullshit. Being told to remove a plot twist or ramp up the emotion was different from receiving orders to clean the toilets or pander to rude customers. Her stomach contracted, not due to hunger. Why on earth had she agreed to work, for five weeks, with the public?

A man with a white comb-over darted forward. 'Welcome,' he said and gave a little bow. 'Someone will be with you shortly.' He showed her to the nearest table. Alex ignored him and went to the one by the plant. She stood her case upright and hid it behind the foliage. Her seat was a couple of tables behind a woman in her late fifties, with a curly blow-dry. Opposite her was a striking member of staff, a little older, with vibrantly dyed ginger hair feathered around her round face. Her arms were crossed in between generous folds of stomach and bosom as if she used to be six-feet tall but someone had pushed her head and feet closer together. She wore a red apron like the man who'd shown her to her seat; he was now talking to a bunch of customers with American accents. He tilted his head and hung on their every word, hips swaying in time to the music. With his white comb-over, pointed nose and eyes magnified by thick glasses, he had a barn owl aspect about him.

Alex's mum regaled her once with facts about barn owls and how they don't hoot, and have lopsided ears. Once retired, her mum became heavily involved with a local bird charity and was kept especially busy in the spring, a time when well-meaning members of the public would turn up with fledglings they'd come across hopping on the ground. Unfortunately they'd interrupted an important part of the baby birds' development on their journey to independence. Their parents would have still been nearby, still keeping an eye and feeding them. Her mum admired birds' parenting skills and had adopted the same mentality, encouraging Alex to spread her human wings, unlike Dad who had been very much against his eighteen-year-old daughter going interrailing. Alex gazed at the Peak District mural, picturing her mum, rucksack on her back, binoculars to hand, searching for a shady spot to eat egg and cress sandwiches. She and Alex often used to go rambling together.

Carrying a notebook and pencil, how old school, the squashed-looking server with ginger hair came over. 'Good afternoon,' she said, as if using a practised telephone voice, cat-eye glasses hanging on a strap around her neck, ruches of good humour around her eyes. 'How are you today?'

'It's morning, actually, which means numerous cups of coffee.' This server needed to pay more attention. 'But I haven't browsed the menu yet. Could you come back in a few minutes?'

'Lovely hair colour, if a little harsh against your pale skin. Do you dye it yourself?'

'Thank you and no.' That was a little rude.

'Me neither. I used to. My sister does it now and—'

'If you could give me a while longer...?'

Alex picked up the menu as her stomach rumbled. Breakfast was served until eleven thirty. She was just in time. Having chosen a dish, she studied the room again. So much for a quirky Northern Quarter vibe. This place couldn't be further from the sophisticated cafés she created in her novels. Her latest release had featured one called Roast Diamonds that served coffee containing crushed crystals. She was about to choose her breakfast when a man caught her attention, whistling indiscriminately, a pen behind his ear, his hair the colour of salted caramel, a flavour she considered highly overrated. He'd stood with his back to her, in the far left corner, but now turned around to reveal, behind him, a large silver cage attached to a stand. Inside, a parrot, with white panda eyes and ruffled grey feathers, swung to and fro on a wooden bar. The bird gnawed the swing's chain with his hooked black beak. Was a pet in a café even legal?

She took out her phone. It couldn't be sanitary. Yet a brief search informed her that no rules had been broken as long as the pet couldn't access the food preparation area. Her mum would have loved to keep a bird and dreamt of building a large aviary in the back garden. However, give Dad latex, rubber, aspartame, anything chemical, no problem, but he'd need mouth-to-mouth if you touched him with feathers, fur or pollen. Or so he said. In Alex's opinion he was more allergic to Mum giving attention to anything but him.

The parrot tossed an empty peanut shell onto the floor as her server with ginger hair appeared again and put down a frothy cappuccino.

Alex frowned. 'I haven't ordered a drink yet. Nor have I drunk cow's milk for three years.'

'Oh. Sorry, must have got the wrong table.' She surveyed the room and then took the mug to a pensioner by the other window and stopped for a chat, laughing heartily within a few minutes, or rather emitting a series of wheezes that sounded like an accordion finding it hard to produce music.

Sloppy service. A resident parrot. What kind of café was this? Hope's tearful face popped into Alex's mind. It was one she was going to have to work in for the imminent future, and it wouldn't do to fall out with a colleague on her first day. She mustn't get sacked for Hope's sake. With a regal manner, Alex waved her hand, for the server to come back.

'Fresh fruit porridge, please, hold the honey. An espresso,' she articulated, as if the woman needed to lip-read.

'"Goldilocks and the Three Bears" was one of my favourite stories when I was little,' the server said. She took off her cat-eye glasses, distracted from her notepad for a moment. 'I used to ask Mum to make me three plates of porridge.'

She was a talker. Alex wasn't used to this. Writing was mostly a solitary profession where she could choose when to answer a phone call, an email or a social media message. Face to face it was far harder to control a conversation. The server scribbled on her pad before heading back to the hatch. Once there, she spoke to the young woman at the till who had short hair with green streaks, a pixie cut they used to call it, pierced eyebrows and she wore dungarees and a checked shirt rolled up to the elbows. Alex flinched as a loud squawk resounded across the room.

'He's very friendly,' said barn owl man, on his way to the counter. 'Never nipped anyone.'

'As long as you don't ask him the obvious question,' said the man with the pen behind his ear. He'd come over. A name badge said 'Manager'. That had to be Tom.

Hope was right. He did have chocolate eyes. Miranda would gag when she talked about manuscripts in her slush pile where authors compared characters' physical features to food or drink. However, as Alex studied his thick hair, cut above the ears, all one length and brushed to the left, salted caramel filled her mind again. His hair wasn't in a man-bun and he wasn't in chino shorts, but a floral shirt hung over ankle-grazer jeans and boat shoes with... odd socks. There was a boyish air about him that she found irritating in a middle-aged man.

'Hi,' he said and gazed into her face, holding out his hand.

'Hi.'

Leave me alone. I'm not at my best before at least my third coffee. Alex averted her gaze; it took more effort than she'd expected.

Reluctantly leaving the more stylish surroundings of Instagram, she slid her hand into his. He made a comment about the weather. The server came over with Alex's espresso; her name badge said... 'Reenie'. Alex took a sip. Not bad. Slowly, Reenie came back carrying a red plate, as if the food were a highly important telegram. She lowered it onto the yellow tablecloth and Alex wrinkled her nose with a sense of nausea that she'd suffered from lately. On the plate lay a perfect circle of egg and neat runways of bacon.

'I ordered fruit and porridge, not a cardiac arrest,' Alex said in an abrupt tone.

The parrot squawked again.

'He's very friendly,' called barn owl man's voice from across the room. 'Never nipped anyone.'

Alex got to her feet and glowered at the cage, the staff and the manager too. 'Why is bad service a joke here?' she asked.

'You do know what this café is called?' asked Tom.

Oh. As it turned out she didn't. Alex had always cut Hope short when she'd tried to give any details, and had simply focused on the directions to get to the building. Then she'd been distracted by her phone outside, just as she was going to read its name.

He picked up the menu and passed it over. Alex read the front. By now the whole room had fallen silent. Contact lenses gave her perfect vision and it wasn't April Fool's Day, so what sort of idiot would call their business Wrong Order Café?

'A café that purposely delivers the wrong orders? Next, in this parallel universe, you'll be telling me that the bird talks.' Alex held eye contact with Tom as she called across the room. 'Who's a pretty boy then?'

'Fuck off,' the parrot squawked.

4

Well, really.

Squashed Woman, Barn Owl, Salted Caramel, the three of them struggled not to laugh. A customer snorted; others exchanged glances.

'Now I understand why Hope kept trying to warn me about working here,' said Alex and pushed away the plate.

Tom stepped forwards. 'Wait, *you're* Alex?'

'Alex Butler. Best-selling author.' She tipped her head and took a signed photo out of her bag. She passed it to him.

He held it in the air with a confused manner. 'But Hope said you worked as a barista across town, that you'd had decades of experience in the hospitality industry.'

Instantly, Hope shot up in Alex's estimation.

'I don't see the problem, especially if your unique selling point is messing up orders. If you could show me to my room, I'll get settled in.' She pointed at the plant. 'You'll find my case under there.' Alex headed for the stairs.

'How about a chat first?' asked Tom, in an even tone. 'Please, do get your bags and follow me.' He gave Reenie a side-hug. 'I saw in the staffroom that you did well in today's crossword, during your morning break. I'll do my best to beat it later.'

She pushed him away playfully. 'Sorry about the order,' she said to Alex. 'Fried, fruit, I got the words muddled.'

Perhaps she needed a hearing aid.

Tom headed past the kitchen towards a room marked 'Staffroom', scrolling down his phone. Inside was an uncomplicated space as bright as the service area, with a red sofa, upholstered armchairs and a large mural on the far wall, designed like a window backing onto a garden. The television in front of it had a giant remote control. On top of the nearby beech cabinet stood an old-fashioned radio, a jar of coffee, tea bags and a tin of biscuits, a kettle, a water filter jug and bottles of cordial. Tom pointed to the sofa and Alex brushed it down before sitting. He sat in one of the armchairs opposite, first removing a blanket with tassels and beads and plastic hoops sewn on.

'How about we start again?' he said and scratched the back of his head. 'I'm Tom Wilson. Manager of Wrong Order Café. May I ask, why do you want to work here? I've just found you online. Clearly you have a successful career already.'

'Because... one of the main characters in my next novel works in a high-end staff coffee shop, in a big company. Research is very important for the authenticity of stories.' She couldn't tell him the other reasons, how she needed the money and that this place was her last chance. 'And Hope needed someone to cover her while she went travelling. This presented the perfect opportunity for me to learn about hospitality from a much more basic coffee business.'

Tom's top lip twitched as if a secret joke was tugging it upwards. 'I hope you're a quick learner.'

Alex made a pfft noise, as if to say how hard can it be.

Hands on his knees, Tom sat, legs slightly apart, looking her

straight in the eye, body leaning forwards. So far so good. Alex
was used to studying body language, to help convey mood in
writing. How folding arms might indicate a hidden secret; how
poor eye contact could reveal lying. Things you weren't aware of
in real life, things you may not even notice if your husband was
cheating. Tom explained how decades ago Stevenson Square
used to be the focus point for open-air speakers, for anarchists;
it acted as the starting point for demonstrators' processions. This
coffee shop was set up way before cafés became such an
intrinsic part of British culture. It survived the First and Second
World Wars, and post-war became a hub for artists, frequented
by the likes of locals L. S. Lowry and William Turner. Business
boomed during the fifties and sixties. The area was seen as fash-
ionable with its quirky hat and clothes shops, but then the
Arndale shopping centre was built in 1975 and tempted shoppers
away.

Alex zoned out a little. Tom would make a terrible historical
novelist; he'd put in far too much backstory.

'In the late seventies the coffee shop floundered and its price
dropped so my parents could afford to take it on. They'd always
dreamt of owning a café. But in 1987 Mum died. Road accident,'
he said in a matter-of-fact voice.

Alex sat up straighter.

'She got stuck in a tailback and a lorry slammed into the back
of her. I was ten.'

For a second she pictured a little boy in front of her, with the
same salted-caramel hair and smattering of freckles, face crumpled as he was told the news. She fought an urge to lean forwards
and brush the floppy fringe out of his eyes.

'That must have taken a long time to get over,' she said, 'especially with so little mental health understanding, back then.' She
nodded encouragingly as he talked about how he was given the

day off school, how he pretended, with friends, that it hadn't happened, how his dad sobbed in bed, every night.

'Sorry,' said Tom and his ears turned red. 'Not sure where that came from.'

'Please, do carry on.' Despite her slightly abrupt manner, Alex had always considered that her greatest asset was her knack of getting people to open up and share their hidden stories. Like Hope admitting she was scared. Like the doorman where she lived still not admitting to anyone else he was gay. Like the aunt who was conducting a secret pen friend affair with a lifer in prison. Mum used to say Alex had been born with the face of someone who'd signed a confidentiality agreement.

Secrets were often seen as dark and deceptive, but sometimes they were simply sad truths that people tried to hide. Perhaps that had been the problem with her third book – readers had worked out that, secretly, her heart wasn't in it. Her husband's cheating was one factor that had pushed her to become an author, to forge an independent, successful existence. During the first year or two that followed, the series of her young lovers, a binge of light-hearted romance, had translated into two huge best-sellers, leaving readers clamouring for more of her heart-breaking heroes and arousing paragraphs. Trouble was, that binge eventually left Alex so sated that by the time she came to write the third novel, simply the word 'romance' turned her stomach.

'Mum had been Dad's life for so long, the two of them were each other's school sweetheart, so the coffee shop became his life instead,' Tom continued. 'My mates loved this place. We'd pile in after school for Coke floats and they'd pester their parents to visit at the weekend. Slowly, by word of mouth, its fried breakfasts gained a reputation. Benedict Cumberbatch came in once when he studied drama at the university. We even served the Gallagher brothers, in the early nineties, when the band started out. Oasis was known as The Rain back then.'

'Has this place always been called Wrong Order Café?' she asked, politely.

'No. My parents named it Susie's.'

'After your mum?'

'Yes. That's when I knew my dad had become really ill. He insisted on changing that name, became fixated on it.'

'You took over the business?' Alex had experienced, first hand, how illness could change people.

'I've always worked here. Dad and I made a good team, him up front, me managing the staff and doing the books. We have two chefs,' he said, 'and three full-time members of staff, alongside me: Hope, Jade – you might have seen her in the checked shirt – and Yash. He's not in today, he's a student and...'

Alex's attention drifted away.

'The café opens from nine until half past five. If I need extra cover for holidays or have a conference or food fair to attend, or a member of staff is ill, I call on Pip, a former employee who's a stay-at-home mum now but happy to pick up a couple of shifts a week.'

Alex suppressed a yawn, a mechanism all bird species employed, to keep them alert if they were sleepy, or cool them down if overheated. Perhaps birds yawned when they got bored as well. 'What about Reenie,' she asked, 'and...?'

'Fletch?' said Tom. 'They don't help out at the weekend, that's really busy, or Fridays, and we're closed on a Monday. But they are rostered in all day Tuesday and then for Wednesday and Thursday Reenie does mornings and Fletch afternoons. Pip is very accommodating and would come in if either of them had a bad day.'

What did that mean? And 'help out'? So they weren't actual employees?

'But that hasn't happened yet. The woman with curly hair is Reenie's sister, Kay. They live together, with Kay's husband, Cliff. She brings her here and usually stays for the shift. Newly retired, Kay enjoys her cross-stitching. Fletch's wife, Val, often stays too. She left her job when he got diagnosed and went freelance with her bookkeeping, so brings her laptop. Val likes the change of scenery but doesn't need to stay for every shift as Jade, behind the counter, is Fletch's granddaughter.'

'What do you mean *diagnosed*?' asked Alex. Perhaps she should have read Hope's text after all.

'Hope really didn't tell you?'

'Tell me what?'

'Reenie has early-onset dementia. Fletch has been diagnosed with Alzheimer's.'

5

Alex sat very still.

'Fletch is seventy and has the same diagnosis as my dad. Jade's parents moved away to London with work a couple of years ago, whereas she stayed here in Manchester, close to her grandparents. He and Reenie might get a little confused from time to time – forget what they were saying or what they were about to do – but are still quite capable of working with a few adjustments. They've become a real asset to the business.'

Dementia? A workplace that revolved around old age would hardly provide the dynamic vibe she needed to revive her career. More than that, those servers were vulnerable people; what if Alex accidentally caused upset or put them in danger? Maybe this stint in a café wasn't the carefree option Alex had thought she was getting. Watching Mum struggle with an illness she'd never recover from had been more difficult than Alex had ever imagined. A hard *no* to going through that again, even if it was with strangers and the medical condition was different. Alex wished herself anywhere but in this building, suddenly desperate to spend time with one of her young boyfriends, so she could forget everything – even for a few hours. Forget that she was getting older with a life quite different now, to the one she'd expected.

'Both have been finally diagnosed in the last year, although they've had symptoms for longer than that. Reenie suffered with mood swings and frustration mainly. She still carries her favourite scissors in her handbag.'

'What?'

Tom explained how it was a comfort thing. Reenie had been a hairdresser and never used to leave the house without a pair. She'd got involved with a homeless charity before she was ill, and in her spare time, would walk around the city's streets at night, with a team, giving free haircuts to rough sleepers. Tom took the pen out from behind his ear and twirled it between his fingers.

'She's been here six months, Fletch about eight. They both replaced previous staff whose condition had deteriorated too much to continue working here. Inevitably, hard as it is, that's the way it goes. Fletch and Reenie's official diagnoses came relatively early in terms of their illnesses, despite how long it took to get them. However, both have changed since I've known them. During the first couple of months neither needed as much supervision, and would even pop out to fetch ice cubes or milk. Their problem-solving skills were better too. Reenie could even follow a recipe and enjoyed helping the chefs.'

'Does your dad live here?' asked Alex. She didn't want to hear any depressing details; she needed to keep her mood uplifted to stand any chance of writing new chapters that zinged.

'A couple of years ago he became much more restless and was up in the night, and the business suffered. It was the toughest decision of my life to move him into a care home. Christ, the costs came as a shock. Mum's brother, Uncle Neil, knew a lot about the stock market and we'd both invested over the years, so now that nest egg is keeping Dad afloat, but it won't last forever.' He ran his arm through the air. 'This place, having servers with dementia, is my small way of giving hope to anyone else going through this challenging journey. If I can help just one other family, it helps me cope with the frustration of not being able to solve Dad's problems.'

Alex didn't want to contemplate losing her own faculties, seeing as now she'd face it all alone, and her failing income wouldn't secure a comfortable ending.

'Dad comes in every week for coffee and cake, usually on a Friday. Sometimes one of the care workers brings another resident. Any change of scene is important, to stimulate their brains, and there's a special disabled toilet in here, at the back.' Tom went over to the cabinet underneath the radio and opened the doors to reveal a trove of jigsaws, colouring books, crosswords and fidget blankets. He neatened a pile of printed-out Sudoku puzzles on top, by the biscuit tin.

'Doesn't it upset him, coming back to the place that used to be home?' Alex asked as Tom sat down again.

'He's not always aware that he once lived here.'

How could he be sure?

Tom explained how his dad, Norm, was diagnosed at seventy too, five years ago. Not keen on retirement, he'd still worked. The symptoms weren't severe and regulars became used to his order mistakes. Norm joked his way through as a means of coping. As the disease progressed, he became stubborn and obsessed with changing the coffee shop's name.

'I only did it to make him happy,' said Tom. 'People with dementia often fixate on something random and it can upset them. Dad was so chuffed when he saw the new name sign and it paid off in the end. A local newspaper got hold of the story and the café quickly became something of a tourist attraction, mentioned on websites listing quirky coffee shops. Tourists provide much of the custom. We've had servers with dementia for the last three years, since it's been up and running under the new name. At least Dad got to help out for several months, with the changes, before he had to go into a care home. The Wrong Order Café, its whole ethos, is as much his project as mine.'

'Great business plan; earnings must have shot up,' she said, admiring his business acumen.

'That's not why I've done it,' he said swiftly. 'The media and tourist attention help me do what matters most, fundraise for dementia charities, and to raise awareness – to show that people with dementia can still have a life. A diagnosis isn't the end.'

Alex put her hand on her shoulder bag, her sense of unease growing with this sound bite. Alex's clever readers would have seen through this fakeness straight away. Philanthropic business people didn't exist, not without ulterior motives. It was all about the money, the author life had taught her that. Nothing extinguished a publisher's cheerleading more quickly than an advance taking too long to earn out.

'Don't you get lots of complaints?' Alex asked as she zipped up her jacket. She couldn't do a job that was about embracing your mortality instead of doing your best to fight it. Hope should have made more of an effort and forced Alex to heed her warnings.

'No. People love coming here. We make sure every menu item is of a high standard, so whatever customers end up with will be tasty. I'd say we get about 40 per cent of the orders wrong and 99 per cent of the customers are happy.' His top lip twitched. 'A complaint is very rare.'

If he was to be believed, that made Alex the 1 per cent. Standing out was a positive, she reminded herself. When she first signed with Miranda, her debut sold at auction for a six-figure amount. At the bank, where she used to work, she'd have talked down her success, but the new Alex wasn't about to do that, not after the crappiest time of her life. Instead, she fed off the attention, the flattery. Fellow authors distanced themselves, old friends stopped returning calls. Alex couldn't blame them for being jealous. At least Mum would have been proud of her, and that was all that mattered. Alex was doing it for her as well.

She would *have been proud.*

She would.

'Anyway, I think I've given you a brief summary of what we're about,' said Tom, as he ran a hand through his fringe.

Brief? If that had been a synopsis of a novel, Miranda's red pen would have run out.

'I'd love to hear about your author career, and what experience you've had working in a café, if any.'

'Apologies, Tom. This has all been a mistake.' She got to her feet.

Brow furrowed, he stood up too.

'I'm leaving.'

'But... your research? What about Hope's job? I can't cover her shifts for five weeks. You aren't even going to give it a go?'

Dragging her case, Alex hurried out of the room; she banged into the café's entrance door and gulped in air as she walked into Stevenson Square.

However, a melodic whistling had followed her out. 'Hope relies on this job,' came his easy voice next to her.

'She should have told me the truth. I gave her every opportunity.' Well, sort of. Hope should have been more insistent, trying to tell her.

'You won't even stay for a few days, until I find a replacement?'

One of her tension headaches threatened.

'Fair enough,' said Tom and stretched his arms, folding them behind his head. 'Not everyone's up to the challenge.'

Alex faced him.

'There aren't many people who would turn down free meals for so long,' he added.

'Do I look like I need handouts?' she asked in a terse tone.

'Of course not, but everyone needs free access to Jade's ruby hot chocolate – a mug of that makes even the worst day bearable.' He gave her a lopsided smile.

Poor lamb. He thought he could charm her into it. 'Why aren't you put off that Hope lied to you about my experience?'

'People have many different reasons for lying,' he said and broke eye contact. 'Not all of them bad.'

That was exactly the sort of thing Alex's ex-husband had said when she found out he'd been sleeping with another woman.

Tom walked back to the café. 'No worries,' he called over his shoulder. 'Hope shouldn't have any trouble finding another job. She's a good worker, a right decent person. Life's knocked her back a few times, but I'm sure she'll survive yet another let down. I'd better get packing up her stuff.' Whistling, he disappeared into the café.

Alex gritted her teeth and surveyed Stevenson Square, not really seeing it at all. Instead, images of Hope turning up to the café to find her bags packed filled her mind. A grey and black feather landed on the ground by Alex's boots. She picked it up and ran a finger along it. The colours and length suggested it belonged to a pigeon. Mum explained once how a ten-year study showed that pigeons had adapted to use roads and motorways to navigate their own journeys, some even changing direction at motorway junctions. Maybe it was time for Alex to take a different route like Hope had, a journey not around the Far East of the world, but in a local coffee shop, for a few days. And she'd promised Hope; she couldn't risk making her homeless. Alex's mum once said keeping fancy possessions was all well and good,

but what mattered most in life was keeping your word. Alex slid
the feather into her jacket pocket, flexed her hands, held on to
her case and clumsily dragged it back indoors. Tom was speaking
to Fletch about doing a stocktake on tea bags, and didn't stop
talking as she passed her case to him.

'I propose a compromise,' said Alex. 'I'll work until next Tuesday. That gives you one week to find a temporary worker to cover
the remaining weeks until Hope is back.' Without waiting for a
reply, she strode straight up to the counter. 'One of your ruby hot
chocolates; make it a large one,' she said to Jade.

From the silver cage the parrot cocked his head and gave her a
fixed stare. Nostalgia for her mother's love for birds evaporated in
an instant. 'What are you looking at?' Alex snapped.

'Silly bitch,' he squawked back.

6

At the top of the stairs was a weather-beaten wooden door, scratched and splintered in places as if rain and gales had penetrated the building.

'Lowry slept in this flat one summer afternoon,' said Tom and passed Alex a set of keys. 'It was the early fifties; he wasn't far off retiring from his job as a rent collector and clerk with the Pall Mall Property Company, in Deansgate. He was known to the owners and called in for a glass of water as he wore a thick suit and was suffering from heatstroke.' Tom smiled. 'Who'd have thought that one day there'd be another artist in residence, this time a famous author?'

The first thing people asked when they found out you were a writer was whether your books had been adapted into movies, as if the carefully crafted words on the page didn't matter. Dad had loved words and was a fan of crosswords, and he'd read to Alex every night. He'd put her to bed while Mum prepared his dinner. *The Tiger Who Came to Tea* was a favourite story. Alex could picture the pages now, and Dad putting on an extra-deep, gruff voice. Sometimes, at weekends, when the three of them had cake in the kitchen, he would lift up the teapot and pretend to drink out of it like the tiger. Fond memories she was surprised she held on to, because as she got older, the laughter with him roared less loudly.

'I live on the top floor,' said Tom and he pointed to another flight of stairs at the end of the corridor. He consulted his watch, a scratched gold face with Roman numerals and a worn leather strap. 'Bread delivery. I'll leave you to settle in.'

Whistling, he slid down the stairs, feet off the ground, holding on to the banisters. Some women might have found that endearing in an older man, along with his trendy beaded bracelet. However it only reminded Alex of how Simon had behaved towards the end of their marriage, as if he'd found a balloon and tied all his problems to it, then let go, leaving himself lighter and less attached to Alex. She turned the key and pulled her case inside, inhaling a mix of zingy fragrances. To the left was a small kitchenette with a collection of herb pots, cosied up together on a white unit – basil, coriander, parsley, mint, all of them labelled. A miniature rose plant took pride of place in the middle of a small dining room table. To the right of the room was a sofa with a colourful throw blanket on it, and a low coffee table that was home to every colour of African violet. It stood on top of a mosaic print rug that lay over laminate flooring. Below a window overlooking the square was a sill strewn with cacti and flowering shrubs, each in patterned porcelain pots.

But more than the plants making the room look welcoming – the trailing ivy hanging in the corner, the dark-leaved plant on a stand that looked like a lemon tree – with the mist spray bottles and mini trowel, were the books lined up along shelves, squeezed into every nook of a corner cabinet, stacked on top of an ottoman, with pages curled at the edges, with bent or faded covers. She crossed the room, passing photos on the walls, like the black and white one of a couple getting married, and one of a younger Hope, her and a small girl side by side. Alex opened a door on the right – the bedroom. More plants. More books. An embroidered bedcover. To the left, a door revealed the bathroom, the tidiest room in the flat with only a few toiletries and no make-up. However, Hope's place wasn't messy, it was simply... full. Full of Hope, even though this flat had represented a life change.

A change of scenery, alone, hadn't satisfied Alex. Her apartment reflected a clean slate, more like a show home with its modern art in frames and perfect artificial plants, with books by other authors stashed into storage drawers, her own on display. Any sign of the old Alex had been discarded. Like a novel that hadn't been written yet, Alex's apartment merely sketched out a story that had never moved forward from proving to the world that Alex was vital, that she mattered. Unexpectedly, this left Alex feeling as empty as her living space.

Thirsty, she headed to the sink and, in search of a glass, opened the cupboards. A jumbled array of food tins faced her – tinned fruit, rice pudding, chopped tomatoes, beans and sweetcorn. Alex dined out mostly but with flagging sales, that was going to have to change. She walked over to the window. Down below, the square had a long, boarded-up strip of land in the middle that street artists had decorated. After knocking back a glass of water, she grimaced; bottled water was a luxury she was loath to give up. Alex collapsed onto the sofa and held her face in her hands. She had no children, or siblings. Alex answered to no one but herself, and that only made things worse. Before they grew apart, Simon used to boost her self-esteem with compliments about her achievements, yet also acted as an objective sounding board over problems at work and promotional opportunities. Mum did too and insisted failures were learning experiences, while offering constructive criticism, like the time nineteen-year-old Alex had her belly button pierced and it got infected. But now, with her writing career flailing, on the cusp of losing everything she'd worked so hard for, Alex had only her inner voice to answer to.

And right now it sounded more like that parrot. *Silly bitch. You've brought this on yourself.*

Miranda's text popped into her head. Alex picked up a cushion and threw it across the room, fighting the sense of not being enough, and the sense of dread that filled her chest. She kept on her high heels and smart leather jacket but compromised her style by tying her hair back. As she headed for the door, a pink and black book cover, under the coffee table, caught her attention. *Glamour Puss*? Hope really had read it. It was even a signed copy, well thumbed too.

Alex recalled the true reason she'd become a writer that is the pain of rejection, and how it morphed into a love of crafting sentences. This creative passion had become blurred when chasing best-seller flags and awards took over. But now she could clearly picture the first time she'd sat in front of an empty screen and typed 'Chapter One'.

Simon had just called from the airport, about to fly to Greece, to holiday with his best friend, Mike, who'd moved there several years earlier. Divorce papers had arrived one week before, the end of a painful process, and Simon had rung to nudge her.

'We've been through this, Lex. It's me. Not you. I want different things.'

'Can't we have different things together? For a while I've considered leaving the bank.'

'Like I've said before, that's impulsive after all the years you've put into climbing the ladder... I'm worried about you, Lex. And wanting life to change, it's not about work.'

'I'd support anything you do; nothing matters as long as we're together.'

His tone had sounded strained. 'I... don't love you any more. I've tried to tell you, Lex.'

'We've been together twenty years, cared for each other.' Her voice had broken. 'Who nursed you through that heart scare when you turned forty?'

'Who's pushed *me* away for months now?' he'd said with an edge. He'd given a big sigh. 'Honestly, Lex, you can do better.'

'That's rubbish and you know it.'

'My flight's being called. Goodbye.'

'I still love you, Si,' she'd whispered.

He'd hung up and Alex's distress had driven her debut novel.

Sentences fell onto the page about a woman who took revenge on a lover who'd wronged her. Alex couldn't write quickly enough. Along the way, her love for crafting a story grew. She'd always enjoyed writing up financial reports for her job at the bank, shaping each sentence. The same day as finally signing the divorce papers, Alex completed the first chapter. Then Mum fell ill. She left the bank, moved in with her mother and lived off savings from the divorce settlement, writing in the evenings, during the night, when Mum didn't need as much attention. Alex had a first draft in four months and the book was published one year later. Her mum never quite got to see it. Si had come to the funeral and Alex took this as a promising sign. On publication day, she'd waited for a call, a congratulatory card, convinced this new Alex could win him back. Instead, she heard via the grapevine that he'd moved to London.

Alex put *Glamour Puss* back under the coffee table, among a pile of Jackie Collins novels. But then she caught sight of a calendar on top of a pile of books, and something made her stop.

Ten minutes later she was still adding up days, wracking her brains about whether she could have made a mistake. She went to the bathroom, and eventually came out, Simon completely forgotten by this moment. Her period had always been more accurate than the Rolex she'd bought herself when her second book got to number one in the charts. It had been late, two weeks ago, and she'd done a pregnancy test then that she'd bought from the chemist. The negative result had made her complacent – what if it had been wrong?

Alex hadn't had sex for... several months before that date night with a dentist – okay, that one-night stand. She remembered that they had laughed together in the dark. They were both drunk. Impatient. Perhaps less careful?

Crap.

That night had actually made Alex consider going on the pill again. Her emotions before her period each month had become increasingly up and down; a new pill might have helped. But she hadn't got around to making the appointment. Her memory had been all over the place recently, her brain too busy trying to come up with the next chart-topper.

A baby, in her forties? In her immaculate flat? Holding her already struggling career back? What a ridiculous idea, Alex told herself, ignoring an inner voice reminding her of the credit analyst she used to work with, who unexpectedly had a baby at forty-two. Alex had never wanted children and hurried to the sink and sipped more water. Stress affected ovulation, that had to be the logical explanation she concluded, despite images floating through her head of prams, dummies and bottles, of a baby with her mum's snub nose.

A whoosh of emotion flooded her body; it made her want to shout the news out the window. She jokingly called her novels her babies; they kept her up at night and she defended them fiercely if anyone criticised so much as a syllable. Alex took a couple of deep breaths and leant her hands on the sink, dizzy from the rush of adrenaline that had confused her for a second. This wasn't news to celebrate. A baby was the last thing her life needed. She made her way downstairs. What was she doing? Serving coffee could wait for a few minutes. Alex stopped outside the kitchen and scrolled down her phone for the doctor's number. She'd need another pregnancy test done, but now didn't trust a home kit. One of the young chefs swore and she followed his gaze towards a broken egg on the floor.

7

Busy with overseeing the bread delivery, Tom thrust a notepad into her hands, with the words 'in at the deep end' and a grin. However, deep it was not; simply writing down orders and delivering food and drink couldn't be easier, surely. Therefore, instead, she focused on brainstorming her chapters. Perhaps the story needed a refresh, a new character perhaps. As of yet, not a single one had strutted up and down in her head pitching why *they* should star in her next book. So far, Alex had based novels in Los Angeles, San Francisco and Paris; this one was to be set in Milan. She'd gone on trips to those locations solely for research, at least that's what she'd told HMRC. Miranda's advice was especially shrewd when it came to tax and claiming expenses.

Alex never did like jumping in the deep end as a child, that sense of sinking, eyes shut, mouth squeezed tight, rigid from the cold, waiting for some deep-sea monster to pounce. Simon had done plenty of research for his midlife health kick, recounting facts to Alex like how muscle was denser than water but fat wasn't, so it was a great thing if you didn't float straight back up to the water's surface. Primary school Alex preferred to sit on the side of the pool at the shallow end, kicking her feet in the cool water until Dad reached out his arms and persuaded her to jump in.

'I'll catch you,' he'd say with an encouraging smile.

Then she'd jump in the deep end like young Adélie penguins did, as they learnt to swim the quick way – but her dad lied, every time. Mouth full of chlorinated water, she'd come up gasping for air, to his laughter, wishing she'd been more like young Gentoo penguins that would take things more slowly, paddling first to get used to the water. Her dad would also challenge her to races, egging her on, reaching the far side way before her and turning to crow about his strength, saying how she'd never beat him. She always hoped he'd admire her for trying but instead he'd encourage her to play it safe, to know when to quit, saying risk-taking wasn't for girls, wasn't for young women. It knocked her confidence and prevented Alex from applying to the top universities, even though her parents were divorced by then. As a youngster, she hadn't hated her dad, believing he was right, protecting her, and she assumed her mum ran around after him because she loved him. Years later, she knew better, so Simon damaging Alex's sense of worth by leaving, as if he'd taken her for an idiot, inspired her to dive, eyes open, into her new life.

Nothing drove her to succeed in the café; she simply needed to go through the motions, for the sake of Hope's position. She stood in the corner pretending to watch the other staff and take notes, while interviewing new characters in her head. *Nice to meet you, Sadie, sorry I've already done a twin sister bitch. Great tuxedo, Carlton, but your style is too old hat.* Frustrated, auditions going nowhere, she eventually headed over to a man poured into a tight three-piece suit. His eyes swept across the menu and he told Alex what he wanted, while she abandoned characters and focused on plotlines instead. Perhaps she'd include a Mafia element; there could be a drug run that went wrong and...

'I'm in a hurry,' said the man, as if he were about to miss the deadline to collect a lottery win. He took out his newspaper. 'Please push my order through quickly.'

Walking more slowly than the coffee machine's flow, she made her way over to the counter. Jade had quickly shown her how the notepad made two copies of each order, one for front of house and drinks, the other for the kitchen. Alex wrote down his table number and tore off the top copy for Jade, who told her to hand the second one to one of the chefs behind the hatch.

A young couple came in and Fletch rushed over.

'Welcome,' he said and gave a little bow. 'Someone will be with you shortly.'

'Soft drinks are in that fridge, Alex,' said Jade, who was at the coffee machine, glancing at her granddad now and again, as he cleared a table and chatted to Captain Beaky, the parrot. Its name felt familiar to Alex but she couldn't work out why. 'You'll find clean glasses in that crate underneath the hatch. When we run out, take that into the kitchen to refill. At the far end, in there, you'll spot two dishwashers; one is for glassware, cups and mugs.' She pointed to another crate on a unit, at the end of the front of house area, behind the parrot's cage. 'Put dirties in there. When it's full take that out the back too. It's our job to run the drinks dishwasher and make sure we have a steady supply of crockery. I make the hot drinks, so do Yash and Pip when they're in. You take orders but can also plate up anything in the counter – cakes, breakfast pastries.'

A glazed expression washed over Alex's face.

'Right now is the lull between breakfast and lunch,' continued Jade, 'but when it's busy, keeping on top of the dishwasher is extra important. You're in luck for now; it's not raining, so many customers will order takeout drinks.'

Jade passed over a latte and Alex put it down in front of the man who continued to read his newspaper. One of the chefs called out Alex's name. This man must have been really thirsty as Jade passed her a banana milkshake for his table as well. Alex put it on a tray and one of the chefs pushed a plate across the hatch. On it lay slices of sourdough toast and two ramekins on the side, one containing jam, the other butter curls. Alex delivered the order but the man frowned and sucked in his cheeks as she placed the tray in front of him. Tom appeared by Alex's side.

'Everything all right?' Tom beamed and rubbed his hands together.

The man shot Alex a disdainful look. 'I took my chances coming in here, assumed the café's name was some sort of joke. I didn't have much choice. I've got an imminent meeting around the corner.'

'Your order isn't right?' asked Tom.

The man's nose wrinkled as he stared at the plate. 'What's the point, mate? Do your customers seek some dominatrix figure who'll decide what they can eat? Is this some kind of fetish establishment, where everyone wants to be mothered?'

Alex's dad would have swung a punch if another man had spoken to him like that, but Tom's upper lip twitched before he burst out laughing and fully explained the concept of the café.

The suit shuffled in his seat, buttonholes stretching as if about to catapult buttons. 'Apologies. Cruel disease, isn't it? My grandfather had it, in his eighties. Whereas early onset, in middle age...' His attention turned to Alex. 'I can't imagine how hard that must be. Look, it won't kill me to have jam on toast for lunch, instead of a ham sandwich, although I was craving banana cake. The last time I drank a shake I was probably doing the Macarena at a school disco.'

So what if Alex hadn't listened properly? It only meant this man's experience conformed with the café's unique selling point. Tom could eyeball her all he liked; she'd be gone in a week. She didn't need to get on with him, unlike Miranda. Every author needed a certain rapport with their agent. She'd sent in the completed manuscript of her debut and Miranda had called her one week later and suggested a meeting. Miranda had stridden in as if she owned the flash bar, wearing a bright red trouser suit. She'd suggested they eat outside, even though an autumn chill hung in the air. As soon as they'd sat down she took out a packet of cigarettes and offered Alex one. Alex had managed not to cough when she inhaled; the glass of champagne before lunch wasn't something she was used to either.

Simon's betrayal, the hurt, how much she missed him, had run through her veins that lunchtime like splintered glass instead of blood. She wasn't going to take crap from anyone, not even a fancy London literary agent. Even though Miranda was the expert, Alex set out her ambitions, raising her hand to stop Miranda interrupting. She described the kind of publisher she wanted, naming a shortlist, her expectations over an advance and what she wanted from an agent, to earn their 15 per cent. She'd sent her writing to Miranda because she worked at a reputable literary agency, but mainly because she was famous for her straight-talking, her transparent style, neither quality apparent in Alex's cheating ex-husband at the end.

Miranda had listened. Smoked some more. Ordered a second glass of champagne. Their partnership was sealed when they both complained to the waiter and sent back their lukewarm mains.

* * *

Taking her morning break, Alex sat down in the corner of the café. Anyway, she wasn't here to learn seriously about the hospitality industry. Aside from helping Hope, she was simply here for extra income and the different surroundings that might somehow inspire her to get on writing.

She took out her phone with the intention of losing herself in her more familiar virtual world, where she blagged about how great her career was going, even though it wasn't now, and only posted her best shots, wrinkles filtered out. Miranda used to post daily about Alex's books, filling her Instagram feed with the two of them meeting for drinks and attending signings. All that ended when the waving best-seller flags went limp, reminding Alex that even though the work felt personal, talking about characters' feelings and motivations, the relationships she had with her agent and editor were mainly driven by the size of the royalties.

Any break was a luxury – as a writer she often worked nonstop throughout the day. A plate appeared in front of her and vibrant colours caught her eye: smashed avocado, smoked salmon, chilli sprinkles. Jade stood by the table, thumbs behind her dungaree straps.

'From Tom. On the house, of course.' She slumped into a seat next to Alex. 'It'll be quieter now until the school run. How are you finding your first day?'

'Nothing to it. Just as well. It gives me time to focus on my career.'

Jade had the greenest eyes, like one of the spiky plants in Hope's room; they matched the streaks in her hair.

Jade put her elbows on the table. 'What do you write?' she asked in a matter-of-fact voice.

'Empowering, glossy women's fiction.'

'Ah, yes. Bonkbusters. My great-aunt loves those. Got any free copies I could pass on?'

Alex bristled.

'I'm a graphic novel fan myself. Manga especially.'

Alex couldn't help smiling.

'What?' Jade leant back, hands behind her head, stretching with the confidence of someone comfortable in their skin.

'Not really reading, though, is it? You're getting most of the story through pictures.'

'And we're done,' said Jade, getting up. 'Enjoy your freebie.' She went back to the till, hands pushed deep into her apron.

Reenie came over in a bright purple blouse. 'Love your nails even if they're a bit stubby,' she said. 'You must have a desk job. The slightest chip on that bright colour would show straight away working here.'

'I work here, too.' A sense of ill ease washed over Alex again. Was it right to put such vulnerable people front of house, in a position where people might mock them or get cross? 'Or rather, helping out. Doing Hope a favour,' she said, in an overly clear voice. 'It's my first day.'

'Oh yes. Hope. She's...'

'Gone travelling. My name's Alex.'

'Nice name,' said Reenie. 'The boy next door was called that when I was little. He used to drop by every day after school. We'd play tag and dare each other to eat chewing gum stuck to the pavement.'

Tom came over, winked at Reenie and pointed to a table that needed clearing. He wiped his brow with his arm and sat down. The parrot squawked.

'He's very friendly,' called Fletch, coming back from the staffroom, 'never nipped anyone.'

Alex cringed.

'Fletch fitted in really quickly here,' said Tom. 'According to his wife, the hospitality atmosphere reminds him of his days running the front desk in a hotel; it's comforting. He's become a real asset.'

'What, by repeating the same phrase every time that bird makes a noise?'

'His comments don't bother anyone and Fletch loves Captain Beaky to bits.' He pushed the plate towards Alex. 'This'll get cold.'

Realising how hungry she was, Alex picked up the knife and fork. 'Wait... Captain Beaky... that was the name of an eighties band, wasn't it? Captain Beaky and His Band topped the charts with poetry set to music.' Simon loved that decade and had played the band's song 'Captain Beaky' more than once. The lyrics came back to her, something about Batty Bat and Hissing Sid.

'Spot on,' said Tom and hummed the chorus to that tune. 'The band was a favourite of Captain Beaky's original owner. George passed away last year.'

'How did the bird end up with you?'

Tom explained how, when his dad moved into the care home, another man, George, did too. Tom saw him for the first time, in the reception area, face red and swollen, it having sunk in his parrot couldn't move in with him. It had been sent to a shelter and every time Tom visited his dad, he'd spot George in the lounge, wringing his hands and talking to the air about his parrot. So Tom asked for details of the shelter, thinking that a few photos might cheer up George. However, the parrot had become depressed, plucked out its feathers and stopped talking.

'It was pitiful to see, and in a way Captain Beaky mirrored George; each had lost their other half. George was well enough to travel at that point, so I got permission to take him to visit; a member of staff came with us. As soon as they were together both cheered up and told each other to eff off.' His face broke into a smile. 'Then George became too ill to leave the care home, so I took Captain Beaky to see him, but by the end George was hardly talking.'

'You took the bird on to make the café even quirkier?' *Clever.*

'I couldn't leave him at that shelter, once George passed.'

I bet, thought Alex.

'Despite his potty mouth, I'd become fond of Captain Beaky,' continued Tom. 'His feathers grew back; it was good to see him healthier. Now he's interested in his toys again, and loves jazz music – we have that in common. If anything by Ella Fitzgerald comes on the jukebox he squawks, 'What a babe.' But, like me, Frank Sinatra is his favourite. He squawks 'New York, New York,' and 'My way,' when those two songs reach their chorus. All his little habits, preferences and phrases... George must have been quite a character, before he got ill.'

Must have been? Did Tom write off people once they lost life skills? Surely he was supposed to be their cheerleader. Alex felt that her publisher had written her off and now it was hard not to think badly of other people in business, even Tom who, so far, had been nothing but nice – just like the editor who hadn't renewed Alex's contract.

Alex cleared her plate of salmon and avocado, begrudgingly admitting it was as good as any of the lunches she'd had in high-end bistros. Miranda had taken her to an oyster bar once; they were basking in the recent signing of six foreign deals at the Frankfurt Book Fair for her debut. Alex had taken photo after photo of the food and posted them on her social media platforms. Simon didn't follow her profiles – she didn't follow his – but mutual family and friends made for common ground. During the first year or two after their divorce, she'd spent many a night in the arms of young lovers, yet was turned on more by the fantasies in her head about the snippets Simon might hear from third parties; about a book signing in a German shopping centre, about the announcement that *Wicked Ex*, her second book, had been chosen for a prominent US book club.

What would Simon think if he could see her now, in a café full of oldies? Alex. Didn't. Care. It had taken a while but she'd finally not wanted him back. What a sense of liberation when she'd stopped checking social media posts, to count how many mutual friends had read her news. In the end, he was right. She did deserve better. Yet... that phrase niggled away, kept her awake at night sometimes. What had her confident, self-assured husband meant by that? Had something happened? Was he hiding a secret or simply fobbing her off?

Jade came over to collect Alex's plate while Tom chatted to a customer at a neighbouring table. 'The dirties need taking through to the back; we need clean glassware before the lunchtime rush,' she said in a curt tone.

Alex almost waved Jade away, seeing as it was the pre-lunch lull. However, something about Hope had struck a chord. Their lives couldn't have been more different on the outside, but Alex felt a connection; Hope shared the inexplicable sense of foreboding Alex had felt grow during recent years. She didn't want to risk making things worse for Hope by her coming back to colleagues who begrudged her travels because of the week with Alex.

Alex put her phone away and got to her feet, feeling oddly motivated.

8

Alex found Hope on Facebook. She sent her a friend request and the message, 'You should have made me listen', adding pensioner and parrot emojis, before she filled up one of the spray bottles and directed mist towards plants in a hit and miss fashion.

Simon used to laugh at how she always managed to kill houseplants. Underwatering, overwatering, she never knew what was to blame, whereas outside, under Simon's care, plant life flourished. Gardening was his favourite hobby and one of the things that had first attracted her to him. Growing vegetables reminded him of his granddad; he said the open air blew away his worries. Any man who could nurture a plant, surely would handle a relationship with care. Indeed he did, for so many years, and she loved caring back. Her friends at the bank used to call her wonder woman, working full time yet preparing home-made dinners every night. She enjoyed it and Simon always washed up.

Alex collapsed onto the sofa, resolving to google houseplant care, and sniffed the arm of her blouse – she smelt like Starbucks instead of Tom Ford perfume. She lifted her laptop off the coffee table and placed it on smart jeans. When she'd first accepted a job in a bank, her mum couldn't understand it, having never been able to follow her dreams herself. She'd imagined her graduate daughter in a global role that would require travelling the world, kicking ass in boardrooms, a life that could have belonged to one of the characters in her novels. However it had stayed with Alex, the stories her mum told, of when her father lost his job at a local brewery during the 1981 recession, not long after Alex was born. For a while money had been so tight her mum had skipped breakfast and bought clothes from charity shops. Alex's dad had outright rejected the idea of his wife getting a job, and this meant her mum had to start from scratch when they got divorced. Alex always swore she'd provide a secure financial future for herself, especially when she got married, with a separate bank account and joint mortgage.

Her mother's disappointment reappeared years later, when Alex and Simon, tired of all the pointed comments and hints, informed her that neither of them wanted children. Alex's dad pushed to know too, during one of their rare phone calls, insisting motherhood was a woman's purpose. Mum would have made a deal with the devil to get Alex pregnant, and always said her daughter didn't know what she was missing. It used to irritate Alex – until she hit her forties. When she and Simon divorced, she pictured her elderly years without a daughter or son to lean on. In the aftermath of her mother's death it brought on crying fits that Alex couldn't explain. She knew from friends that becoming a parent gave no guarantee you'd get on with your offspring. Alex had always had her mum, and Simon, and then her new job as an author, a new best friend, until she didn't. Now she had no one, nothing at all. She'd alienated friends from the bank, they didn't understand the pressures of being a public figure, and her friendship with Miranda wasn't sealed with a history together, but a signature on a contract that could be torn up at any moment.

One thing today had shown was that perhaps she'd taken her writing career for granted and perhaps working in a café was more challenging than she'd thought. Having no one but her fictional characters for company was a definite plus of her author life, back in her own apartment. Alex opened her laptop and gazed at the first chapter. Perhaps she should completely rewrite it. She opened a new document, typed 'Chapter One', and didn't know whether two knocks at the door caused her irritation or relief. Tom stood in the hallway with a book in his hand, like a student expecting a fine. Without his apron on, she faced his floral shirt in its entirety; Laura Ashley and Jackson Pollock might have teamed up to design it.

'Just returning this to Hope before I forget, if things get hectic and I have to pack up her stuff because I've only been able to find a permanent replacement who'll want to move into her flat. I'm going to miss having a lodger who doubles as a library.'

She opened the door wider, noting the novel was women's fiction as he carried it over to the dining table and slid it onto the shelf on the wall. Her dad would have told him to man up.

'Great story,' he said. 'She's one of my favourite authors. I know they call it women's fiction but I love it too. Why *do* they call it that anyway?'

'You really have to ask?' said Alex and sat back down on the sofa.

'You mean elements of patriarchy and sexism, that are still around?'

'Oh, well... yes,' she said, unable to hide the surprise in her voice as he sat down beside her. 'What men write is automatically considered mainstream. And don't get me started on how romance is side-lined by the media's yearly *best of* lists...'

It turned out Tom's niece was a marketing assistant for a very forwards-thinking, independent publishing house and her talk about the industry fascinated him.

'It's patronising, not only to romance writers but their millions of readers,' Tom said and shook his head.

'You do spend a lot of time with your niece.' Alex gave her first genuine smile since walking into Stevenson Square.

'With Hope, too. We both enjoy a good romance. Gives you that warm glow, doesn't it, experiencing second-hand all the special feel-good moments love causes? I'm a sucker for a happy ending. You don't always get those in real life. Hope and I often sit right here, of an evening, with a bottle of wine, reading or talking about books. In my opinion, they should keep women's fiction as a label but create a men's fiction one as well. That would give lads a place, in a bookshop, to browse, with covers and relationship storylines more targeted at them.'

Those chocolate eyes – Hope's description, not hers – unsettled Alex with their intensity. Might there be romantic feelings between him and Hope?

'Sorry, bit of a book buff; perhaps you need to take a break from publishing out of hours. Mind you, I'd be tempted to work through the night if it meant matching the earnings of top authors.' He gave a low whistle. 'Although I know it's harder for many writers, the difference between my café's income and that of The Ritz.'

A realistic take – how refreshing.

Sitting next to her now, Tom caught sight of her screen and his face lit up. '"Chapter One". You must love this stage, faced with endless possibilities.'

'Couldn't have put it better myself,' she said in a flat tone.

Tom gave a laugh, rich and warm; she wanted to join in. However, Alex couldn't shake off the discomfort created by a business owner who took on people with dementia but paid them nothing; after all, he had said they 'helped out' which didn't make them sound like full paid-up members of staff. Despite its rudeness, she also felt for the parrot, stuck it in a cage 24-7.

'Writer's block?' Tom asked. 'Isn't Hope's workplace inspiring? Why don't I tell you more about it?'

She closed her laptop, unable to think of a polite excuse. 'Okay. What about Reenie and Fletcher?'

'Fletch,' he corrected. 'You'll fit right in as they're artistic types too. Reenie used to do amateur acting. Fletch played the guitar.'

'Can't they follow their passions any more?'

He explained how Reenie had been hit the worst, in terms of her hobby... At first she'd stumble over the odd word, then would lose her way in a long monologue. In the old days, she was often designated the lead role and played an amazing Joy Davidman in *Shadowlands*, and Gertrude in *Hamlet*; the community theatre company she belonged to was as ambitious as her. Fletch could still play the guitar as he'd learnt as a small boy, formed a band with some mates while at school, and rarely a day had passed since then, that he didn't pick up his instrument.

'Dementia means you lose the skills you picked up last, so he's managed to hold on to this childhood hobby. However, lately, he's become more disgruntled if he messes up, and doesn't bring it in as often. He's quite brilliant at it and closes his eyes when he plays, as if it's his heart, not his brain, sending signals to his fingers. His wife reckons the years of practice mean that his body kind of takes over.'

Writing was like that sometimes, when Alex was really in the zone. She couldn't type fast enough, as if the story was telling itself.

'On the photo wall there's a shot of him playing. We take a lot of snaps, with customers' permission, then on any days Reenie and Fletch are a bit lost, they see the photos of themselves working here before, and it's reassuring. I'll have to get one of you, too.' He pointed to the laptop. 'Has it helped? Me talking about the staff? Please tell me to go, if you're itching to type. Or tell me about your fictional coffee shop.'

Tom stretched out his legs. Alex had zero inclination to impress a man wearing sandals.

'My last book didn't sell well. It all went downhill after a damning review on a highly respected book blog. My contract hasn't been renewed. My agent is hopeful about one publisher we could submit to, with just the opening chapters, if I thoroughly rework them. The story has a staff coffee shop in a fracking company.'

'Oh. Right. That's bad luck.'

'It's make or break time. I've got until July when my agent gets back from her holiday, and the publisher's submission window temporarily closes. If I can't renew my passion and inject it into my opening chapters, I might actually end up working somewhere like here full-time.'

'Wouldn't that be terrible,' he said.

'Exactly.'

'Perhaps you need to change your writing direction completely.'

'You mean write fantasy? Horror? I wouldn't know where to start. And it's too late for that.'

'No, nothing so drastic, I meant... the Wrong Order Café, it's very different to Susie's but in lots of ways it's the same. Customer care is still important, as are quality products. The function of this place hasn't changed, that is serving people with amazing food and drinks, but the journey to reaching that end point is different now.' He shrugged. 'What's the main function of your stories?'

'Oh... well... to provide readers with... escapism, I guess, with a gripping plot, sex, romance too, female characters they can relate to or wish they could.'

'Perhaps there's a different way to deliver all of that? Plenty of books have a gripping plot but they aren't thrillers, for example.' Tom's eyes had dropped to his watch. He stood up and swept his fringe out of his face. 'Always happy to help you brainstorm, even if the only things I write are customers' orders on notepads. But feel free to use me as a sounding board. I'd love to be part of the process.' Tom gave her a thumbs up and went to the door.

'What's the real reason you called by?' she asked.

'To try to persuade you to stop for the full five weeks?'

Alex folded her arms.

Tom's lips twitched. 'Seriously... I was curious, I guess. One shift might have sent you packing straight back to Deansgate.' He gripped the door handle again. 'Right, I'd better get back to the man in my life.'

'I didn't know someone else lived here.'

'My life won't be worth living if I'm late for our movie date. Let me know if the television is too loud, it's *Legend of the Guardians* tonight.' Tom gave one of his boyish grins and closed the door behind himself. His whistling eventually faded out.

9

Quarter past nine and Alex appeared at the counter, inhaling the rich aroma of coffee beans, which awakened her senses. Her stomach grumbled. To her surprise she'd slept well, but then since her divorce she'd got used to relaxing in beds that weren't hers.

Alex would never forget her first one-night stand since splitting with Simon. It was after her book launch in London. She'd got a little drunk with Miranda, who disappeared with her then girlfriend not long after their crowd arrived at a nightclub. Alex had danced with her editor, who shot off at twelve, pleading an early start, as did the bookseller shortly afterwards and Alex found herself sitting alone with only a vodka spritz for company. A barman, who loved her Mancunian accent, made it a threesome. He was from Essex but supported Man United. After clocking off, he took her hand and invited her onto the illuminated tiled floor to dance to 'Don't Leave Me This Way' by The Communards, the club's regular end-of-night song. Mortgage and marriage free, his chat was about Netflix, music and eating out.

There was no awkwardness the next morning. He kissed her on the cheek and left a spare key on the pillow before heading to the gym, telling her to make herself breakfast and post the key through the letterbox when she left.

Sex with Simon, at the end, was like a fizzy cocktail gone flat. She'd lost interest; she didn't know why. Mum said many birds had childhood sweethearts they paired with for life, as if it were a good thing, despite the fact that her and Dad's story was that they'd split up.

'Hope's shift starts at nine o'clock sharp,' said Jade, jolting Alex out of the past.

Tom mouthed 'It's okay,' to Jade and passed Alex an apron with a name badge attached. Bless. He must have been star-struck, taking her side against a long-standing employee. Alex shot him her best author smile. She could use Tom's fandom to avoid the dirtier tasks.

Reenie plated up a pain au chocolat.

'My mum's favourite,' said Alex, not sure what to say. 'I prefer the pain au raisin myself. Which is the most popular here?' The question flustered Reenie. Of course, she wouldn't remember previous days' sales. Jade sent Alex an eye roll. Alex helped herself to a slice of fruit bread. 'It's not busy yet so I'll have a double espresso please, Jade.' She sat by the big plant like yester-day, when she'd been undercover. Tom brought in a crate of clean glasses, from the kitchen, and put it under the counter. After a quick chat with Jade he went over to Alex.

'Breaks are scheduled, I'm afraid. Your first fifteen-minute one is at half past eleven.'

She took out her author smile again. 'But you understand how it is, Tom, for us writers. We can't be time constrained. An idea has come to me for the next novel. I need to think it through immediately.'

If only.

'I'm afraid that can't be helped. It's especially important with staff like ours that we all stick to a schedule.' He lifted up her plate. 'A shift here can't be anywhere as stressful as a day at your desk meeting deadlines, leaving you plenty of energy to get that idea down, this evening.'

Alex appreciated him understanding her challenging life. She tipped her head as if she were royalty. Shrieks of laughter came through the door, when it opened, from a group of mums at one of the wooden benches in the middle of the square. Tom had explained that the Wrong Order Café didn't have outside tables. Even though it was unlikely at their early stage of the disease, he couldn't risk Reenie or Fletch getting distracted and wandering off. Ignoring a long raspberry blown by Captain Beaky, Alex went over to a table and took an order from three backpackers.

The day progressed, a mix of delivering food and drink, Alex feeling her way through which conversations worked with Reenie and Fletch, and how best to react to the parrot's swearing. Alex thought less about her deadline. *Less about myself*, she concluded, after an especially busy patch of latte and scone orders. It felt unfamiliar.

Her lunch break was to be late every day, at half past two, after the rush. Alex sat down with a sparkling water and a ham sandwich. She took a large bite. The suited man yesterday would have enjoyed it instead of the jam. Reenie had finished her shift so Alex studied Fletch, who'd started a couple of hours ago. A casual observer might not see his illness. A man with bags under his eyes as black as his sun cap called Fletch over. He must have been in his late thirties. Fletch leant his notepad on the table as he wrote down the order.

'Perfect, cheers, mint writing. I do love a mocha.' The man

rubbed his half-shaven chin, went to say something, changed his mind.

'I'm always doing that,' said Fletch. 'My mouth gets into gear before my brain.'

The man rubbed his chin again, as if he hoped it were an oil lamp and a genie might pop out and speak for him.

'Spit it out, man.'

'You don't seem... miserable,' the man blurted out. 'Despite... my dad, you see, recently... he's been diagnosed with dementia.'

Fletch paused. 'Go on, lad.'

'He played amateur football until his forties, then coached until way past his retirement. Perhaps all that heading has had something to do with it.' He sighed. 'The upshot is, he's only in his early seventies, yet reckons his life is over.'

Fletch leant in.

'I came in here last week, sat for a while. This café has made me more positive about his situation.' His fists clenched. 'We got his diagnosis last month. None of us were expecting it. Dad, Mum and me, we assumed the mistakes he was making were simply part of getting older. The consultant told us straight, no build-up, no reassurance. I'll never forget Dad's face. He and Mum cried. The consultant gave us a leaflet, thrust a prescription into Dad's hand and ushered us out of the room, telling us to contact the Alzheimer's Society.'

Alex strained to listen and her jaw clenched as she imagined the anger the man must have felt.

Fletch's face reddened. He took a minute. 'I understand,' he said eventually. 'I used to believe there was nothing to look forward to until Tom gave me a job here, as if I were a burden with nothing to offer. I had all these plans. You see, I didn't retire at sixty-five, loved my job and had carried on working part-time.'

Fletch stared into the past for a moment. 'I was going to do charity work. I enjoyed driving and wanted to... that was it, get involved with transporting people to hospital or day care centres. But then this happened. A few months after finally leaving work, driving made me panicky. I left the engine running for over an hour once while I went shopping, left the keys in numerous times and once I found myself sitting at traffic lights and my mind went blank...'

The man hung on every word said by a different Fletch to the one Alex had seen so far.

'I wanted to play my guitar more often too, but...'

'My dad has always loved singing. We grew up with a karaoke machine, and he and Mum would go to sing-along tribute nights for their favourite bands. But his heart isn't in it now.'

Fletch put his hand on the man's shoulder. 'It is tough going but things get better, as long as you don't give up and sit in your chair all day. With this café, I've got a purpose again. It was just a matter of finding it. You should bring your dad in, son.'

'Can I take a selfie with you? To show him?'

Fletch crouched down and put his arm around the man.

Jade dropped into the seat next to Alex and slid over a book. On her finger was a silver ring with a black stone in the middle. '*Heartstopper*,' she announced. '*Volume One*. A friend lent me the books. The Netflix series has been a massive hit. It's a gentle introduction to graphic novels. After this you can try *Attack on Titan*. I've got the whole series myself.' She got up. 'Only then will you be qualified to criticise the type of book I love.'

Alex studied the novel and then her phone, a choice between taking up a reading challenge or posting another disingenuous Instagram story? Alex opened the book and briefly admired a sketch on a piece of paper used as a bookmark, drawn with biro, of a girl with spiky hair asleep on a school desk. She continued reading the book on her last fifteen-minute break. A thin, tired-looking teenage girl, whose anorak had holes in, was eking out a Coke in the corner. Alex went over and gave her the muffin she'd been about to eat, despite the apple and cinnamon smelling so good. Her dad never used to believe in pocket money, perhaps this teenager had a parent like that.

'I can't afford this,' said the girl.

'It goes out of date tonight. We'd only throw it away.' Alex shrugged. 'I can't bear to see waste.'

When she sat down again, at her own table, Fletch hovered at Alex's side, his magnified eyes staring at her.

Alex pointed to her badge. 'I work here.'

'I know that, lass.' Fletch jerked his head to the girl. 'Kind gesture. How many kids of your own have you got?'

'None.'

He rubbed his forehead. 'Sorry, I'm always asking questions I shouldn't.'

Crap. She'd almost forgotten. 'It doesn't matter,' she mumbled.

She nipped to the toilet, but her period was still late. Waiting for anxiety to arrive, she rubbed a hand over her stomach. Since she'd lost her muse, she'd felt a vacuum inside. A large hole existed that used to be full of hate-driven inspiration. Had Mother Nature filled that gap with something far more life-affirming?

Fletch had finished his shift and left when she came back out. Jade pulled on her coat and said goodnight to Captain Beaky, making kissing noises at him. He perked up, having become quieter since the café had emptied. It couldn't have been much fun for him, alone every night, downstairs, in his cage. Mum would have insisted on sleeping in one of the chairs, to keep him company.

Alex rushed upstairs and came back, out of breath, catching up with Jade who was outside the front, unlocking her bicycle. Alex thrust the copy of *Glamour Puss* into Jade's hands.

'Checkmate,' she called over her shoulder as she went back inside.

10

Jade gave a big yawn as the breakfast rush eased. Alex never did understand why people got tongue piercings. Alex had muddled through the morning, the first day of June, her third in the café. She'd spilt drinks as she carried them on trays and dropped a croissant onto the floor. Jade clearly relished telling her neither Reenie nor Fletch had ever done that. Yet, she gave her a tip on the best way to hold the tongs; she was as patient as Tom when it came to mistakes. One of the chefs had dropped a whole salmon on the floor – money wasted – and Alex had waited for Tom to let rip like the kitchen managers did on reality programmes. Instead, through the hatch, she saw him pat the mortified chef's back and explain that only yesterday he'd dropped a glass himself.

Alex leant against the wall, scribbling down writing notes, when a group of German tourists entered the café. Reenie headed over and complimented the dreadlocks of a man in a T-shirt with a palm tree on the front. Jade nudged Alex and pointed to tables that needed clearing. Alex nudged Jade back and pointed to an old receipt on the counter, next to the till. A doodled girl stared out from it with large eyes and long black hair, drawn in clumps not strands. She held a spear and bore a fearsome expression.

'I'm not the only one who enjoys putting pen to paper.' Alex's eyes narrowed. 'Cool illustration, a bit like the bookmark in that *Heartstopper* novel.'

Jade shoved the receipt into her apron pocket. Alex made her way out from behind the counter. Guttural German accents took her back to the book signing in Hamburg and the amazing apple strudel she'd treated herself to afterwards.

'Did you drink Rauchbier, our smoked beer?' the man with dreadlocks asked Reenie.

'No but I tasted black bread... Schwarzbrot. It tasted more like cardboard.' She crossed her arms under her bosom as wheezes of laughter escaped her chest.

'Like your floppy white bread,' he replied, humour softening his German accent. 'But I am happy to risk a couple of slices. I would like a ham and cheese sandwich.'

'I had ham for breakfast when I lived there,' said Reenie. 'Chinken?'

'*Ja, Schinken*. We eat a lot of it.'

As she stacked plates and cups onto a tray, careful not to break her nails, Alex listened in. Reenie had done an exchange at school, in the eighties, near the Black Forest. She talked of the photos in her old albums of the Triberg waterfalls.

'I'd get muddled up with the words *München* and *Mönch*,' she recalled. 'Every time someone talked about going to Munich I prepared to see a monk.'

While the customers talked about Bavaria's medieval castles and baroque churches, Reenie took the group's orders.

Half past eleven approached and Alex took her break. A twinge of pain indicated how her back was unused to her standing on her feet for so long, tangible proof that she'd spent the morning productively. In a job like this she got to see the results of her efforts, such as customers enjoying food or a clean table, unlike a day as an author where she simply filled a screen with words, which – certainly during the first draft – weren't always that good. Alex sipped her coffee and bit into a slice of tiffin, having eaten more carbs in the last few days than the whole of the last three years. She'd needed them after an email from Miranda, already asking how the rewrite was going. Also one from the bank had arrived, to tell Alex what they'd told her before, in letters as well. If she defaulted on another mortgage payment, they'd point her to independent debt advice, and if there was no realistic payment plan, and she couldn't sell the apartment, they'd be forced to begin repossession proceedings.

Repossession. Losing her home. Alex bent her head and stared at the floor, pushing down a surge of panic.

Reenie delivered the sandwich, then a full English breakfast and two bowls of cereal. One woman looked at her friends' plates and then back at hers.

'Everything okay?' asked Tom, who'd been talking to Captain Beaky. He flicked a tea towel over his shoulder.

'*Wunderbar,*' the young man said.

'I didn't order the full English breakfast,' said the woman, 'but I've never tried a hash brown. It looks delicious.'

'The rest of our orders are perfect,' said one of the others. '*Danke,* Reenie.'

'*Bitte,*' she said and clasped her hands together. Fiddling with her cat-eye glasses, she joined Alex at her table. 'The German word for "you're welcome" came to me straight away.'

Alex didn't know what to say. Perhaps nothing was best. Or *congratulations.* But was that patronising? Before she could answer, Reenie gave a big sigh.

'Whereas I don't even know what I had for dinner last night. I can't chat in the evening about my day with Kay and Cliff. The details are gone. I used to love mulling over everything my clients told me, and it means things have changed with my friends because when we meet up for a catch-up...' She shuffled her arms under her bosom.

In that moment Alex longed to be in a nightclub dancing until her feet hurt, being blinded by strobe lighting, and jostled by other revellers, because anything would be easier than not knowing how to make Reenie feel better, including blagging her way through a chat about *Love Island* and N-Dubz.

'But I still keep myself busy, living new experiences. I know these short-term memories will be stored somewhere and that's comforting, despite the fact I can't get to them. Like a favourite book that gave a lot of pleasure and is kept on the shelf, even though its owner may never reread it...'

The man with dreadlocks called Reenie over, and talked more about the Black Forest. Reenie described a wooden cuckoo clock she'd bought on her exchange. She struggled for a moment and then called it a cuckoo wall watch, but the Germans understood. Alex noted how the word 'cuckoo' was onomatopoeic, sounding like the noise that bird made. Another example was the word 'cliché', Miranda had taken great pleasure in once explaining. In the 1800s, a French printer created a plate bearing common sayings, so that they wouldn't have to be constantly rewritten. The noise the plate made when printing the words sounded like *cliché*. *Cliché, cliché, cliché*. Being an author was all about the detail. However, Miranda reckoned the most important thing was being able to walk in the shoes of others. Alex googled the word 'dementia'.

She imagined Reenie's day, waking up with no memory of the evening before, going downstairs to make breakfast knowing that some day in the future, she'd never know whether she'd already eaten or not; recognising familiar faces, most of the time, but dreading the day that she couldn't – and going to bed not always quite sure how she'd spent the last twenty-four hours. Alex gave a shudder and tapped into Instagram and the feed of a trendy young band she'd been doing her best to like.

When the German group finished, they left a tip and each bent down to give Reenie a hug. Outside, they took photos in front of the café, pointing to the red-lettered name above the window. Alex put her empty cup up to the counter. Jade gave another yawn.

'You ought to go to bed earlier,' said Alex.

'I did but... couldn't drop off.'

'On YouTube, I suppose?' Like Alex's string of young lovers who'd scroll until three in the morning.

'No, I was read... I mean... it was too hot. Manchester might have another heatwave this summer.'

Alex smirked. 'Did you enjoy spending the night with Tabitha Stallion?'

'I've no idea who she is and my girlfriend wouldn't approve of a one-night stand,' said Jade, suddenly interested in the till roll.

'Admit it! You loved *Glamour Puss* as much as your great-aunt.' Alex readjusted her claw hair clip as a heady sensation ran through her veins.

'Okay,' muttered Jade, with the look of a child who'd been caught reading after lights out. 'Granted, it's a page-turner, but I wasn't so taken with the ending.'

Alex stopped fiddling with her hair clip. 'You read the whole thing in one sitting?'

Jade concluded it was an easy read, that Tabitha's journey deftly hooked readers in. Her transforming from country girl to city starlet, along with how she returned to her hometown and was an absolute bitch to the former school bullies, had kept Jade engaged. 'The way she stood up to her old middle-aged boyfriend, that cattle herder, Maverick, who'd kept her in the shadows before and abused her youthful innocence was brilliant.' Jade hadn't seen the plot twist coming, about her car accident caused by Maverick taking revenge, and Tabitha ending up disfigured in hospital, facing a jail term because he made it look as if she'd driven dangerously and killed that pedestrian.

'But instead of fighting back, she gave up, went back to being a wallflower,' said Jade, 'and let that smarmy old surgeon treat her like a fifties housewife, submitting to his every whim. Tabitha deserves a better ending than moving in with that creep while on bail.'

'Didn't you read the blurb on the book's back cover first?'

'Nah. Dived straight in.'

'What about the pages after the last chapter?'

'No offence, Alex, but I pushed the book to one side pretty quickly after a last chapter like that, where the main character simply ends up where she began, her life being controlled by a misogynist dickhead. I mean, what's the point?'

'Then you missed finding out that my second book, *Wicked Ex*, is actually a sequel.'

Jade's face lit up before she could hide it.

'There's a reason Tabitha befriends – and ultimately seduces – a much older man who's still one of the most skilled plastic surgeons in the whole of Los Angeles,' continued Alex. 'She hasn't quite finished with Maverick.' Maverick was Simon's nickname from high school; friends reckoned he could be Tom Cruise's double. The character was handsome, charming – Alex had still been trying to win Simon back at that stage.

* * *

Later that evening, finding herself stuck in front of the laptop, on Hope's sofa, staring at the empty page of the new rewritten chapter one, with a packet of Hope's biscuits for company, Alex picked up *Heartstopper* again and soon found she'd read almost half of it.

She'd not been in long, after seeing the doctor, the private one she used for emergencies. A luxury she'd have to give up. The doctor had checked her blood pressure and asked her a whole range of questions about symptoms such as headaches and mood swings, poor sleep patterns too. Simon's sister had struggled with all of those during the first trimester of her pregnancy. As for the anxiety, that was nothing new, Alex's career was stressful. The doctor asked her to fill a urine bottle and took a blood sample, added that a natural pregnancy at forty-three wasn't common, yet wasn't impossible. The term 'geriatric mother' made Alex wince. Miranda's cousin had had a baby last year; she'd been thirty-eight, and, as a columnist for the local paper, had lambasted the hospital for making her feel ancient. Miranda would roll her eyes and talk about how her cousin now ate picnics in the park instead of dining in bistros, and loved parties in soft-play areas instead of five-star hotels. Alex imagined how a baby might turn back time to the happier years when she had a family unit with a husband and a mother, both of whom loved her.

Her phone pinged. Alex braced herself but it was only a Facebook message from Hope.

Arrived in Bangkok. Concrete and crowds everywhere. About to risk my life in a tuk-tuk. Working at Wrong Order Café can't be more challenging than that.

Alex sent back:

Want to bet?

The night-time photo Hope had attached was of her and Leah standing in front of a neon-lit shopfront, a selfie of them with their arms entwined around each other.

Alex went into Hope's bedroom, opened the wardrobe and stood in front of the mirror hidden away on the inside of the scratched door. Even though drinks splashed and the contents of dirty plates stained, she'd worn a silk blouse tucked into designer jeans for her work day, with her usual foundation loaded with retinol and her lips overdrawn with red pencil. As seconds passed, her reflection's posture became stooped, the eyes dulled as the truth stared back.

One failing career. No significant other. A home under threat. The real possibility of single motherhood.

Alex felt like that little girl jumping off the swimming pool's edge, realising too late that there was no one to catch her.

Her phone pinged again.

Fancy dinner upstairs, with me and my better half? Tom

11

Alex climbed up one floor, without her usual leaving home puff of perfume and re-powdered nose. She knocked on a door, wooden and scratched like Hope's. A floorboard the other side of the door creaked as it opened. A loud, wet raspberry announced her arrival.

'This is Alex. Aleeexx,' Tom articulated, speaking to his left shoulder. 'Come on in, Alex. I hope you like risotto.'

'*Captain Beaky*'s your better half? Doesn't he stay in the staffroom overnight?'

'Downstairs? On his own?' asked Tom in an incredulous tone, as if she'd suggested they roast the parrot for dinner.

'I assumed... his job is to attract customers, right, rather than being a pet?'

'First and foremost, he's my boy,' said Tom as he closed the door behind her. 'I only keep him caged up during the day because I can't keep an eye on him, and he loves being among the hustle and bustle. He's the reason I installed the jukebox. As for up here, he's only caged if I'm in the shower, or asleep – I can't risk him settling next to me in bed, I might accidentally crush him.'

Fighting down the sense of nausea that resurfaced due to the aroma of garlic and lemon, Alex surveyed the flat. It had a similar layout to Hope's. Yet it was free of clutter, with clear surfaces and cord concealers around wiring. A play stand stood in the far right corner, made up of a perch with a bowl at each end, one filled with water. A little wooden ladder descended on the right, down to a high-edged tray to catch food bits and droppings. A bird swing hung on the left, next to the ladder. Tom approached the stand as the parrot rubbed his beak against his long fringe, chewing the ends, before hopping off.

'Doesn't he mess everywhere?'

Tom took two wine glasses out of a cupboard in the kitchen. He raised one to Alex and she nodded. 'Not often. Some parrots relieve themselves every fifteen minutes but George trained Captain Beaky. Apparently George would say "poop"...' He'd said the word quietly and smiled at Alex '...before allowing him out of the cage, or say it and hold him over the bin. These days such a process isn't recommended as it can lead to problems with birds only doing it on command, but Captain Beaky has never had an issue with that. It made sense to stick with the same system, as long as he's happy.' He stopped pouring wine as the parrot began plucking at its feathers. Tom frowned and picked up a discarded broccoli head from a chopping board. He hurried over to the play stand, bit off a small bit of the vegetable and made appreciative noises. Captain Beaky tried to swipe the small green floret but Tom ate another small bit and made more pleasurable sounds. The parrot jumped onto his wrist and Tom allowed him to peck at the vegetable, before he dropped it into the food dish. The parrot jumped onto that end of the perch and continued eating.

'Everything okay?' asked Alex.

'Captain Beaky doesn't pluck his feathers often these days. It's a sign of stress. I should know better than to mention his previous owner by name. It still upsets him.'

Simon didn't like birds in his garden, said their droppings ruined the aesthetic and their song destroyed the calm. He would never harm a living thing – he'd moan about slugs but couldn't bring himself to put down salt – however he did buy an ultrasonic repeller to put off the birds. Alex turned a blind eye when Mum swapped its battery for a dud one.

Alex sat down and studied the shelves of neatly lined-up books, and the top-of-the-range music system next to a collection of CDs made up of Dean Martin, Nat King Cole, Billie Holiday...

'The parrot must like you cooking – the noises, the smells, like in the café.'

Wearing mismatched socks, one green, one red, Tom strode over and handed her a glass.

'No. He knows not to come into the kitchen area. Following advice at the rescue centre I did a lot of research before letting him fly around. I threw out my Teflon pans, the coating is dangerous to birds when heated. I also avoid candles and aerosols, hide medicines and vitamins, and I keep the toilet seat down to avoid risk of drowning. I've covered most of the visible wiring and I fitted blinds so that he didn't fly into the glass. When my radiators are on in the winter I make sure he stays away...'

'He sounds high maintenance.' The best thing about splitting from Simon was that she only had her own needs to consider. In the early months she missed the routine of going to bed with him at eleven – he insisted on eight hours' sleep – and making sure he never ran out of his favourite porridge oats with added blueberry flakes in the cupboard. Her string of young boyfriends showed how picky Simon had been, with their propensity to stay up all hours and ability to eat anything for breakfast, even old takeout.

'Nah, he's good company. George must have been a gamer,

like me, because when I'm playing and a character dies, Captain Beaky bobs up and down and cackles. He loves *Match of the Day*, rocking from side to side when the theme music comes on, shouting "Balls" at the screen.' Tom clinked her glass. 'It's very cathartic living with someone who can get away with saying whatever they want.'

'Like swearing at me when I asked who's a pretty...'

Captain Beaky looked up from his snack.

'Would you like it if I asked who's a pretty girl? There's much more to Captain Beaky than his striking good looks.'

Captain Beaky wasn't so unlike her agent, Miranda. 'Imagine how much easier life would be if we all said what we were really thinking.'

Tom said he didn't think Reenie or Fletch would completely agree as sometimes they couldn't help sounding insulting or hurtful. 'Day by day, they're losing social niceties, the subtleties of language everyone else uses automatically. A couple of weeks ago, in front of everyone, Fletch commented on a breakout of spots on Jade's cheeks, told her to stop eating chocolate. He couldn't understand why she looked upset.'

Reenie had called Alex's nails stubby and Fletch assumed she had children, but then receiving thoughtless or critical comments from strangers was part of her job.

'Dad's got no filter now.' Tom ran a finger around the rim of his glass. 'When he started to forget Mum had died, I'd bring up the funeral but soon realised I needed to find a kinder way of handling her not being around any more. If it hits Dad that she's actually dead, he'll say how he had nothing left to live for when she passed – even though he still had me.'

'That must be hard to hear.'

'I tell myself that's not the dad who brought me up talking, although the day after Mum died, I knew I'd need to be strong.'

'Aged ten?'

'I'd never heard anyone cry like that, not even in the school playground. Dad always had my back and couldn't have been more loving, more encouraging, however hopeless he felt inside. But once you've seen pain like that you can't ever forget it.'

'My dad couldn't have been more different.'

'How so?'

Alex sipped her wine and it came out, how, more than once, her father had said what a disappointment it had been not to have a son. He'd dress his insult up, say it was only because he worried more about a daughter and whether she'd find a man to take care of her. As she talked, Tom focused completely on her in a way her dad never had. Her dad never had a filter either, however *his* thoughtless comments were made on purpose. After her divorce and Mum's death, Alex lost some of her social niceties. Perhaps being a mother would bring them back again. She placed a hand on her stomach. Tom got up to put cheesy bread in the oven and set the table. He took the wine bottle over to her.

'Sorry to be difficult,' she said, 'I really don't fancy wine after all. Could I have water?'

Did Alex just turn down alcohol out of concern for another person? Miranda wouldn't have approved of a sniff of compassion. She once said Alex was a breath of fresh air, her only author who didn't require hand-holding. Others suffered a crisis of confidence down the phone, if a book didn't get a deal or an editor wanted big changes making to a story. Whereas Alex would simply digest the news, then work with Miranda to plot their next move, like one of the hardened characters out of her stories, such as Silvian Glass, the scheming love interest from her last novel.

Alex relished the first home-cooked meal she'd eaten in a very long time. Afterwards, they settled on the sofa and Tom put on a

CD. She dodged out of the way as Captain Beaky flew over and nestled on his lap. Alex reached out to touch the parrot's back but he went to peck at her finger.

'It takes him a while to get used to new people, that's all.'

'Not bothered,' she said, trying not to show disappointment on her face. She consulted her watch. 'In fact I'd better—'

'Don't leave yet. Humour me, Alex. As a complete amateur, I've had an idea about your next novel.'

A fan who thought they could write a book? God help us. But then Alex inwardly chided herself. She'd started off as a reader, and her fans could certainly be clever enough to write, going by their well-thought-out reviews.

She had mulled over her and Tom's last conversation about her writing, and how his café had changed its name and style but still kept customers satisfied. *Heartstopper* had also made her consider a new direction. Unlike her blockbusters it was a small story. It dealt with big issues and the TV series had achieved huge viewing figures, but essentially it was an emotional journey about a group of teenagers in a high school. Alex had kept all connections with people at a distance these last few years, real and fictional, and her books focused on action rather than contemplation. If her friends on the page suffered a bereavement she swiftly made them take revenge. If their self-esteem had tumbled, she gave them plastic surgery, a new wardrobe or a pistol. *Could she really focus on their depths instead?* The possibility had fired her up inside, in a way writing hadn't for the longest time.

Captain Beaky caught her attention, his head swaying ever so slightly, to notes of 'Beyond the Sea'. Tom whistled along.

'Go ahead,' she said.

'I used to love *Dallas* as a young teenager, in the eighties,' said Tom. 'The wealth and extravagance, the storylines to match... but back then anything felt possible. I dreamt of one day being Bobby

Ewing, owning a big house, with money rolling in. People hadn't just been through as difficult a time as the last few years, with the world's health, war, living costs and climate in crisis. Full-on escapism like that won't ever lose its popularity, but perhaps some readers might like a character they can relate to, these days, a more grounded plot and setting that offers them hope about their own situation.'

'I've been thinking along those lines myself. You don't want to write it for me, do you?' she joked.

Tom yanked a handkerchief out of his trouser pocket and sneezed loudly. Alex jumped as Captain Beaky did the same thing immediately afterwards, mimicking the noise.

'No thanks,' he said and blew his nose. 'Three thousand words were hard enough.'

'What do you mean?'

'Dessert?' He went to get up.

'Tom?'

Ears red, he sat down again. 'Back in March I wrote a short story, for a newspaper competition. Every now and then Norm insisted I should have been an author; he had a memory of a parents' evening where the teacher raved about my writing. He mentioned it again, out of the blue, and I thought why not? Anything to make him happy.'

Often people asked Alex to critique their work, as if she had nothing better to do, as if writing novels to meet a publisher's deadlines was more like a hobby. She'd refuse point blank, politely of course, explain her workload, point them to literary consultancies. But now and then if someone let slip they'd put pen to paper, aghast at showing it to anyone, she'd recognise that air of low confidence and insist on taking a look.

'Go and get it.'

'Good lord, no. I didn't even finish it and never sent it in. It's not very good.'

'How about I decide that?'

'Shut up!' said the parrot.

'Sorry. That's his way of saying he's tired. He often sleeps on my lap, but if I've got guests or the television has played loudly all evening, it's too much. I'll pop him into his cage, in the spare room. It's dark in there. Then, after dessert, I must prepare for tomorrow. My ad went up on a couple of recruitment websites. I've already got an interview for someone to replace you...'

His voice petered out and she forced herself not to look at him, avoiding the hopeful look she knew he'd be wearing, him worried about Hope potentially losing her job and wanting to change Alex's mind about leaving. But Alex couldn't worry about that. She'd have given the job a week, longer than some might have.

'No dessert for me, thanks,' she said, her appetite having disappeared, due to thoughts about Hope and Tom's news about the interview, which created a hollow feeling she couldn't explain. Captain Beaky was rude, Jade offhand, customers spilt drinks and stacking the dishwasher ruined her nails.

'And first get that story.' Alex went to take out her phone, but was suddenly overwhelmed by a wave of sickness and covered her mouth with her hand, until it passed. Tom came back holding a sheaf of papers to his chest; they were covered in longhand. How quaint. She reached out and waved her hand. With a sigh, he passed them over. Alex read and he cleared the dishes and washed up. She reread it while he dried crockery and filled the kettle.

'Terrible, isn't it?' He placed two coffees and a plate of biscuits on the solid wood table in front of the sofa, its shape that of an upside down drum.

She put a finger to her lips as she finished the last paragraph for the second time, before tossing the papers onto the table.

'It's a typical story by a beginner writer – autobiographical in the sense that it's set in your workplace. Every writer thinks their personal story is the most meaningful. The main character of my first novel worked in a bank. Miranda, my agent, got me to change it, said if you based anything on a life you knew well, it made the writing lazy because you weren't using your imagination.'

'Told you it was rubbish,' he said in a bright voice. He reached forwards, for the plate, but she took his arm, excitement flickering inside her stomach.

'From the first paragraph I couldn't put it down. A man and a woman meet randomly in a Buddhist centre, each there to seek momentary refuge from a life that needs turning around... then traumatic events take place and lead them to let slip their deepest secrets to each other, believing they will never meet again... I already want to read a novel of this.'

'You're just being nice, right?' He rubbed the back of his neck.

'Do I seem like someone who flatters people if they don't deserve it?' She picked up the pages again. 'How did you imagine the story panning out?' she asked. 'No story, short or long, is truly over when you write "The End". As the author or reader you always continue it in your head. I read *Romeo and Juliet* at school and imagined a fantasy sequel set in the afterlife, where they met up again and both lived happily ever after. I'd plot it in bed every night, scene by scene. I do that with my own books, before they are complete.' She picked up one of the mugs.

'My brain works like that in bed sometimes too, except it's about work and how I can further the café's objective of spreading awareness of dementia.'

Mid sip, Alex swallowed her drink the wrong way.

'What?' he asked.

'Nothing.' She wiped her mouth as the coughing eased.

'Alex?'

'Okay... you're an entrepreneur, your main aim is to turn a tidy profit. Reenie and Fletch, on paper, are just free help. Marketing sound bites are all well and good but you don't need to give me your business spiel in private.'

'Free? Who told you that? Reenie and Fletch may have challenges but they still deserve respect.'

Wait. How had he turned it around and stolen her line?

'Some might think that they don't do the job properly, so why would you pay them?'

'Their work is perfect. They give the place a warm-hearted ambiance that wouldn't exist if they left. They earn no less than Jade or Yash. I've had to be quite firm with both Reenie and Fletch about that.'

An altruistic business person? Alex hadn't met one of them in publishing or banking. She felt like a bird that used the moon and stars to navigate, knocked off course by an unexpected burst of light pollution.

He squeezed her arm. 'It's okay,' he said, gently. 'People who think the worst have usually been through a difficult time and their trust has gone.'

She made her excuses and hurried into the bathroom, closing the door behind her. Alex sat on the edge of the bath and pressed her fingers against her eyes. It took five minutes to gather herself. Back in the living room, she finished her coffee and read Tom's story once more. The male protagonist owned a coffee shop that came under threat when a construction team turned up to convert the empty building next door into a trendy brunch place... The property developer in charge was the female lead, the woman he'd confided in at the Buddhist centre. Alex loved the way Tom's short story ended, with them coming face to face, having hoped never to see each other again.

'If it carried on, the story would see a turbulent journey of the two main characters blackmailing each other with their secrets,' he said, 'him to see her development project closed down, her to push it through. However they'd fall in love and—'

'Write me a synopsis of the whole story. Five hundred words, no more, no less. Wrong Order Café is closed on a Monday... you could get it done for then and we'll meet up to talk through your ideas.'

'I appreciate the interest, but what's the point?'

She clutched her hands together. 'Miranda wanted me to add the old sparkle to my current project but the spark inside me, the one I need to write my best... I've felt it again, these last few days, but only when I consider working on something different. This is it. A heart-warming, funny, yet emotional romance, a smaller story in terms of setting, but one that nevertheless packs a punch, with alternating chapters, one written from the point of view of the man, the other of the woman. And Miranda does love a dramatic opening.' The 1 July deadline could be met, with its remit of handing in unputdownable writing, but not with the story her agent was expecting. 'Four weeks. Three chapters.' She paused. 'And two authors. You could be published, Tom. I get a feeling it's a dream of yours too, not just your dad's.'

Tom's jaw dropped.

12

It was as if the whole of Manchester had decided the weekend started first thing Friday morning. Jade was rostered on, Yash too, and part-timer Pip. For Alex, the café lacked a personal vibe without Reenie, who'd cut straight in to conversations with a comment on beauty or fashion, or Fletch, who'd talk about the current jukebox tune if a guitar was playing, or with tourists about hotels and his tales from the front desk. Tom was right about what they brought to the business. However, Captain Beaky was on his usual form. Only to prevent waste, Alex fed him a grape left on the plate of a customer, through the bars. She tried to get him to say, *Thank you, Alex*. Five minutes of her life she'd never get back. He blew raspberries at a delighted toddler, and in perfect Robert de Niro style, kept asking a couple at the table next to him, 'You talkin' to me?'

Eleven thirty arrived and Alex took her break in the staffroom; she needed the quiet. Norm had arrived at eleven and Tom was in there with him, on the red sofa, going through photo albums. Norm didn't look up when Alex walked in. His hand held Tom's and shook slightly.

'Dad, this is Alex.'

Hooded eyes, beneath a forehead mapped with deep lines, inspected her.

'Ginny know you're cheating? You always did have an eye for glamorous lasses,' he said, a twinkle in his eye.

'Dad, this is an employee, Alex, she's working in the café for a few days.' He lowered his voice and turned to her. 'Ginny is an old girlfriend; we dated for over seven years. Dad's convinced we got married.' Tom's phone rang. He shot Alex a hopeful look and walked over to the window mural, at the back, as he talked to the caller.

Crap. Reenie and Fletch were easy to talk to, still aware, still able, but what would Alex say to Norm? What if he got angry or upset, or wanted to leave the staffroom?

Norm looked her way. His mouth dropped. 'She was a fine-looking lass like you. Kind too. I should have told her the moon is beautiful.'

Tom put a hand over the phone. 'I need to check something in the kitchen. One of the chefs is having problems with his land-lord and he was on the phone to him when Dad arrived.'

'Understood. Disciplining staff is important; they shouldn't bring personal problems to work.'

Tom looked confused. 'No. I've got some advice to pass on. I rang a regular supplier, last night – his sister works at the council and he's found out a bit about tenants' rights. Will you be all right for a few minutes, with Dad?' He reassured Norm he wouldn't be long and left.

Alex hesitated before sitting down on the sofa next to the old man. 'Who should you have told the moon is beautiful?' she asked. 'Were you talking about Ginny?'

'No.' He shook his head vehemently.

She picked up the album and put it on her lap. The open page showed a snap of a boy in shorts and a T-shirt, with salted-caramel hair, chocolate eyes. He sat on a Raleigh bike that had a birthday balloon attached to the handles.

'Tom,' she said and pointed to the photo.

Norm's glasses had slipped down his nose and gently Alex pushed them back up, trying to imagine the man who used to run this café, the man who'd been there for his young son, despite his fractured, widowed heart. Her eyes dropped to his shaking hand, the prominent veins, the raggedy brown age spots, a mosaic representing a long life led. She turned the page of the album to a photo of a woman in her thirties, with Tom's strong nose and freckles, wearing a boa and a twenties flapper dress in front of a group of people done up in fancy dress. A young Tom stood in front of her in a cowboy outfit; her gloved hands rested on his shoulders. Alex lifted the album for Norm to see but the beech cabinet topped with refreshments had caught his attention. Alex fetched the tin of biscuits and removed the lid, offered him one, but Norm didn't respond. So she poured a glass half full of water and added cordial, sat next to him again, and a shaking hand reached out. Gently, she helped guide the glass to his lips, not sure how much to tilt it or how much he could drink at a time. He downed it in one go, Alex praying he wouldn't choke.

'That hit the spot,' he said to the room and gave a big grin.

She pulled a tissue out of her pocket and wiped his mouth, and was about to turn on the television when Norm became agitated, pulling at his slacks. *When was Tom going to get back?* Norm stood up, with an unsteady manner. She slipped her arm through his but he moved away and glared, pulling at his trousers once more. He needed the toilet. *What was she supposed to do?* She couldn't leave him alone, so in a panic Alex went to open the staffroom door, to call for Jade or Yash, when it opened and Tom hurried in.

'Sorry, Alex. I just needed to—'

'Your dad needs the toilet. I didn't know what to do. He doesn't know me, and...'

Tom headed straight over and led Norm to the disabled toilet at the back, rubbing his dad's back. She could have done that but what if he needed help undressing and cleaning himself afterwards? Mum had needed personal care and had hated every minute, but Alex hadn't minded; she loved her. But a pensioner she barely knew? The old Norm would, no doubt, have been equally mortified at the prospect. It was midday now and the end of her break was well overdue, but she wanted to wait, check he was okay; she felt responsible, somehow, for the upset.

'Sorry,' she said, when Tom and Norm finally emerged. 'I felt pretty useless. I'll get back now and...'

'Alex,' he said softly, 'the others are managing, it's the pre-lunch lull. Don't apologise. Every stage of this illness takes a while to get used to. I never feel I'm getting it right.' He switched on the radio. Smooth FM. 'Come on, Dad,' he said, and held his hands, swinging them to and fro in time to the music, the scene emphasising Tom's irrepressible light-hearted attitude. Norm's eyes brightened and he moved his feet side to side. A ballad came on.

'I should have told her the moon is beautiful,' he said, shoulders slumped, feet moving more slowly.

'Who?' pressed Alex, but Norm had zoned out again.

Tom continued to swing Norm's arms a little higher. 'He's been fixated on this for months.'

'It's not this Ginny?'

'No. She and Dad never really got on. He never trusted anyone who didn't like coffee. I hoped this moon thing might pass. It came out of nowhere, a bit like when he wanted to change the café's name. He's even cried about it. Captain Beaky's owner,

George, he developed a fixation about being adopted. It made him very sad and not even his brother could convince him otherwise. No one knew what triggered that either.'

'Yet this is quite specific, telling someone the moon is beautiful; it's a small detail.'

Small details so often hid a bigger picture. Like the receipt in Simon's wallet; she'd needed cash to pay the window cleaner and Si was out in the garden digging up weeds. It was for a bunch of roses, one week before. He'd always told Alex he preferred seeing flowers growing and had never bought her a bouquet during their twenty years together.

Alex headed back into the café, midday sunshine streaming through the windows. She took the order from a young woman tapping on her phone, arm through a Chanel handbag.

'Someone's tired today,' said Jade, as she set about making the customer's mocha coffee and Alex suppressed a yawn.

'Late night planning my next novel,' she replied, as a sizzling noise came through the hatch.

'You didn't spend the early hours with *Heartstopper*'s Charlie and Nick?'

'Early enough. They kept me company during my breakfast.'

'Still think graphic novels aren't proper reading?' Jade put the mocha on the counter.

Alex lifted one of Tom's popular chocolate orange scones onto a plate. 'They are nothing like reading normal books that don't have pictures.'

Jade's face tightened.

'No, it's a whole different experience and... I loved it.'

'Really?' She'd never smiled at Alex like that before.

'Even though the setting, the plot and characters are visual, you still use your imagination and simply take all of those things to the next level. Because of that I quickly formed an emotional connection to the main characters, totally investing in them from the first few pages.'

Jade passed her a tray. 'I'll bring in the other volumes then.'

Alex had her faults. Miranda would happily point them out. Her propensity to email too often. A competitive edge that made it difficult for her to gain the support of other authors. But she'd always been able to admit when she was wrong and, more often than not, that left her with an advantage, as it threw people off balance – unless, like Jade, they had that skill as well.

'I downloaded *Wicked Ex* onto my Kindle last night. Halfway through, great sequel,' said Jade, not meeting Alex's eye. 'Crushing big time on Tabitha, don't tell my girlfriend.'

A tattoo of a cherry blossom stood out on Jade's neck. Alex wasn't a fan of inked skin, but this design was crisp, realistic, yet delicate with the pink colour. Alex took the scone over to the woman with the designer handbag. She had her phone at the ready but her face fell when she saw the plate.

'That's what I ordered,' said the woman.

'Correct.'

'But this place is called Wrong Order Café. I've primed my followers on Insta, they're waiting for the next instalment of my story, messaging with their guesses of what I receive instead of the scone.' She gave Alex a belligerent look. 'Your café's title is false advertising; I should report it.'

'The staff with dementia don't work on a Friday,' said Alex politely.

The woman beckoned with her finger and Alex bent down. 'Couldn't you pretend to have it? Just for a short video?' she whispered.

Alex's eyes narrowed. She couldn't even admire the pure gall of the customer. 'Absolutely not; that really would be an act Advertising Standards wouldn't approve of.'

'I won't tell if you won't,' she said and winked.

'I'm sorry, no can do, but you see our parrot over there?' She pointed to the cage. 'Bless his heart, he's a real character, and oh so polite. Your followers would love him. Do go over and film him talking. Perhaps pay him a compliment, like saying "Who's a pretty boy?"'

An uncomfortable sensation nestled in her chest and Alex walked away. Not everything was as it seemed on social media, she knew that better than anyone else lately. Her last book signing wasn't well attended, but a skilful photo implied there'd hardly been room to sit; the bookshop's team, including the cleaners, inadvertently helped. Her mum once talked of how clever mockingbirds were, mimicking the call of other species to keep them away, by making their own territory sound overpopulated. It wasn't so different to Alex's tactics with her media platforms, carefully engineering them to give her a strong image.

* * *

At four o'clock a young man arrived for his interview with Tom. Alex went into the staffroom. Norm had nodded off on Tom's shoulder, empty plates in front of both of them, the blanket with tassels and beads on their laps.

'I know it's not part of your job, but would you mind staying with him for the next half-hour?' asked Tom. 'He's only just dropped off and went to the toilet about ten minutes ago.' He fiddled with one of the tassels. 'One last shot... is there any way you'd consider staying on? Hope's more like a friend. She's going to be devastated if she comes back to find her life here packed up, even though she and I discussed the possibility that I'd have to take action if things didn't work out with you. I was given no notice about this trip; Hope understood the risks. Yet that doesn't make it easier and with any luck this candidate will be prepared to stay temporarily until she's back, but if I can't persuade him... perhaps we should warn her.'

Alex risk being asked again to pretend she'd got dementia? Spend the whole of June being reminded of her mortality? 'I'm sorry, Tom. This job isn't for me. And why worry Hope when she's enjoying the trip of a lifetime?' *Why admit to Hope that Alex had let her down?*

Tom mentioned how the fidget blanket helped Norm settle, and they swapped places, Alex feeling restless too, as she sat next to Norm. The lucky diamond charm she'd given Hope sprang to mind, along with her mum's comment about how keeping promises was far more important than keeping wealth. After Tom left, Alex took out her phone and tried to come up with a title for her and Tom's book. He didn't know it yet – his laughter last night had proved that he thought her suggestion had been a joke – but she was deadly serious about them co-authoring. She could see it now, the two of them bouncing ideas off each other. If she were to be pregnant, sharing the workload would be invaluable. Alex. Pregnant. It would turn her world upside down.

A damp patch formed on her shoulder. Norm, dribbling. Alex would hate to end up like that. Gently, she nudged him, hoping he'd straighten up, but he woke with a jolt and blinked rapidly.

'Oh. Sorry. How about a biscuit?' she asked.

'You're a good girl. I do love shortbread.' His hand raised in the air, fingers moving as if looking for something. She fetched him a biscuit and he wolfed it down as if he hadn't had lunch. His fingers became restless again and for a while he fiddled with the blanket. He gave a long sigh. Alex paused before taking his hand in hers. She held it tight. He had a strong hand, one that would reach out in a swimming pool, a hand that would stay outstretched and catch you.

'I should have told her the moon is beautiful,' he said, in a raspy whisper. Frown lines disappearing due to a brief lucid moment, he stared her straight in the eyes. 'You'll help me, won't you? I can see you take it seriously.'

'Of course I will, Norm,' she found herself saying. 'Can you remember anything about her?'

His face crumpled, the focus gone, and he pulled away, reaching for the fidget blanket.

Alex yawned and rubbed her eyes. A day off. Imagine that. Being self-employed, the job never released its grip. The café had been busy all weekend. Tom couldn't understand why so many young-sters had come in on Saturday morning, talking about Instagram and asking Captain Beaky if he was a pretty boy. Her phone buzzed twice and she focused on the bedroom. Day six and none of the potted plants had died. On the bedside table lay the stack of Jade's *Heartstopper* novels. She'd finished the penultimate one at two in the morning.

She got up and drew the curtains open. A parliament of magpies strutted up and down in Stevenson Square, debating with each other among Monday commuters. As a species, it was misunderstood, so-called thieving magpies weren't actually attracted to shiny objects but repelled, hence farmers hanging CDs in their trees to scare them away. Simon once mumbled that Alex didn't understand him, didn't try. Like when his best friend, Mike, moved to Greece, Si suffered a low mood afterwards. Alex said it was only natural to miss him and feel a little envious. He said it wasn't that and tried to explain, but she'd cut him off, irritated. Perhaps she shouldn't have. She collapsed back onto the bed and picked up her phone. Two messages. The first from Miranda.

Deadline now less than four weeks away. How's it going?

It's going.

She pressed send.

Message two. From Hope. She'd attached a photo of soup with... tadpoles in?

Less than a month and I'll be back. I can't wait. How's it going?

What to say?

It's going.

She pressed send.

Before Alex moved out tomorrow evening, to go back to her flat in the glass tower in Deansgate, she'd take extra care to water the plants. Although a few wilted plants would be the least of Hope's problems, if she came back to find her belongings packed up and someone else living in her flat.

The phone flew to the end of the duvet and Alex closed her eyes, tempted to spend the whole day in bed. She'd lived the last week one day at a time, instead of thinking forwards to the next round of edits, next release, next blog tour – or reflecting on the last bad review, the last poorly attended signing. In Hope's modest flat she'd established a routine her glossy characters would have sneered at, taking a well-deserved hot shower after work, chilling with one of the herbal teas she'd found in the kitchen, cosying up on the sofa in front of decades-old TV sitcoms. Alex's own flat felt like a friend you had to live up to. She slept in expensive Egyptian cotton sheets and silk pyjamas, hung incomprehensible modern art on the walls, and installed brash statement lighting, a free-standing bathtub you couldn't lie down in and a sharp-edged, cold marble floor. Whereas Hope's little home, with its warm carpet, throw blankets and dimmed lighting, felt like a friend you could wear no make-up with, and share ugly crying.

Another buzz vibrated up the mattress. With a dramatic sigh she sat up and retrieved her mobile.

Breakfast at ours? Tom's synopsis is ready. Silly sod. Captain Beaky.

Her face smiled back at her from the phone's glass front. Re-energised, Alex washed and got dressed.

* * *

'Just in time,' said Tom as he answered the door, not dissimilar to a pirate with the edge of a tattoo visible underneath the arm of his T-shirt and a parrot sitting on his shoulder.

A loud wolf whistle rang into the corridor. She folded her arms at an unapologetic Captain Beaky, although the sound fitted with the seafaring theme, as legend had it that the wolf whistle originated from a boatswain's call during noisy storms. Yet the more likely truth was it came from shepherds warning each other about an approaching wolf. Truth could so easily be twisted into fake news. Alex knew that better than most.

Tom deposited the parrot at the play stand and indicated for Alex to sit at the table, in front of a basket of warm croissants. He carried over two plates of scrambled eggs on toast, then fetched slices of melon. He placed a slice in one of Captain Beaky's bowls.

'This is quite a spread,' said Alex.

'I treat myself on a Monday. It's the only day I truly get to myself, what with the café actually closed.'

'How do you normally spend it?'

'A quick stocktake in the morning, later my laundry, and I visit Dad in the afternoon. He's often tired after lunch but in the summer I try to get him in the garden and it's warmer after lunch.'

It didn't sound like a whole day to himself, to recover from a strenuous week. Working in the café took its toll – Alex had blisters on her feet, lower back pain and stiff shoulders. At least tomorrow her week was over. She'd miss a couple of hours in the morning, too; Tom had agreed to cover while she had her follow-up appointment at the doctor's. Not that she needed the result of a urine test. Her period still hadn't made an appearance. During the months preceding her debut release, she hadn't believed it would really happen, terrified the book might bomb or she'd become a laughing stock for thinking she had talent. The prospect of a spring baby brought concerns too, like sleepless nights, colic, like being a bad mother...

Tom unravelled her spiral of concern with news that the lad he'd interviewed would start on Wednesday. He'd wanted a permanent position but needed the money and was happy to work until Hope returned. Tom had snapped him up; he was overqualified if anything and used to run his own pop-up coffee shop until recently. Hospitality was struggling to recruit at the moment and because his pop-up was so new, he couldn't keep hold of the staff, who left as soon as a more stable position elsewhere came their way. They could pick and choose. 'We're lucky to have him; he's full of ideas. Thanks for staying this last week, it's appreciated. Keep in touch, won't you? There's a free coffee for you whenever you want.'

'Of course I will. We're writing a book together.'

'Ha! You'll have to get up a little earlier to catch me out. I wrote the synopsis so do with it what you want.'

'Tom.' She put down her knife and fork. 'Your short story showed real talent, and I don't feel qualified to write from a man's point of view, not for so much of the story, not for this genre that's less about action and more about emotions.'

'Come on, Alex, a joke's a joke, and we both know it wouldn't work,' he said through a mouthful of croissant.

'Why not? I was dropped in the deep end in the café and, okay, so I've only been here for a week, but I managed to carry out Hope's duties. What's the difference? Consider it a job share.'

He stopped chewing. 'But you're a best-selling, award-winning author.'

That used to mean so much.

'Wouldn't have the time, anyway,' he said and carried on eating.

'Yes you would. Evenings. I'll come over. Edit your work. We've just got to come up with three chapters. If Miranda likes them, if we get a deal, we can negotiate the deadline for the whole manuscript.' She leant forwards. 'If it sells well, with the extra income you could combine writing with running the café, split your work hours, get in an assistant manager.'

'That's a lot of ifs.'

'It's my last chance, Tom.'

'You're *serious*?' said Tom, in a voice that sounded equally horrified and delighted.

'Please consider it.'

'Please' wasn't a word Alex used often with work, not in her calls, or emails. Not after Simon had betrayed her and she'd felt like a fool. She worked damned hard and deserved edits on time, outstanding covers, PR staff keen to book tours and events. Some might call it entitled, she preferred well earned. For the first couple of years she'd liked this new Alex. When Mum died and she found out about Simon's cheating, she'd felt like a fledgling pushed out of a cosy nest, forced to learn to fly and fend for itself. She'd succeeded. It had filled her with confidence. Alex truly believed no one knew what they could achieve until they tried. Simon didn't believe she should leave the bank. Her dad had never believed in her, but as she'd matured, Alex had realised that that was his problem, not hers. Sometimes people doubting you was all the motivation you needed.

'Forget it,' she said and smiled. 'Dream-chasing is a brutal business. You need a thick skin to cope with potential rejection or failure. I can see what a safe, secure life you have here. Like you say, you haven't much experience. It was a stupid idea.'

She gave it three seconds to him agreeing to co-author. Three, two, one...

Tom reached for the jam. 'You're absolutely right, Alex.' He took a bite. 'Best of luck with it.'

Her teeth snapped into a semicircle of melon and juice spurted onto her chin. 'Right. I'd better not hang around. I've a novel to write.' She wiped her chin with the back of her hand and went to get up but he topped up her coffee.

'Dad would have been so excited about your proposal; I'd do anything for just one day with him, talking about the past, telling him about everything the café has achieved...'

She hesitated and then reached for the drink. 'The beautiful moon fixation... any idea what it might mean?'

'Maybe Mum did a drawing of one; she always had a pencil in her hand and hoped one day to make her own gift cards, although animals were her speciality.'

'Have you looked through them? Perhaps Norm wished he'd encouraged her more.'

'Or like George believing he was adopted, it could simply be his brain playing tricks on him.'

After they'd eaten, Alex persuaded him to dig out his mum's old drawings. Authors liked mysteries, she insisted, it's what they worked with day in, day out, subplots, plot twists, big reveals, foreshadowing to help the reader work out the ending, bombshells to knock them off course, subtle clues. Tom carried in a cardboard box and the two of them sifted through them. Foxes, rabbits, a pond with ducks, woodland trees, a hedgehog under a bush... Tom explained how those within a setting, like a forest, used to take her ages as she made sure everything was in the right position and in proportion. She'd spend ages refining her sketches and only got around to painting a few in.

'The pond one is my favourite; such detail, like the way the light falls on those lily pads.'

'Dad was always telling her to go part-time in the café, that we'd manage.'

'My mum died a few years ago,' said Alex. 'Cancer got her, but it was quick in the end; she caught pneumonia. Her lungs couldn't cope.' She sat with her thoughts for a moment, how the divorce settlement had enabled her not only to give up work and look after Mum, but also explore various miracle cures when traditional treatments had run their course. Like the healing water from a spring in Greece, the expensive herbs and supplements, the last-ditch trip to a medical centre in the States; she pretended to her mum that her settlement money had been much bigger than it was, when in fact, by the end, she'd spent every penny. 'One of the last things she said to me was to find my true calling and follow it with a passion. She never did. That's one reason I became an author.'

Tom wanted to know about her mother's dreams and Alex talked about the rescue centre for injured birds she'd wanted to set up.

The two of them flicked through the last of the drawings. 'There's no sketch of the moon. So much for that idea. On Friday, your dad mentioned it again and in a lucid moment, he really made it sound as if there was a true story behind this fixation.'

Tom put the lid on the box. 'Unbreaks my heart when I get my dad back, just for those few seconds of clarity, but then he's gone and it breaks all over again. He apologised once, got really upset, said he was sorry I had to look after him, sorry to be a burden. I told him not to be silly but he'd already gone.' He put the box on the floor, reached to the drum-shaped coffee table and picked up a sheet of paper. 'I've spent hours working on this. Here's the synopsis.'

Her eyes skimmed the page. It took less than five seconds. 'Only one paragraph, covering the two main characters meeting in the Buddhist centre and then, weeks later, coming face to face outside his café on the first day of the building work... they get together by the end. Tom, where is the detail? We know all this.'

'I'm not much of a planner. I go with the flow.'

'But you can't write a whole novel like that. I don't, anyway; my writing is always plot driven so I get down the detail for each scene before starting.'

'This book is going to be different, right? Why not take a chance?'

That spark of excitement lit up inside her again.

'Initially we've only got to come up with three chapters,' he continued.

'Wait... *we?*' This was new, someone who could play her at her own game.

'A slip of the tongue.'

Was he trying not to laugh?

'A Freudian slip, more like. Admit it. You're excited.'

'Extra income would take away some of the pressure about paying Dad's fees. In fact, I might have already thought of a title, related to the emergency in the Buddhist centre,' he said. '"Coming Up For Air" by Alex Butler and Tom Wilson.'

14

At nine o'clock sharp, Alex walked past the gold plaque outside and entered the three-storey high, private doctor's surgery. She checked in at the polished reception desk on the ground floor, and sat down on the leather couch in the waiting room, next to a pile of glossy magazines. She went to take out her phone but changed her mind, having noticed a missed call from the bank yesterday afternoon. She'd need to work all hours in the coming months to garner a publishing deal with Tom, and potentially an advance that would cover her bills during six months' maternity leave – and save her apartment. Her first ever advance paid for the deposit to buy it – the divorce settlement had gone and Mum had rented so there was no inheritance. Alex couldn't lose it; that glass tower represented a new beginning and everything she'd worked so hard for.

With renewed panic over the 1 July deadline, even though they'd had breakfast together, she'd invited Tom over last night. He didn't like to leave Captain Beaky alone, so she ordered in takeout, her treat, and they ate upstairs at his.

'Why don't we have a prologue containing two very short

scenes,' she'd suggested, 'to introduce both characters and give their first impression of each other?' They'd spend next Monday critiquing each other's introduction. Tom suggested they use the seaside setting of his short story; he'd always dreamed of falling asleep to the sweet talk of waves. Alex agreed and also approved of his main characters' names, Jack and Clara.

'Ms Butler?' asked a clearly articulated voice, dressed in a starched white coat.

Thank goodness Alex hadn't become an author while she was still married, leaving her stuck with Simon's surname for eternity. She left the comfortable waiting room and followed the doctor upstairs. Alex sat on the black chair, next to an orderly desk. The room was elegantly decorated in magnolia and pale green. The doctor tapped on her keyboard with long nails before turning to face her. Alex's blouse clung to her armpits as she prepared to be told she had options, options she'd already considered. Having suffered two losses, gaining a baby might be the universe's way of redressing the balance. An unexpected chance to embrace something she never thought she'd wanted. Dummies, dirty nappies, sleepless nights, yet an incredible bond, perhaps a friend forever, a person to fill the gaps in her life left by her mum and Simon.

'How are you today, Alex?'

Nervous. Petrified. 'Fine, thanks.'

'The results of your bloods and urine test have come in, and you're...'

Her heart thumped inside her chest, as if hosting a celebration. Parents said kids stopped you focusing on yourself. Perhaps that was what Alex needed, the ultimate distraction. Last night she'd browsed on the internet and had already picked out a Moses basket.

'You're not pregnant. The home test you did was correct.'

It had different height settings and a rocking mode, and...
What?

No baby?

That couldn't be right. Even if it was by far the more sensible outcome; she was single after all, with an uncertain financial future and career to relaunch...

So why did she want to cry?

'I must be.' Her voice wavered. 'My period still hasn't arrived and I've felt sick.'

'With the symptoms you described last time, I wouldn't have done blood tests on a woman over forty-five, but given your younger age I felt it necessary... and they have, indeed, explained your condition. You see, as I suspected, you're in peri-menopause. You really had no idea?'

Alex almost stopped breathing. 'I'm only forty-three.' A young forty-three at that. Everyone said so. With or without clothes on, boyfriends could never believe her real age. This was *not* fucking happening.

'It can start at anywhere from the mid-thirties; it's the period of transition into menopause. If you cast your mind back over recent months – or years, even – have you had sleepless nights for example?'

'Like I said before, my career's a stressful one. That surely explains the mood swings, the anxiety we talked about.'

'How about brain fog – muddling up words or having memory problems?'

She didn't reply.

'Hot flushes?'

'No. That means it can't be the menopause, right?'

'Not necessarily. What about night sweats?'

'They... they were linked to anxiety, lying awake panicking about my books bombing.'

The doctor tilted her head, nodding in a sympathetic manner. She talked about irregular periods, nausea, how important exercise was, along with a good diet, how Alex shouldn't overdo alcohol. However, mentioning HRT was a step too far. Alex was a vital woman, a glamorous author, not about to embrace hairs on her chin, a middle tyre or bingo wings. She should never have trusted a private, money-grabbing doctor, keen to misdiagnose in order to dish out expensive tablets. Alex had plenty of her own hormones, thank you very much. Fumbling, Alex picked up the leaflet the consultant slid across her desk and charged out.

'Menopause' was one of those misleading words, like 'inflammable' that actually meant something *could* catch fire. It was an *end*, not a pause, of the dynamic life she'd carved out for herself.

Alex had never wanted to be a mother, but that was when she had choices. Like the boyfriends she'd carefully selected for their energy and lack of emotional baggage, a baby might have staved off that one-way road to a care home, keeping her young, keeping her fun, preventing her from being alone...

An image of the Wrong Order Café popped up in her mind and Alex shuddered. She couldn't work there another minute, surrounded by people reminding her she was one step closer to their destiny, and a parrot that insulted and patronised her. Mum told her a story once about a cockatoo who lived to the age of 119. Born in the late eighteenth century, he'd travelled the world on his owner's ship before settling in a hotel where he became quite the celebrity. By the end he was featherless, gnarled and skinny, but still entertained human companions. It reminded her now, of Reenie and Fletch, still laughing and chatting with customers, despite the damage done not to their bodies, but their minds. Yet what was the point when they couldn't remember a single thing about their day?

Blindly, she walked. The weather was sticky for the beginning of June and she ended up in the cooler Arndale. Around and around she went, passing the same shops several times – Next, Lush... Mamas & Papas. Schools were out when she eventually ended up back in the Northern Quarter, feet sore, throat parched. A white feather blew against her feet. She picked it up. The rachis up the centre was bent and the barbs scraggy. She shoved it into her chinos pocket, stumbled inside, almost knocking Fletch over as he darted forward.

'Welcome,' he said and gave a little bow. 'Someone will be with you shortly.' He hovered. 'Lex, isn't it?'

Alex blanked him and veered around Reenie, who was talking extensions to a young woman in a wrap dress. Alex avoided Jade's eye. Tom came out of the kitchen.

'I expected you back at lunchtime. Everything okay?'

'Never better,' she said stiffly.

'Can't say the same here. Our new member of staff called. He's been made a better offer. Is there any way you can carry on working for a few more days?'

The gentle lilt of his voice drew her in, but not enough to help out. 'No. Sorry.'

'It's just. I'm desperate.' He pulled the tea towel off his shoulder and mopped his forehead. 'On top of being short staffed, one of the dishwashers has packed in and—'

'Ask someone else.'

He shrugged. 'I can't, Alex. Yash has exams, Jade works full-time as it is and Pip—'

'This really isn't my problem.'

His eyebrows raised and she broke eye contact.

'Well, I'm afraid I won't be able to write that prologue scene this week. My non-fiction life will have to come first.'

'Because my job's a joke, isn't it? I'm a joke. So let's forget the whole thing.' She rushed upstairs, slammed Hope's door behind her and fell into the sofa. Her rattan handbag landed on the other side of the room. Knocks sounded on the door. Alex closed her eyes and put her fingers in her ears, feeling as old as she had the moment Simon told her who he was leaving her for.

'What's her name?' Alex had demanded. 'Do I know her?'

'No. She's called Megan. We're moving in together, today.'

'How long has this been going on?'

'Long enough,' he'd said, in a quiet voice. 'We met at the gym. She teaches fitness classes.'

She'd sounded young at heart and athletic, unlike Alex who spent all day, every day, at her desk in the bank, eating too many snacks.

Alex opened her eyes and stared at the plants she'd succeeded in keeping alive, hands bunched in her lap, not as smooth as they used to be. Her waistline had filled out, her hair thinned, and now and then, like in the Village with Hope, she'd cried in public, but she'd put that down to several fraught years, not hormonal changes. Alex threw her clothes into her case, scooped up her toiletries from the bathroom shelf and tossed them on top. Despite the warm weather, she pulled on a jacket and hurried towards the door; her hand reached out, but... she just couldn't press down on the handle.

Caring was shit.

Clumsily, she filled the mist sprayer. The jet of water missing most leaves, she gave the plants one last drink. Alex blew her nose and pulled her case downstairs. Tom came out of the kitchen as she descended.

'What's happened, Alex?'

She pushed past him, into the café, failing to navigate the chairs and tables as her case knocked into them. It was empty apart from Jade and Yash behind the counter and Kay and Reenie chatting near Captain Beaky – and Fletch in the far corner, by the window, serving a couple of teenagers. She went to pull open the front door when the lad, whose tie hung loosely around his neck, sniggered.

'We ordered meat, not something sweet,' said the lad and he pointed at the cookie Fletch had brought over. He grinned at his friend and she winked.

'Yeah and turkey, not jerky,' said the girl.

'Not pies or fries,' said the boy, with a serious nod.

'Not cheese, not peas.' The girl spoke with an innocent air.

Confusion filled Fletch's face and he picked up the biscuit plate.

'Hey, what are you doing, mister, I was looking forward to that.' The boy grabbed the plate back, while the girl took a photo of Fletch as he walked away. Fletch scratched his head, messing up his neat comb-over, his expression reminding Alex of her own despair from earlier, sitting on Hope's sofa trying to make sense of what the doctor had said. A tide of heat erupted within and flowed into her cheeks. Fletch had lost a bit of himself, so had Alex, but he wasn't in a position to put up a defence. She let go of her case, strode over and picked up the girl's phone from the table.

'Oi! What ya doing?' The lad stood up and glowered.

Alex opened the phone's photo gallery app; she deleted the snap.

'You can't do that,' protested the girl. 'We were only having a bit of fun; it's not like he'll remember, so where's the harm?'

'Get out before I track down that uniform and ring your head teacher.'

'We didn't mean anything by it,' said the girl, and sulky expressions crossed her and her friend's faces.

Alex bent down and hissed at the teenagers, 'You may not believe it at your age, but we're all heading the same way; none of us avoid grey hairs and forgetfulness.' She went over to the door, yanked it wide open and pointed. 'Clear off,' she said, in a loud voice. 'Don't ever come back.'

Tom stood by the counter; Jade had gone to get him. Fletch stayed in the corner by Captain Beaky, as if that spot of the café was a safe homing point. The teenagers slunk out. Alex slammed the door behind them.

'Did I do something wrong?' Fletch muttered to Jade who'd gone to his side.

Alex spun around. 'You were super professional. They were just troublesome customers. You must have dealt with plenty in your hotel job and have still got the knack.'

'Hotels, gawd, yes.' His face relaxed. 'The trashed rooms, the unpaid bills, the room service flashers...'

Alex turned back to the front of the shop. She held on to her case, preparing to leave, but for some reason couldn't move her feet; her palm felt sweaty against the metal handle. Commuters passed by, outside, with a home to head for, and groups of friends, loved-up couples.

Leave for what? A flat she couldn't afford? A book she couldn't write on her own? A life with no one who mattered? And Hope's life here left in tatters?

The parrot squawked.

'He's very friendly. Never nipped anyone,' said Fletch to no one in particular.

A sob ripped through Alex's body. Footsteps shuffled. An arm slipped around her waist and Alex looked down at Reenie.

'Let it out, love. Not all of us here know what we're doing but at least, in this building, we've got each other's backs.'

15

Alex sat by the glossy-leaved plant, next to her suitcase, like she had on the first day. Jade brought over one of her ruby hot chocolates. An elderly couple came in, regulars by the way they greeted Fletch, even though he didn't recognise them straight away. They ordered pots of tea and fruitcake after their names came back to him. Alex focused on the colourful mural that featured the town hall. Many times she and Simon had walked past as they'd spent a day, just the two of them, shopping and eating out. 'Dream a Little Dream of Me' came on the jukebox. Alex stirred her drink, milky bubbles floating on the top before bursting. The idea of having a baby had been nothing more than a dream she'd got carried away with, blocking out the reality of her age, of the fact she'd never felt remotely maternal.

Having a baby to fill in the cracks left behind after a divorce and bereavement would have been utterly unfair on the child. She could see that now.

A colleague at the bank, a father of twins, had implied once that Alex was weird for not wanting kids. If he'd grown up watching her mum's life, at the beck and call of her father and domesticity, he might have felt differently. Over the years, people said she'd regret it or change her mind eventually, suggesting she must hate children or implying she was selfish. Yet she'd always appreciated visits to the niece on Simon's side, and selflessly looked after her husband and Mum over the years, from giving them small unexpected gifts to nursing him through shingles and caring for her 24-7 at the end. Alex took out her compact. Since becoming an author, she'd not cared for anyone else and didn't much like the person staring back from the small, round mirror, a person who'd have brought a baby into the world merely to make herself feel better. Despite the heat, Alex shivered. What had she been thinking? Had her life become so self-involved? Sugar and cream calmed her down as she sipped the hot chocolate. What had she become since turning forty?

The answer came clear and loud as one word popped into Alex's mind. It grew bigger and bigger until she felt she might explode.

'Lonely,' she whispered to herself as if afraid the walls might hear and tell the room. She sat with the word, surprised to find it felt a good fit, like a jacket you didn't consider your size or style that turned out to feel just right, once on.

But how could that be? She'd filled her flat with important things like awards, designer clothes, admired art, loyalty cards to top restaurants.

She dabbed her eyes. Get a grip. Alex Butler was not menopausal, and she wasn't some lonely saphead either.

A message pinged.

Tomorrow we're off to Hanoi to hunt for a mythical turtle. Still getting used to Bangkok's delicacies.

Hope had attached a photo, another soup, this time with chicken feet in it.

Alex sniffed and directed her camera at Captain Beaky. She took a snap and sent it.

Don't give me ideas.

If Hope could be brave enough to backpack across the other side of the world, then, right here, in Manchester, Alex was going to work her way back to finding her old self – the one who never forgot colleagues' birthdays, the woman who cut Mum's toenails and brushed her teeth when she couldn't, a woman who looked for strength in herself and not in a flash career, nor a string of romantic flings, nor in a potential pregnancy.

Doing a terrible job of pretending to be busy, Tom stood behind the counter. She beckoned him over. He arrived with a scone and set down the plate. Alex cut it in two, slathered on cream and spooned on a huge dollop of jam before offering him half. She took a large bite.

'Is there anything I can do to help?' he asked in a gentle tone.

For a brief moment he lay his hand on hers. Readers pulled her close for selfies and Miranda went through the motions, with her air-kissing, but she missed the way she and Mum always used to link arms really tight, or walk hand in hand, fingers interlocked. Friends at the bank used to give the best hugs. She shouldn't have lost touch. Her phone pinged again. Hope had responded with a laughing emoji and... a kiss. No one in her life signed off like that, not any more, apart from Miranda, but she didn't count; she'd have sent a dozen kisses to her worst enemy if she thought they had a new writing voice the market would pay thousands for.

'No. I'm not ill, though, if that's what you mean,' she blurted out. 'And if the offer's still there, I'd like to stay working here, until the end of the month.'

Tom looked as if Frank Sinatra had come back from the dead.

'I expect your half of our prologue written by Monday.'

'I'm on it. Captain Beaky is helping, so the language might be fruity.'

'Fly Me to the Moon' came on the jukebox and the parrot swayed from side to side, eyes closed, wings flapping, while Tom hummed along.

'How about I chat more to Norm on Friday?' she said, her voice becoming steadier with each mouthful of hot chocolate. 'I'm determined to get to the bottom of this *beautiful moon* anxiety of his. Like any story, I'm convinced if we unpick the past we'll find the answer and maybe stop him upsetting himself. Was he or your mum into astronomy?' she asked, warming to her subject.

'No.'

'How about astrology?'

'Nope, not that either; she wasn't a cynic, had books on spiritualism, and I've got vague memories of her going to yoga classes way before they became popular. But Dad said she used to tease him that astrology was a load of rubbish, knowing that he was addicted to reading his horoscope every day.' Tom finished the last bit of his half of scone. 'My last girlfriend, Kate, she read hers too and said our zodiac signs are sun signs and reflect people's personality. Whereas moon signs exist that reflect our inner emotions and to find out what yours is, you need to know exactly when and where you were born. It was a few years back. She and Dad used to enjoy talking about it.'

'Is it possible that Norm is talking about Kate when he says, "I should have told her the moon is beautiful"?'

'No idea.'

'Ask her.'

'Our contact is only sporadic, now, but she comes in for a drink occasionally. I could give her a ring.'

'Did you part on good terms? Invite her over for a free lunch. Tell her an author friend has got some research questions about astrology.'

His eyes concertinaed at the corners. 'Okay, I'm on it, but I'm not convinced you'll discover anything.' He rubbed his palms together. 'Right. Better get back to the dishwasher. I reckon I'm going to need to call someone out. It's not draining properly.'

'You've checked the filter?'

'Yup, and the drain hose.'

Alex took out her phone and went into Contacts. She texted Tom a number.

'Trev owes me a favour. I recommended him to the Italian restaurant next door; it's part of a family chain in the north-west and now he's the on-call plumber for all their emergencies.' She blew her nose and knocked back the rest of her drink. 'Could you take my suitcase upstairs, Tom? If it's okay with you, there's something I've got to do before the shops close.' She paused. 'Please.'

A serious look crossed Tom's face, unusual for him. He brushed a strand of hair out of her face. Her mum used to do that and say she should get a fringe cut. 'No problem, Alex. Consider it done.'

Sunshine fell onto her cheeks as she walked out of the door. She shoved the phone back into her pocket and her fingers touched the scraggy feather from earlier. Alex took it out and peered into the sky, before she turned right and hurried off in the direction of Market Street.

16

Alex applied a sweep of blusher, having not slept well. She pulled on a T-shirt and cool harem pants that she'd normally only wear as loungewear. At five minutes to nine, she tied the blue apron around her waist and pinned on her name badge, having already eaten a bowl of cereal. She'd nipped out this morning, early, to grab a basket of essentials. Now she was staying, Alex had examined Hope's fridge properly. The milk she'd been using was well out of date and that could have partly explained the nausea.

Downstairs, the charcoal aroma of toasted bread welcomed her. Alex greeted Jade and walked behind the counter. She placed the notebook she'd bought last night in the far back corner of the room, behind the dishwasher. She swiped a raspberry from a breakfast tray Reenie was about to take to a customer and, ignoring Jade's tut, pushed the fruit through the parrot's bars. Mum would have approved, would probably have been amused by the rude comment Alex was bracing herself for. He cocked his head and took it with his beak, without a word. Tom said good morning and hurried out of the front door. The candle and crystal shop next door had flooded and he'd offered to help. Alex removed dirty crockery and crumbs from one of the tables. Nearby, Reenie patted the shoulder of a young woman with green hair that stuck out from under a cap.

'I asked to go from yellow blonde to ash, had it done two weeks ago, but it's slowly turned green.' The woman pulled her cap down tighter.

'I'm sorry. I shouldn't have mentioned the colour but I'm a hairdresser – or used to be.' Reenie stood on tiptoe and peered closer. 'Have you been using purple shampoo?'

The woman nodded.

'It sounds like...' Reenie peered closer. 'I think... the stylist used the wrong, now what is it called? Toner.'

'What if they charge me to fix it? It cost more than my weekly food bill to get it done.'

'You have three choices, chickie.' Reenie gave a wide smile. 'You go and complain, stand your ground. Or visit the salon I used to work at. They'll sort you out. My treat, I insist.'

The woman shook her head. 'It's too generous. What is the other option?'

Reenie frowned.

'You said I had three choices.'

'Yes... your eyes, that's it... Such a lovely shade of brown. Are you a natural brunette? Would you consider going back to it?'

'Oh...' The woman put down her spoon. 'I don't know. I've been dying it blonde since I was old enough to persuade my mum.'

'Your skin has a beautiful peach undertone that must suit your natural colour.'

A loud cough carried across the café and Jade gave Alex a pointed look and jerked her head towards a group of pensioners who'd come in. Alex put her dishcloth back by the sink and headed into the corner and scribbled furiously in the notebook there, first.

'Really?' said Jade and slipped her thumbs behind the straps of her dungarees. 'You can see we're busy but are still going to prioritise your writing, putting more pressure on me, but worse than that, on Reenie?' She sighed. 'I get it. Creatives have big egos, they need to believe in themselves, but you've got two jobs now. So much for Tom saying you were really keen to stay on until Hope comes back.'

Keen was taking it a bit far. Alex flipped the notebook shut. 'It's out of my control, Jade, I have to write when inspiration strikes.' She strolled over to the pensioners. Trev the plumber came in shortly after the woman in the cap left. Pip was in today and in the kitchen helping one of the chefs wash crockery by hand. Already Alex had a sense of how the staff worked as a team. Mum once stood up for geese when a woman at the park called them 'noisy greedy-guts'. She'd explained how they were the epitome of teamwork. They flew in V formation, so that the ones behind had a better view. The wings of the geese in front also created lift for the ones at the back, making it easier for them to fly. For that reason the hard-working lead would regularly change. The honking in the air was an act of encouragement, to cheer each other on, during a long journey, and if a goose fell sick, others would break formation to offer support and fly by its side.

She and Mum used to agree that often it was the humans who were bird-brained.

Tom strode into the café as Alex went on her morning break, his jeans wet, hair mussed up. He nodded at her before going upstairs to change. She rubbed her back and collapsed into a chair at one of the tables. In between sips she wrote in her notebook, carefully considering each word. Jade sat down next to her and crossed her arms.

'You still aren't taking this seriously, are you? You've been nipping to that notebook all morning.'

'You doodle.'

'That's not the same. I save my proper drawing for after hours or during my breaks.'

'You're an artist, then? That sketch on that bookmark is amazing.'

'It's just a hobby,' she muttered. 'And don't change the subject.'

'I've still served customers, haven't I? Cleared tables?'

'You think this kind of work is beneath a highfalutin' author?'

Alex put down her pen. 'This work is harder than I ever could have imagined.'

Somewhat mollified, Jade fiddled with her dungaree button. 'How are you going with the *Heartstopper* books?'

'I hope the ending's going to be as feel-good as the writing. There's nothing worse than a story finishing on a sour note.'

'But I assumed authors wrote what they loved to read. I went around to my great-aunt's last night. She loves the page-gripping element of your novels but says they don't all end well.'

'They don't?'

'Doesn't one finish with the main character finally finding love, but then her boyfriend dies?'

'Yesss, but during the course of the story she's overcome her browbeaten past, become a strong, independent woman and can now survive anything.'

'Another book's main character develops a drink problem by the end.'

'Getting revenge is stressful work. Watching her cheating husband get locked up for a crime he didn't commit made all the fallout worth it, even if that is addiction.' A customer went to the till to pay and Jade got up. Alex put down her pen. She'd never really thought about her books that way.

Tom came out from the kitchen and chatted to Jade, passing her a cup as she went to make a drink. Since leaving the bank, Alex hadn't felt like a team player. After Simon taking her for a fool, she'd approached everything as if she had a fight on her hands – with cover designers who simply wanted her books to fit in with the market, with social media assistants who didn't give Alex's books enough space. Or so she thought. And Alex had got on with her editor, but underneath resented questions about her characterisation, plot or pace.

A niggling voice, at the back of her mind, had sometimes asked why, at her publisher's parties, she'd often found herself talking to the waiters. That voice occasionally piped up with an answer too: Alex had an overly sensitive ego that had made her difficult to work with.

The lunchtime rush was almost over when Reenie prepared to leave. Fletch arrived with Val, laptop in her hand.

'I'm sweating buckets, here,' said Reenie and fanned her face, after giving a nonplussed Fletch a hug.

'Wait till you're outside,' he said. 'Never known a hotter July.'

Should Alex point out it was June? Was it kinder to let the mistake go? But then Fletch was still in the earlier stages of the disease, it wouldn't be right to simply humour him. 'June,' she said, 'but what's the difference? All months roll into each other in the summer.'

'Too right,' he said and smiled.

'By the way, could you bring your guitar in tomorrow?' Alex asked him. 'I'll ask Jade to remind you.'

The smile dropped from his face. 'No point. Can't play it as well.'

'It's important. Please?'

Captain Beaky blew a raspberry and, distracted, Fletch headed for Val who had taken his apron out of a bag. Reenie stood by the door and grabbed the handle.

'Hold on a minute,' said Alex. She hurried towards the corner and came back carrying the notebook. It was gold and black and covered with images of hairbrushes, nail varnish bottles and toiletry bottles. She handed it to Reenie. 'This is for you.'

Reenie looked at Kay, and then back at the notebook. 'I don't understand.'

The three of them moved out of the way of customers leaving. Reenie turned to the first page and read out loud, slowly at first, with the odd stumble.

Wednesday, 7 June – morning working at the Wrong Order Café

Another blazing day without a cloud over Manchester. Despite the hot weather, I told Alex I couldn't believe how many customers were still keen to sit indoors, even ordering hot chocolate, instead of going elsewhere with outside tables, but she understood, not being an outdoorsy person herself.

Tom spent the morning in the kitchen helping next-door clear up after a flood. Our dishwasher was broken and Alex's friend, Trev, came in to mend it. He had a lovely tattoo on his arm, and wore the biggest smile when I complimented it. It was unusual, coloured in yellow, a big sun with rays going all around it. The ink spread across his whole arm and was in memory of his mum, who used to call him her sonshine. Before he lost his hair, Trev said he used to be ginger like me. He used to get called 'carrot top' at school. I told him the other kids would call me 'pumpkin head'.

Later, I chatted to another customer about their hair, a young woman, she was upset because...

An unfamiliar, warm feeling swamped Alex as she listened to
Reenie read.

...money was obviously tight and she couldn't have been
happier when she left, even giving me a hug after I got her
phone details and said I'd send her my salon's number later. I
asked Alex to get Kay to remind me.

I had a slice of Lotus Biscoff cake mid-morning, a new
recipe of Tom's. I reckoned it was even nicer than my favourite,
chocolate fudge. I told him how much I loved the cinnamon
taste. Later, a crowd of Australian tourists came in and we had
a long chat about Neighbours. Like me, they were sad it had
ended. They recommended other Aussie soaps and Kay said
she would look them up for me. One of them, a man in his
forties, Wayne, had found the café online. His aunt had
dementia and had just been diagnosed and gave up work,
even though her boss said they would accommodate her
changing needs for as long as possible. His aunt was worried
about making mistakes. I said I could relate to that. This Wayne
was going to tell her all about his visit to the café and how the
wrong orders didn't matter. I couldn't believe it when they left a
five-pound tip. For excellent service, they said. Afterwards, I
told Alex that, in that moment, I felt like a hairdresser again.

Then it was time to go home after another busy, productive
shift at Wrong Order Café.

'I'll be writing in this notebook during every one of your
shifts. It's for you to read in the evenings, so you know what's
happened,' said Alex. 'You can talk about your day, then, to Kay
and your brother-in-law, and all those friends of yours. You could
meet up with them for coffee, take your notebook, have a proper
catch-up about your week, like you told me you used to.'

Reenie read the page again. Finally, she closed the notebook and hugged it tightly as if it were a lost relative. 'It's like proof that... I'm still me.'

Jade had come over, as had Fletch. He slipped an arm around Reenie's shoulders.

'That notebook's brilliant, to keep memories alive,' he said and pushed his glasses up his nose. 'If you want to, that is. The biggest hotel I ever worked in was down in London; we're talking chandeliers, uniformed bellboys and valets. The Queen visited once, I can't remember why. The front desk staff had a photo taken, Her Majesty stood right next to me in it, I was so proud.' His voice faltered. 'I've put the photo away in the loft now. It's too painful to have out on display as the whole event, it's just a blur.'

'I've kept my hairdressing awards out,' said Reenie. 'The ceremonies are a complete blank but those two glass stars are proof I've achieved something.'

Mum had known other people with cancer and their experiences were individual too, neither right nor wrong. In the end she accepted her fate, with grateful thoughts about her life, whereas a friend from the hospice was angry until the day she passed.

Reenie leant her head against Fletch. 'I wish we'd kept notebooks all our lives. None of us appreciate the good times enough, we're always thinking ahead to the next goal. I spent my whole career wishing I had my own salon. I don't know why. Compared to now, I always had everything I needed, enough money to pay my own way and go out with friends and on holiday. I boosted customers' self-esteem and comforted them through divorces and bereavements. My life's been pretty, bloomin' terrific, really.'

'Too right, gal,' said Fletch. 'I earned so many tips from customers whose comfortable stay, with excellent service, provided a much-needed break or helped push through a lucrative business deal… I was part of that. I made a difference. Yet I used to doubt it was all enough.' He shook his head.

Alex looked back on her life. She'd been promoted in the bank, topped book charts, spent unforgettable moments with her beloved mum when it counted. Yet she still wasn't happy, still wanted more.

A troublesome sensation rose in her chest. *When on earth was she ever going to be satisfied?*

'Why didn't you just tell me what you were doing earlier?' asked Jade, when the two of them were left alone.

'Because you were right, it was work. I might include diary entries in my next novel, so doing this is simply good practice.'

'Mate, is that honesty the only reason you're doing it?' Jade raised an eyebrow. 'Or is the truth that you're actually a sweetie?'

Alex pulled a face. 'Out of all the insults you've ever thrown my way that's 100 per cent the most offensive.'

17

Despite another restless night, words easily flowed into Reenie's notebook the following morning because Kay told Alex how cheerfully Reenie had read snippets from it at dinner the previous evening. Talking about the Australian customers had led to a chat about her brother-in-law's work trip to Sydney, when he was younger. For the first time in ages, the table conversation had blossomed more easily between the three of them, like in the days before Reenie had memory problems. Listening to Kay, Alex felt good about herself in a way she wasn't used to.

Grateful to sit down for lunch and take another hit of caffeine, Alex opened the notebook again and stopped dead at yesterday's page. A small illustration accompanied the entry that had mentioned the Australians, a manga-style kangaroo wearing a suit and tie, and a hat with corks swinging from it. Once more, Jade's sketching really caught movement. She must have done it during her morning break. Tom approached in his usual sandals that made him look as if he were permanently on holiday. He also wore a black T-shirt with the galaxy depicted across it. He brushed his fringe away, sat down, eyes closing for a second.

'Bad night, too?' she asked and bit into a basil and mozzarella panini.

'Too many sirens. Then that group of drinkers came past. I love living in the city but occasionally dream of owning an isolated farmhouse. About three in the morning, a car parked up with music pumping out. Youngsters sang along to a dance track, something about a "baby Benz", and "it's a short life".

'Ah yes. Drake,' said Alex.

'Then a slower one about being "out of time"...'

'That one's by The Weeknd.'

'Wow. I'm impressed,' he said and rubbed the back of his neck. 'How have you kept up with modern trends?'

'Um... clubbing, I guess, with boyfriends who've educated me.'

'Just like that I feel a lot older than you.' He gave a sheepish look.

Not possible. Not since she'd seen the doctor. Life, since her late thirties, might be starting to add up. She couldn't get the doctor's diagnosis out of her head. Friends had always joked how suited Alex was to working in the bank; she was even tempered, sensible, kept to the safe side of life. But Simon's cheating and Mum's terminal illness had skewed the balance. At least that's what she'd concluded. However, the anger, the frustration, the uncontrollable crying fits would often be triggered by something innocuous... On reflection, her moods had swung up and down before those two life-changing events. Like the time a few months before Simon announced he was leaving, he'd forgotten to buy salmon for dinner. The rage swelled up in her as she'd called him useless and slammed the door as she left for the supermarket. Once her mum called around, she'd been into town, and happened to call into a retro sweet shop. They'd sold Flying Saucers, Alex's favourite sherbet sweet when she was a little girl.

Alex had opened the packet and promptly burst into tears. She claimed PMT but that sort of thing never used to happen. And one Sunday, outside in the back garden, Simon had stood up with the empty watering can, shrubs revived, a hazy afternoon. He'd touched her arm and suggested the two of them went upstairs. Not understanding her sense of repulsion, she'd shaken him off.

'You've changed, Lex,' he'd said.

She took a large bite of the panini. That was no excuse for him to screw his gym buddy. No excuse for him to leave her with questions about the self-deprecating comment he'd made about her being able to do better. He was a successful software engineer. Fit for his age. Caring. Had a great sense of humour. They'd had a nice house. Great holidays. Apart from his two-timing, on paper, Simon was a catch.

Was he a secret gambler? A drug-taker? Porn addict?

'Can't say I've ever heard of The Weeknd,' said Tom and he stole one of Alex's crisps. 'Talking of music, why did you ask Fletch to bring in his guitar today?'

She tapped her nose. 'Meet me and Fletch in the staffroom after work and you'll see.'

* * *

After the last customer had left, Alex went into the staffroom and sat on the sofa. She took out a writing pad and pen. Tom came in and then Fletch. He went to his guitar at the back of the room and brought it over. Jade was sketching in the café, happy to wait until Fletch was ready to go home.

'I've got a favour to ask,' said Alex.

'Everyone helps me these days,' said Fletch. 'This will make a nice change, Lex.'

She flinched at the shorter version of her name he seemed to have adopted. Simon used to call her that.

'I'm an author. I'm only working here until Hope gets back from her trip. I've got a new book to write. In fact, I'm writing it with Tom.'

Fletch tidied his comb-over. 'I still enjoy reading, even if I can't always concentrate and can't hold all the clues in my head. Thrillers are my favourite genre, you see, but it's hard to keep track of all the twists and characters.'

Alex didn't know how to reply, so she simply nodded and squeezed his arm.

'My main character, Clara, plays the guitar,' she said. 'I was hoping you'd play a few tunes. I can make notes, observe your fingers and arms, build up a picture.'

Fletch put the instrument down. 'I'm no good any more, I make mistakes.'

'Clara does as well, so that's perfect. What was the first song you ever played properly?'

Fletch's face relaxed. '"Love Me Do" by the Beatles, still one of my favourites. It only uses three chords. Only two for the intro.'

'Great songwriting,' said Tom.

'My mum would agree, she loved the Beatles, had a huge crush on John Lennon with his sexy accent,' said Alex.

'She's dead?' asked Fletch abruptly.

'Yep. Pancreatic cancer.' It had been shock enough to be told her mum's diagnosis, but right at the end a revelation scared Alex even more, that her gran had suffered from colon cancer when she was younger. Death had crept around the corner, as if fate were biding its time, choosing a cancer for Alex. The end of her own life had waved hello.

'It would be lovely to hear you play it,' she said, brightly.

Fletch's eyebrows knitted together.

'I love a Beatles track,' said Tom, as he sat on the sofa's arm.

Fletch hesitated and then took his guitar out of its cover. He put the strap around his neck and fiddled with the tuning pegs. 'I don't know where my plectrum is.'

Tom searched inside the cover and took one out. 'Val must have put it in.'

Fletch adjusted his glasses and strummed. Alex watched his fingers on the strings and how he created rhythm with the plectrum. The lines on his face became less deep. His shoulders loosened. His foot tapped.

'My sister used to sing along,' he said.

'How about I google the lyrics?' said Alex. 'Tom, you up for a bit of singing?'

Silly question, he was already whistling the chorus.

A hopeful look crossed Fletch's face. Tom shuffled up to Alex on the sofa and their two voices soon accompanied the guitar, becoming especially loud when Fletch's notes stumbled. The door flew open and Jade came in, pen in her hand. Her face broke into a smile as she saw Fletch playing.

Alex clapped at the end and scribbled for a few moments while Jade stood entranced. 'That was great, Granddad!'

'Right. Research,' said Alex. 'Why do you enjoy playing, Fletch?'

He shrugged.

'It will help with my character, the book I'm writing.'

'Entertaining family at Christmas, seeing them happy, I suppose. Also, lots of popular songs are easy to play and a guitar is portable. I used to take it to friends' houses. We formed a band and would have jam sessions with other musicians. But then life got busy, I guess. I miss those times.'

Alex wrote more notes. An hour had passed so quickly.

'Would you be happy to do this again? It's really useful,' she asked, suspecting that he might not remember committing.

'Let's perform "Love Me Do" one more time; Jade can join in,' said Tom.

Fletch messed up a chord and dropped the guitar onto the sofa. 'I'm tired now,' he muttered.

'Come on, Granddad. Gran's making your favourite steak and kidney pudding.' Jade packed up the guitar, linked her arm with his and closed the door behind them.

'That was kind of you,' said Tom and pushed Alex's shoulder gently.

'Kind? Fletch was the one doing me a favour.' She hurried to the door. 'Shall I fetch Captain Beaky?'

'Good idea. I'll wash up our mugs.'

Alex went into the café. Jade had left her a sketchbook behind, open, next to a dirty mug on one of the tables. She must have forgotten to take it on the way back out. Alex went to close it but sat down instead. The drawing could have come straight out of a graphic novel, of a woman with long, jagged brown hair and a rucksack on her back spilling books. In her hand she held a sword made to look like a quill. Alex had googled the Japanese manga style Jade loved so much, and, like the kangaroo, this drawing was in that style, the face with large eyes, a small mouth, and hair that defied gravity. Alex couldn't help turning the page and came to a storyboard. The same woman had gone into a coffee shop. Behind the till was a girl with spiky green hair, with narrow eyes and a pointy nose. She held out a mug with steam swirling out of it. On the coffee machine in the background, the word 'poison' was written. A one-eyed giant parrot sat at one of the tables; it had a huge, gnarled beak and sharp talons. Tom's whistling brought Alex back to reality and she put the sketchbook behind the counter, where Jade would see it, before picking up the cage.

'In trouble, in trouble,' Captain Beaky squawked.

18

'Are you sure you don't mind me taking a longer lunch than normal?' asked Alex, during her late-morning break. She sat in the staffroom, on the sofa, next to Norm. Tom stood in front of them, tapping on his phone.

'You're meeting my ex, Kate, to help Dad, and I appreciate you trying. It was good to catch up with her, to be honest. When I called last night, we spoke for almost an hour, even if she did grill me about how much red meat I'm eating lately.' Tom met Alex's puzzled face. 'She's a freelance nutritionist. I guess a love of eating is what brought us together.'

Alex passed Norm the fidget blanket that had slipped off his knees. Norm lay his hand on top of hers and patted it for the rest of the time she sat drinking her coffee. Mum used to do that, when she was ill. Tom left to make a phone call about a late delivery, and arrived back just in time as Norm had been asking why Susie hadn't visited him. Tom knelt down in front of his dad and pointed upwards.

'Mum's up there, keeping a beady eye on us. So we'd better behave ourselves.'

Norm blinked and then went back to the fidget blanket.

When Alex's mum got her diagnosis, the two of them had refused to acknowledge that she might die. But as time passed, Alex noticed a change. Mum would switch off when Alex talked of new treatments she'd googled. They enjoyed the trip to the States, despite Mum worrying about how much Alex was spending, but things changed from the point the consultant there emphasised just how experimental his drug trials were. He'd tried to explain this over Zoom, before they travelled, but Alex hadn't wanted to listen. In the end, Mum decided not to go ahead and they simply enjoyed the rest of their time there, seeing the sights as far as Mum could manage. No more miracle cures, she'd told Alex.

'Lexie, love, come and sit down.' Her mum had patted her bed, a few nights after they got back to England. 'I... I know I'm dying. I've accepted it. You need to as well.' Her voice broke as tears streamed down Alex's cheeks. 'You've been so supportive, giving me – us – hope, as best you can. But it's too painful now, the thought that you might still believe there is a way out of this. We need to face the inevitable together.' Alex hadn't been able to speak. 'I'm okay about it – with you by my side. Let's just make the most of the time we have left.'

As the memory shook her, Norm's hand stayed on hers, warm and shaking, unlike Mum's that final time, cold and rigid.

She entered the café and Jade pointed to a drink that had spilt onto the floor, still not talking to her, furious after Alex had owned up to flicking through the sketchbook. Alex mopped up the mess and then cleared tables. One customer had left a couple of blueberries on their plate. She picked one up and went over to the cage.

'Legs!' Captain Beaky squawked.

She glanced down. What was the bird going on about? She pushed the blueberry through the bars. Alex caught Jade's eye. 'Look, I'm sorry. Honestly.'

Jade grimaced. 'That sketchbook was private.'

Alex placed her palm on her chest. 'Aren't I the one who should be angry? In that story you poison me. I like to think that giant parrot saves the day and knocks the mug out of my hands.'

Jade snorted and Captain Beaky immediately mimicked it. 'No, he's in on it, because he's a magical bird and to make your sword quill you stole one of his feathers.'

Alex leant against the counter. 'You're very talented,' she said quietly. 'I'd love to know how that story finishes.'

Jade had already turned away and the hiss of the coffee machine gave her answer.

As two thirty approached, Alex's stomach rumbled. She had never felt so hungry, still unused to being on her feet nine till five. The only daily exercise she'd get, especially while writing a first draft, would be half an hour in the glass tower's basement gym.

The entrance door opened and several customers came in – a young couple, both wearing aviator sunglasses, a father with a baby strapped to his chest, and an older woman with shoulder-length white hair underneath a floppy hat. Alex consulted her watch as Tom opened the staffroom door carrying an empty glass.

'Kate!' he called and deposited the glass on the counter before hugging the woman in the hat.

What? But she looked old enough to be his mother.

'This is Alex,' he said.

Kate held out her hand and gave a firm handshake. Alex couldn't stop staring at the bright eyes and glowing complexion.

'I do hope I can help sort out this worry for Norm.' Kate turned to Tom. 'Talking of which, can I say hello? You mentioned he was here.' She reached into her bag and brought out a tray of colourful sweets. 'These are special jellies, 90 per cent water and made especially for dementia patients to make sure they keep hydrated. I bought them a while back and kept meaning to call in.'

'Don't ever change, will you, Kate?' said Tom and he took her hand and kissed it, using a tone he'd never used with Alex, a tone that stabbed her inside, like when Simon had first talked about Megan. Alex had no idea why. Tom wasn't anything like her type.

Fifteen minutes later, the two women sat at a table; they'd both ordered and Yash brought over another espresso for Alex, a green tea for Kate. Tom sat nearby, with Norm, who rocked to and fro.

'It's hard every time I see Norm, like this,' said Kate and she stirred her drink. 'He was always such a livewire and a terrible flirt, in an old-fashioned way, you know? Charming, polite, with a twinkle in his eye. A legion of older ladies would come in here for morning coffee with a side of compliments.' She cleared her throat. 'But he's well cared for and lucky to have Tom.' She caught Alex's eye. 'Tom's a special person.'

'It's great that you're still friends,' said Alex. 'I'm barely on talking terms with my ex-boyfriends. I don't know how you manage it. In my experience, age gaps make it even harder to remain friends afterwards; without the romance, there's little common ground.'

'Granted, twenty-five years is a lot.'

Alex gasped and Kate gave a small laugh.

'Sorry,' said Alex. 'I didn't mean to be rude but you don't look your age.' Kate had to be in her late sixties.

'Friendship was never a problem for Tom and me. Our relationship, at first, was platonic. He used to joke he slowed me down, but truth be told, I found his constant ambitions for the café inspiring.'

'Well, to paraphrase a well-known saying, you're as old as the man you feel.'

Eggs Benedict arrived for them both.

'I don't agree,' said Kate and she unfolded a napkin. 'I believe you're as old as the *fear* you feel.' In between mouthfuls she spoke about a friend who dreaded losing her looks. She'd been a model in the eighties, hanging out with celebrities and top photographer David Bailey. When work dried up, she turned to fillers and Botox and somehow all the procedures ended up making her look older and more unhappy. Kate wiped her mouth. 'Whereas take my yoga buddy, Jude, her biggest fear is living in the past... I don't know too much, she just said her brother does and is never happy. Jude works really hard to move on from upset, getting therapy, and she's always challenging herself and taking on new hobbies. We're very much alike.'

'What are you most scared of?' asked Alex and she put down her knife and fork. 'Surely, if we're all honest, it's becoming old and incapacitated, like Norm?'

'No. Far more frightening would be reaching that point having wasted the previous years worrying about it. My biggest fear is that I'm on my deathbed without having achieved everything I want to. There's still so much more I want to learn – about other countries, new hobbies, people. I want to make a difference, in some small way. Recently, I've helped out at a charity shop once a week.' Kate laughed about how she'd taken up chess and hadn't won a single game yet. 'Anyway,' she said, as she pushed away her empty plate, 'what exactly can I help you with?'

Relieved to change the conversation, Alex told her about Norm's fixation. 'Is there anything specific to do with the moon being beautiful in astrology?'

Kate drained her cup, taking her time. 'If your moon sign is Taurus that's fortuitous, as that's when the moon is making most use of its potential. But Norm's isn't, so I can't see how the moon would have a special meaning for him.' She talked more about moon signs but could come up with nothing relevant.

When they'd finished chatting, Kate sat with Tom and Norm, and Alex went back to work as the after-school rush began. Several cake slices and milkshakes later, as Alex's shift came to an end and the café cleared of the smell of stale PE kits and clumsily sprayed aftershave, she sat down by the jukebox, perspiration running down her back. She took out her phone and searched for words connected to 'moon'. Tom had just got back from taking Norm to the care home; Norm had fallen asleep shortly after Kate joined their table. Moonseed was a climbing vine, moonwort a small fern, mooncalf a word for a fool, moonwalk brought to mind a dance move...

She beckoned Tom over. 'It's a long shot, and I've no idea what the link would be... I can tell Norm is born and bred Mancunian, but a person born in the county of Wiltshire can be known as a moonraker. Was your mum born down south?'

'Nope. Wilmslow, the posh side of Manchester.'

'Was she a fan of James Bond films?'

'Yes, but didn't like that one.'

Alex pushed ahead. The name Luna means moon; did his parents ever own a cat or dog called that? They didn't. Nor did his mum ever own jewellery made from moonstone, and none of her favourite songs had the word in, such as 'Fly Me to the Moon', or

'Moonlight Serenade'. Freddie *Mercury*'s music was the nearest she'd come to liking anything to do with outer space.

Tom yawned. 'Captain Beaky and I are going up. Fancy dinner tonight, so I can pick your brains about writing? I could throw together an omelette.'

She gave the thumbs up, and as he left, Jade came past, apron off.

'Jade, come and sit down for a moment.'

'Why would I want to do that?'

'To allow me to apologise properly.'

A chair scraped back and Jade dropped onto it, arms folded, a defiant look on her face.

'I'm truly sorry but I'm bowled over by your talent.'

'I'll accept your apology if you stop talking rubbish.'

'Believe me, don't believe me, but I can tell you've got a gift. That storyboard is incredible, the characters jump off the page, the detail of the drawings sucks you in.' Alex raised an eyebrow. 'So what are you going to do about it?'

'*Do?*'

'A gift like that should be shared.'

'I'm an amateur, Alex.' She swept an arm around the room. 'My real talent is for making amazing hot chocolates.'

'Creatives aren't born as professionals, Jade. I worked in a bank before my first novel. I got a deal without a degree in creative writing. Google "Imposter Syndrome" when you get home. All artists suffer from it at one point or another.'

'Are we done?' asked Jade and she stood up.

Alex leant back. 'Sure. Unless "the moon being beautiful" means something to you.'

Jade raised an eyebrow. 'As it happens, that phrase does – but only if we're talking anime, that's the animated version of manga. I keep meaning to watch a series called *Tsuki ga Kirei*. It's about

two high school students and their romance – an original series
not based on books. It has a sweet innocent edge to it, apparently,
a bit like *Heartstopper*.'

'And...?'

'Its title means "the moon is beautiful, isn't it"?'

19

Half an hour later, Alex stood in the shower, the jukebox's last song of the day playing in her head, 'The Girl from Ipanema'. The toucan bird lived in Brazil, with its striking black body, white throat and huge yellow-orange bill. The bill looked heavy but was actually light, due to tiny air holes in it. Alex's whole body had felt heavy these last years, the sense of loss dragging her down. Yet light and airy was the image she projected, in real life and online, laughing with fans, flirting with boyfriends, the queen of funny GIFs.

Alex pulled on jeans and a shirt; she hadn't felt this excited about writing for months. It brought in a different dimension, having someone to brainstorm with who wasn't market or money conscious. She sat on the bed to examine her feet. Recently the soles had been dry and itchy. She'd moisturised at night but that made no difference. She picked up her phone and hesitated before opening up Chrome. It didn't take her long to discover that body itching was one of the symptoms of the peri-menopause, along with everything else the doctor had mentioned. Her search went further. Forty-seven was the average age for peri-menopause to begin but it could be up to a decade earlier. Websites popped up with chat rooms and women sharing advice and experiences. If only Mum was around, she'd ask her about it. On and off during the school years Alex had found Mum crying in the kitchen. She'd laugh it off, saying it was nothing, that she didn't really know why she was so upset. Alex always assumed her dad had been mean again but perhaps, sometimes, there had been another reason.

Alex brought up her contacts list and tapped on Hope's name. Her finger hovered over the message box. She shook herself and shoved the phone in her back pocket. After grabbing a notebook and pen, she headed upstairs. Tom opened the door.

'Legs!' squawked Captain Beaky.

'He said that earlier.' Alex examined the lower half of her body again.

Tom deposited the parrot on the bird stand. 'No doubt George would approve, for all the wrong reasons, whereas, for once, my feathered friend has innocent intentions. *Legs* sounds like *Lex* and Fletch has been calling you that, hasn't he, and in front of Captain Beaky? All I can think is that this clever lad has connected the words Lex and Alex together, and realises they are about you. He's certainly intelligent enough. You must have made quite an impression on him.'

A comforting sensation spread through her chest. She passed Tom a bottle of white wine and went over to the play stand. The bird cocked its head and then... Alex crouched. He'd flown up and landed on her head. He bent down and chewed on a lock of her hair. Tom came over and held out his arm. Captain Beaky jumped on it and he placed the bird on her shoulder instead.

'He was trying to preen you. That's an act of affection.'

She turned her head sideways and the bird did too, his panda eyes coming into view. Very slowly she raised a hand and stroked his chest. Each equally surprised, the parrot and the author stared at each other.

* * *

After eating, she and Tom lounged on the sofa, Captain Beaky settled on Tom's lap.

'So whose scene should come first in the prologue, Jack's or Clara's?' asked Tom.

'As mostly women will read this book, Clara's? What do you think?' This was new, taking into account someone else's opinion, without going on the attack or putting up defences.

'That makes sense,' he replied. 'Her first chapter should lead, too.'

'For my opening scene, the events in the Buddhist centre will be revealed, and Clara will mention her secret but not what it is. That will raise the reader's curiosity.' She put down her pen. 'What inspired your short story, Tom? A secret of your own?'

Captain Beaky's eyes closed as Tom stroked his feathers. 'The devastation of the last few years, I suppose. Everyone will have secrets about how they've coped in private. It's relatable, right?'

The act of actually writing was the one area of her life where Alex was scrupulously honest and often her characters' emotions mirrored hers. However, discussing those feelings out loud, with another person, was something altogether different. She gripped her pen. 'Yes. I've had extremely low moments, where life has felt like a spinning wheel and I've wanted to peel off my public smile and hide under the duvet.'

'Losing a parent is tough.'

'I'm sorry for you too, now losing Norm, but in a different way. I know that's life, the ups and downs, but I never knew it could get so bad.'

Tom shuffled up and slipped an arm around her shoulder. For a second she went rigid but then relaxed. It had been so long since someone had done that simple act, without making a joke or hoping it was a speedy step towards having sex.

'Simon left me for a younger woman. She's only twenty-six, a personal trainer,' she found herself saying. Kate's words had rung in her ears, *you're as old as the fear you feel*. Getting old... had that become Alex's fear, because it meant being rejected or replaced, it meant loss? 'After finding out about Megan,' she continued, 'I felt written off, like an old car with too much mileage, scratched bodywork and worn tyres.' So she'd traded herself in for a shinier version, painting over any flaws and injecting them with Botox. Everyone knew vintage cars were worth the most, as long as they looked as if they'd just come off a production line. 'When Mum died, I worried about my future in a way I never had before.' Old age had loomed before her like a wake of vultures. Her mum had come home from a bird sanctuary once, over-flowing with vulture facts – how they'd vomit if threatened so they could fly off more easily, how they'd urinate on their feet to cool them down in hot weather. Becoming an author had fought off the fear for a while, of the ravaging, scavenging years ahead. Her new career had given the coming years structure and purpose, and the prospect of funds far beyond her banking salary so that she'd be in a position to make comfortable choices in her later years.

Tom pulled her closer. 'Come here, colleague. Look how you used those hard times to build a career. Okay, like any other, it's going through a sticky patch, but I've got a good feeling about this project of ours. I can't wait to get the prologue done.'

She wanted to snuggle closer, to bury her head in his chest, but mustn't get used to that human warmth that had been missing for so long, only to have it disappear on 1 July. And he had called her 'colleague'. She liked that about Tom; you always knew where you were.

'It certainly has been a bumpy ride. The Eternal Springs blog hasn't helped – that's the blog I mentioned to you before that left a damning review for my last book.' She explained about its reputation, number of followers, and how a bad review on there had caused her downfall. They talked more about the prologue and how it could be a little flash forwards. Jack would reveal he had a secret, like Clara did.

'Then chapter one will go back and cover a scene from Clara's life as it is at the moment, to give the reader context, before she escapes into the Buddhist centre in distress, not knowing where to turn due to her life being a mess.'

'Great,' agreed Tom. 'Jack's first one, the book's second chapter, could deal with his context too, before he meets Clara. Then the dramatic events will unfold.'

'Their secrets are...?'

He rubbed his hands together. 'Clara has been hiding the fact she has a young son; she feels having a child held her back, in her last job, from promotion, so hasn't told a single co-worker. Whereas Jack's restaurant was built on the premise of traditional home cooking, but due to the cost of living crisis he's been using ready prepared bake mixes.'

'Tom! That's genius. Both those scenarios are going to provide plenty of scope for humour. We can't avoid planning ahead a hundred per cent, but to keep the process fresh we can consider just a few chapters ahead at a time.'

'Don't you think it makes more sense to sub four chapters to your agent, instead of three, two from each character's point of view?' He smiled. 'I'm all for equality.'

Mum would like that. She'd always been keen on how many bird species defied the idea that it was a female's natural role to do the child-rearing, with both avian parents caring for the young, equality at its very best. In fact, male Emperor penguins alone incubated the eggs. A teenage Alex felt secretly grateful her dad didn't show more interest in her mum's passion for birds and get ideas. She didn't want to spend any more time than necessary with his tempers and unkind comments.

Despite a bit of beak grinding, Captain Beaky slept peacefully, as Tom asked questions about the craft of writing. She passed on the tips she always gave aspiring writers, the basics about show not tell, keeping firmly in point of view and not overusing adjectives or adverbs – yet making it clear so-called rules were to be broken if necessary. Mouth dry, she fetched a glass of water. Saturday had already arrived. Alex yawned and slipped her shoes back on, reluctant to get up from the cosy sofa. At least that's what she told herself, but it was more than that. The thing she missed most about Mum and Simon was that sense of home, and just for a moment, the three of them sitting here, had reminded her how that felt. She studied the parrot's mottled grey colouring and striking red tail feathers.

'He really is a pretty boy,' she murmured.

Captain Beaky snapped one eye open.

20

Fairy lights lit up the dim bar in Deansgate, one of Alex's favourites. Or was it? These days she was used to the calmer atmosphere of the Wrong Order Café, with gentle jazz in the background broken only by customers' laughs and Captain Beaky's pronouncements. Due to the humid weather, it had been a busy Saturday and more than once she'd had to charge out to the supermarket on Market Street to buy bags of ice cubes for Jade's frappés. After the meals at his, Alex felt she owed Tom dinner and invited him out. Blow the expense, the two of them might be about to write a best-seller, and she couldn't wait to tell him what she'd found out thanks to the animated series Jade had mentioned. She'd resisted the temptation to go back to her own glass tower flat and pick up a glamorous outfit. Seeing her desk and the old four walls again, which had begun to feel like a prison, might have killed her renewed enthusiasm.

R'n'B songs played and people drank colourful cocktails in bodycon dresses and muscle-fit T-shirts. Alex had simply slipped into a pair of linen trousers with an elastic waist, and a loose white blouse. Her hair was still scraped back into a ponytail but

she'd powdered her face, surprised by the relief at not feeling
obliged to get dressed up. It was only Tom. He was meeting her
there at seven, after driving to the care home to give a box of
birthday chocolates to one particular carer who treated Norm like
family. Alex had popped into the big Boots at the end of Market
Street and asked the chemist about cream for her itchy feet. Her
visit there took longer than expected as she ended up in an aisle
full of menopause products, with supplements for joints, and
skin and nails, with special shampoos and intimate gels. Perhaps
it was time to register with an NHS doctor and find out more.

More about the next stage of her life. More about getting
older.

Mum believed in facing your fears, like telling Dad she was
leaving. No one had expected his tears, but by that time Mum had
no sympathy left, not when it came to him. The dikkop waterbird
had partly inspired her. It laid its eggs next to the nests of the Nile
crocodiles, to protect its offspring from other predators. The two
species cohabited, the bird sometimes protecting the crocodiles'
eggs as well, with its wings. So even though her mum was scared
of life ahead, like the dikkop bird, she bravely embraced the
necessary challenges.

Alex took out her phone, brought up her contacts and tapped
on Hope's name. She selected the camera option, held the phone
in the air, took a selfie and sent it.

I borrowed your shirt, it's nice and baggy, all of mine are too clingy for
this weather. Same with the trousers. I bet today Manchester is hotter
than the Far East.

She paused, thinking about the kiss Hope had signed off with
last time.

I hope the food has got better. x

She pressed send but then typed again.

Remember telling me you were scared of everything? How you wake
in the night, over-thinking and worrying? Have you heard of the peri-
menopause?

She deleted the last word and went to drop her phone back in
her handbag but instead typed the word again.

I thought I was pregnant. Turns out I couldn't have been more wrong.

She pressed send again, before she blurted anything else out.
Opening up wasn't easy, but speaking to Tom yesterday... It was
the first time she'd been that honest with anyone since Mum and
it had left her lighter inside.

Five past seven. She'd give Tom ten more minutes and then
order a drink. Waiters strode past with beers and cocktails, and
wooden boards bearing stacked burgers and metallic mugs of
fries.

'Yo there, Alexandra.'

Alex felt like a customer who'd been caught trying to make off
without paying. Only one person had ever called her that, a guy
who had latched onto her at a book event in Salford. Turned out
he was an aspiring writer. Turned out he was great in bed. But
even that wasn't enough for her to keep seeing him for longer
than one week. In his head his novel was going to be the next big
thing. She'd read the first 5,000 words, told him it needed work,
that opening chapters full of backstory weren't going to pull in
readers, you needed to dive into the main plot from the off.

However, he wouldn't stop pushing, asking for her help, asking for an introduction to Miranda. Alex ghosted him in the end.

'Hi, Hawk.' *Was that even his real name?*

He brandished an almost-empty flute. 'Fancy seeing you here,' he said, raven hair longer now and tied back in a man-bun. He wore sunglasses even though it was dark inside. 'The extra curves suit you, babes.'

An insult with no imagination wasn't going to upset her.

'I followed your last book going up in the charts – shame it fell so quickly.'

'Hawk, I'm sorry we lost touch but—'

'*Lost touch?* That's some way you've got with words.'

'I needed more me-time.'

'That was the coolest way to end it?' He waved a hand in the air. 'But no matter, I got my deal and am going to be published next month.'

He was?

'Guaranteed success. I've paid the publisher one thousand up front for the most amazing advertising campaign; they've reassured me it will work.'

Don't say it, don't say it. 'Hawk, publishers pay you, not the other way around.'

His thick eyebrows scrunched together and he took his sunglasses off. 'I didn't take you for the jealous type.'

Despite him being an idiot, she'd never forget the thrill of writing her first novel, that sense of achievement – and sense of entitlement she could now see she'd had. Who was Alex to judge him? A hand rested on her shoulder. Tom.

'Everything all right?' he said pleasantly to Hawk.

'Whoa, steady on, Granddad.'

Alex stood up. 'It's okay, Tom. Why don't you go and get our drinks? I'll have what you're having.' She nodded at him and he left.

Alex turned to Hawk. 'I'm sorry for the way things ended. It was cowardly of me. But I found your requests for help overwhelming. Ours was supposed to be a personal not professional relationship, a bit of fun.'

He opened his mouth to protest but changed his mind, slipping on his sunglasses again.

'You ought to know you're dealing with a vanity publisher; it's a scam. Many aspiring writers are caught out this way and I'm sorry you've already paid out. You deserve better, Hawk. Don't let them publish. Report them to the Society of Authors. Then learn more about writing, buy how-to books, listen to podcasts. I did all of that while writing my first story. There's nothing special about me. If I can do it, so can you.'

Tom had appeared and set down their drinks. Hawk rubbed his arm, in an embarrassed manner, and swiftly took his leave. Alex let out a deep sigh and picked up one of the red wines. She clinked glasses with Tom before taking a large mouthful and sitting opposite him. She liked the casual waistcoat he wore.

'Don't ask,' she said.

He gave a mischievous smile. 'But as writers, working together, on a story that features romance, surely we should know a little more about each other's dating history? You've already met Kate.'

She rolled her eyes, yet found it easy to tell him about her first taste of romance, after Simon, with the barman at her book launch in London. She'd dated men in and out of the publishing world, from a shoe shop owner to a librarian. Not all of her dates were memorable. In hindsight, some were desperate. Her longest relationship was with Ryan. That ended last Christmas. They'd been seeing each other for six months.

'Why did you break up, if you don't mind me asking?'

Alex sipped her wine. 'I was afraid of letting him get close.'
Afraid of letting him see the real me.

The conversation swung to Tom, how he and Kate broke up three years ago, a year before his dad had to go into a care home. They'd been together five years. She wanted a partner who could go travelling with her, be more spontaneous, but Norm was becoming increasingly reliant on Tom. When a six-month volunteering trip came up working as a public health assistant in Costa Rica, educating people about nutrition, Kate couldn't stop talking about it. Tom encouraged her to go and they grew apart.

He took a handful of peanuts from a nearby bowl. 'Looking back, we weren't a good match. I could never grow old with someone who doesn't eat chocolate.'

'You've never married?'

'Married to the business when I was younger... and then it all seemed too late; my social life dwindled as friends got engaged, married, had kids. Then Dad's memory problems surfaced.'

'Dancing in the Moonlight' played.

'Thanks to Jade I've made a breakthrough about his moon fixation,' said Alex, stomach fizzing in the way it used to when she had a new idea for a novel. She told him about the animated series *Tsuki ga Kirei*, a romance, its title meaning 'the moon is beautiful, isn't it?' She rubbed her hands together. 'Imagine you are Japanese, dating me and—'

'So I'm twenty years younger with no laughter lines? Okay, I can do that.'

'As I was saying, we're seeing each other and go outdoors later, imagine we come from very traditional families and are very polite, a little old-fashioned. I might gaze into the night sky and shyly say "*Tsuki ga kire*" – "the moon is beautiful, isn't it?" I googled it and it has a double-meaning, Tom. It's code for "I love you".'

'What?'

'I know! So charming, isn't it?'

'So... Dad being upset that he should have told someone the moon is beautiful, could really be him worrying that he should have told someone he loved them?' His brow furrowed. 'I'm not sure it can be that. He told Mum at every opportunity. Her brother, Uncle Neil, used to say as much; he'd been a little envious of their relationship, over the years, said it was nause-ating how often they declared their feelings for each other. They used to both say they were each other's one and only loves, first and last. Plus, neither of them is Japanese. Although occasionally Dad used to talk about serving sushi in the café; he's always loved Japanese food.'

Alex broke eye contact and picked up the menu. 'It's as you thought, then, Norm's fixation must be one of those random things. Right, let's get food. They do great kebabs here.'

'Alex?'

'The chipotle chicken burger, here, is fantastic.'

'Come on. Out with it,' he ordered.

She hesitated. 'I'm probably wrong, but... could Norm be talking about something he wished he'd said to another woman?'

21

Hi Alex, yes, I read about the peri-menopause in a magazine at the hairdresser's. But my mum simply got on with all that, my auntie too, certainly my grandmothers. I never heard it being discussed, so what right have I to complain? Isn't it just part of a woman's lot? A natural process? But it is tough. If someone had been rude to me, like you were, in the Village, the last thing the old me would have done was cry. Ten years ago the bookshop I'd worked so hard to build went bust…

Wait. She owned a bookshop? But then that made sense in light of how passionate Hope had been talking about her favourite authors, back in the Village. When Alex had asked her what made her happy, Hope had said *books and more books*.

It couldn't cope with online competition, and what with having to stay closed in 2020… However I got through that bankruptcy, but have never doubted and questioned myself as much as I do now. Leah's ace, does her best to support me, but is too young to really understand, plus I don't want to sound like I'm complaining all the time. And middle-aged celebrities look so young these days, talking about their sex lives or the latest triathlon they've completed... most days I feel like it's just me.

We're in Cambodia now. No one warned me about tarantulas the size of hands. But I'm eating the most amazing sticky rice cakes. Ask Tom to make you his walnut and maple syrup pancakes. Hope x

Alex ran a finger over the message as she sat at the small dining table in Hope's flat. She'd been polishing her prologue scene since it was Monday and the café was closed.

My mum didn't talk about it either, Hope. I wish someone had warned me. Perhaps I wouldn't have given myself such a hard time these last years. Perhaps my world falling apart hasn't only been down to Simon, to Mum's illness – to me. Maybe I've not been failing and I'm not a bad person, getting so angry and irritated by small things, crying over trivia, forgetting people's names, forgetting words, going into a room and not knowing what for. Deep down I've worried I had early-onset dementia, that's one reason finding out about the Wrong Order Café was a shock.

Good luck with the spiders. Alex x

A knock rapped on the door and Alex grabbed her notebook, slipped on trainers and opened the door. She followed Tom upstairs and into the flat, carrying a plastic bag.

'Legs!' came a squawk.

Alex reached into the pocket of her baggy shorts – well, Hope's – and pulled out a bag of almonds as she headed over to the play stand. Captain Beaky took one from her palm. Tom sat on the sofa, quietly reading his notes. She went back to the door, lifted the plastic bag and shook it.

'I brought food. Don't get too excited. Cheese and coleslaw sandwiches. Crisps. Apples.' A meal she would have turned her nose up at a couple of weeks ago. Lunch, at her desk, was sushi or a black coffee and small bar of Green & Black's. Dinner was out, or a box from Bernardo's next door. 'How was Norm?'

'He enjoyed the sunshine. Luck was on our side with it being less humid today. The odd cloud meant we could stay out there longer, even though he slept after twenty minutes.' He stood up and stretched, disappeared into the spare bedroom and came back with a small bird carrier. 'Let's eat outside.'

But the building had no back garden. He must have meant out the front. It might be noisy but Tom wasn't his usual cheerful self so she went along with it. The parrot squawked and flapped his wings before happily hopping into the carrier, as if he knew where he was going. Alex followed Tom out into the hallway and... Oh. Up the flight of stairs at the end of the corridor. They came to a door at the top. Tom took a key out of his pocket, opened it and they walked into a rooftop garden. Alex placed the bag on a small wooden bench and admired the array of plants in brightly coloured pots. There were pines and small palms and lavender bushes. Trellis panels with sprawling artificial ivy covered the metal railing going all around, giving privacy. The small bench partnered with a picnic table. A ceramic bird bath stood at the far end. She went over to the trellis and admired the eclectic skyline, with its space age skyscrapers contrasting a crusty old factory, and a green square of park providing relief from grey buildings.

A noise disturbed her and she turned around to face the most prominent feature of the roof space, on the opposite side, an aviary as tall as Tom, with a variety of stands, of fixed and swinging perches, a hidey-hole box and toys with bells. Tom had stepped inside and closed the door behind him. He put the carrier on the floor and Captain Beaky strutted out before flying up to a swinging perch.

'Out and about! Out and about!' the parrot squawked and whistled.

Carefully, Tom came out and sat down at the bench, while Alex unpacked tea.

'Sometimes we come up in the evening and enjoy the sunset together,' he said. 'It depends on the wind and, of course, we don't venture out in the winter.'

'What a treat for him,' she said and passed Tom a sandwich wrapped in a napkin. 'I hope these are okay.'

'You had me at coleslaw.'

They sat in silence, or rather not talking, the soundtrack of Manchester playing, with car horns, aeroplane engines and police sirens. Captain Beaky wrestled with a rope toy as a blue tit landed on the edge of the bird bath. One day, when Alex was old enough, Mum had shown her how to open child-proof medicine bottles and spoke of the phenomenon, documented from the late sixties, of blue tits teaching each other how to open the old-fashioned British doorstep milk bottles with foil tops, to access the cream that had floated to the top.

Shadows under Tom's eyes curved deeply. Alex wished she could show him how to cope with the slow, painful loss of the dad he loved, but like caring for her mum who was also never going to recover, Alex knew Tom would have to find his own way.

Still. That didn't mean she couldn't try to help, and to do that she needed to channel plain-speaking Reenie and Fletch.

'Friday. The beautiful moon. Let's talk about it, Tom. Your whistling has been even more out of tune than usual since then.'

He smiled, put down his sandwich and stretched out his legs. 'I must be distracted. It's just... I'm struggling with the possibility that Dad, my dad, might have been having an affair... or had been seeing someone after Mum passed, but was scared I wouldn't approve so hid it from me. I thought he and I told each other everything, that he knew all I wanted was for him to be happy.' Tom bit into the bread again. 'Although I'd find it difficult to believe. I can see why you might have suggested it, not knowing Dad like I do. He was never one for keeping secrets. Either way I need to address his fixation. Dad mentioned it again today. It makes him so bloody sad.'

'Is there a close friend or other relative he might have confided in?'

'No. He's an only child. Uncle Neil became the sibling he'd never had, but died shortly before Dad became ill.' Tom chewed slowly. 'Although... it's a long shot, mind... an old best friend of his, from school, Jimmy, still lives in the north-west, in Liverpool, last I knew. I wouldn't say they've been as close in recent years, but they met up now and again. I got the impression Dad would have liked to see him more often, but Jimmy was a chef for a cruise ship company and often abroad. They went to catering college together.' He shrugged. 'His phone number will be in Dad's address book.'

Alex gave a thumbs up and headed over to the edge, gazing down at Stevenson Square. 'What's that covered area all down the middle?'

'Underground toilets, disused now, originally built around the time of the First World War. You know, about ten years ago a void was discovered underneath the Arndale; there were once plans to build an underground rail system in Manchester. The idea was shelved in the seventies due to government spending cuts. Dad prided himself on knowing all sorts of trivia about the city.' Tom smiled to himself.

'What's so funny?' she asked, leaning on the railing.

'Oh... nothing.'

'Tom?'

'Dad used to laugh really hard about one particular fact.

Manchester was founded by the Romans. They built a fort in between two hills that they thought looked like, well... breasts.' His pale cheek pinked up under the day-old stubble.

'Go on...' she said, finding his embarrassment oddly endearing.

'This led to the name Mamucium meaning "breast-shaped hills", then later the Normans arrived and across the UK, at the time, all of their settlements used the word "chester". Hence Manchester.'

'I think your dad and I would have got on. I love discovering trivial facts while I research, like San Francisco being built on more than fifty hills.' She shrugged. 'Let's ring Jimmy.'

'*Now?*'

'Research comes above all else.'

They ate and then Tom went to fetch drinks. He came back with two cordials and a leather address book tucked under one arm. He settled next to her on the bench and dialled Jimmy's number. The two men chatted for a bit as Alex relaxed and enjoyed her drink.

'No, honestly, that's fine, Jimmy. I understand. Yes... great... okay. Cheers. See you then.' Tom ended the call and turned to Alex. 'He felt bad about not visiting Norm since his diagnosis. Jimmy worried he might not handle it well, might say the wrong thing, he's never dealt with anyone who's had dementia.'

'Several of Mum's friends stopped calling when she got her terminal diagnosis. It hit her hard.'

Despite her anger, Alex had understood how difficult it was to know what to say to someone who knew they were dying. Even though Alex wasn't religious, as Mum lay in the hospice bed, right at the end, Alex had whispered that they'd meet up again, in a heaven populated by birds. The two of them would sit, tandem-style, on the backs of large geese and fly through the sky. Rainbow-coloured birds would sit on their shoulders as they fed them berries and strolled through forests dusted with glitter. In the evenings they'd bathe in sparkling lakes alongside a flock of Mum's favourite waterbird, the Mandarin duck. Safe in the knowledge that mother and daughter, hand in hand, would be together for eternity.

Mum had slipped away so quietly, Alex didn't notice.

'Jimmy is over in Manchester at the weekend; his wife's sister lives here and it's her seventieth birthday. I explained the café was closed on Monday so he suggested he accompanied me to the care home to see Dad then. We'll meet here first. He'll tell us what he knows.'

'You reckon he can help?'

'Maybe. He mentioned something about sushi, but then had to go as his front door bell rang.'

22

Alex put down her cordial as a leaf waltzed across the rooftop. 'Time to crack on with our book. Let's read out our prologue scenes.'

'You first,' Tom said quickly, unable to leave his beaded bracelet alone.

She picked up her notes and the friendly summer breeze lifted her top sheet of paper.

'"Feeling oddly light-headed, Clara took off her pumpkin beanie and, through the street-facing window, peered up into the sky where seagulls swirled as if painting a Van Gogh. She struck up a conversation with a man next to her who couldn't keep still..."'

Tom listened intently as she read through the scene that ended with someone screaming. By then he was perched on the edge of the bench.

'You've really hooked the reader in, leaving them to guess what on earth is happening. Love a little less that I've now got to read my own work out,' he said and pulled a face.

'Any criticism?'

'Oh, I don't know, I mean, I'm only an amateur.'

'Honestly. Go for it.' Reenie and Fletch made mistakes all the time and didn't cave in when they were corrected. A wave of heat swept up her body. Perhaps Alex Butler the author had become too sensitive.

Jack mentioned a couple of points and Alex found herself agreeing.

'After telling her secret to Jack, Clara talks about there being two kinds of people – those who take risks and open up, and those who keep themselves to themselves.' Tom tilted his head. 'Which are you, Alex?'

The swimming pool from her childhood, her dad's outstretched arms, came to mind straight away. 'The second; even family can't always be relied on. What about you?'

'I believe that when people are at their lowest they feel very much alone and make black and white generalisations – "everyone is against me", "the world is a terrible place"... Phrases like that, weirdly, act as a comfort. However, I reckon the truth is there's plenty of good out there if you look for it; plenty of people more than willing to help save you, if you'll just let them in.'

Avoiding his eyes, she picked up an apple and took a large bite.

'Let me make a few tweaks to my opening scene, so that it fits,' said Tom, 'because that's going to be the process, isn't it, for co-authoring? At least for us, as we aren't planning much.'

'I know as much as you on that score.'

Alex took another bite while he crossed out a couple of words and scribbled in new ones, Tom's comments persisting in her mind. *Simon was a bastard. The world was unfair for taking Mum. Publishing is a cut-throat business.* Those three generalisa-tions had seen her through tough times; feeling hard done by eased any pain. But maybe Tom had a point. Simon had suggested counselling at the end and been more than easy-going regarding the divorce settlement. As for her mother, the world had actually dealt Alex a great hand, by giving her Mum in the first place. Then publishing... why should she and Miranda be best friends? It was a business relationship and Miranda had helped Alex reach heights other authors could only dream of. Her editor, too, only suggested changes to make work stronger – she'd always suspected that deep down and could see it more clearly now.

'Be gentle with me,' said Tom. 'I've only got one short story to my credit. Well, a half-finished one.' He gave a nervous smile as if about to read out a defence statement. Alex focused completely while he spoke. As he finished, an ambulance siren sounded in the distance.

'Tom!' She grabbed his hands. 'Your writing's bang on the mark! Engaging, tightly put together. I'm so impressed considering how new you are to this game.'

'Me writing a novel... it feels more real, now we've started. Is this really happening?' he asked.

'You'd better believe it,' she said and let go of his hands, baffled as to why she'd grabbed them in the first place. She'd never done that with a manager or co-worker before, especially one who couldn't match socks, and day in, day out, whistled with such alarming cheerfulness. 'I'm curious, why does Jack go to the Buddhist centre instead of drowning his sorrows in the pub, or talking things through with a friend? Clara acts on impulse, while passing, but he seems to have planned it.'

'His mum died recently. Throughout her life, when she'd had a problem, she'd go to the Buddhist centre and said she always came out of the building with the solution. Jack went there to feel closer to her spirit, hoping she'd be hanging around, listening to his thoughts, offering advice like she always used to.'

That was quite lovely and the spark that had ignited inside Alex's chest, since changing writing direction, grew bigger.

'Let's get together again next Monday, in the morning before Jimmy arrives,' she said, 'each with our first chapter.' She cleared her throat. 'Thanks, Tom. This project is really going to help me rediscover my love of words.'

'Does that mean my name goes first on the cover?'

'Absolutely not.'

They leant back, elbows touching. His arm wrapped around her and he squeezed. Alex relaxed. Tom was a hugger, the way he greeted Reenie and Fletch each morning was proof of that. She wasn't used to it. The work culture in the bank had been more formal and publishing types were fans of the air-kiss.

'I found that Eternal Springs blog you talked about and read the review you felt was "damning". For *Parisian Power Trip*, wasn't it?' Tom asked.

'Carnage.'

'The blogger felt you were simply ticking boxes.'

'Please, don't remind me.'

'I only bring it up because, the way I read the post, the author of the blog came across as if they were a genuine fan. They spoke about how much they'd loved previous books, what skill you had for creating characters that jumped off the page, but that this was the first book of yours they'd been able to put down midway. In their opinion the ending was rushed; usually you were the queen of denouement. Those are compliments in a way, right? They ended by saying they still couldn't wait for your next book, hoping you were back on form.'

'More like they couldn't wait to tear it apart. Even if there were positive elements – and I don't agree – that's not what the blog readers saw. Did you scroll through the comments?'

'But that's the internet, people with nothing better to do.'

Alex didn't answer. That review had been mean-spirited and led to a wave of bad publicity that, in turn, made her career spiral, but... had Alex lost perspective? She'd allowed writing to become her whole purpose, it was how she measured her success, not only as an author, but as a person. No wonder she took every criticism to heart.

'Thanks once again, Alex, for giving me this chance. It's a real honour to work with such an established author and I'll give it all I've got,' he said, as if swearing his allegiance to his country.

'You could repay me by making your walnut and maple syrup pancakes. Hope mentioned them. We've been texting.'

'Deal. Let's just give Captain Beaky a bit more fresh air.'

Alex leant into him; evening sun rays landed on her skin as she breathed in the calming fragrance of lavender. Bliss. The noise in her head drained away, as if she'd taken a sedative. Captain Beaky was hanging upside down. Tom explained how it meant he was very content. Parrots were at their most vulnerable positioned like that, so it meant he was very comfortable with his surroundings, very comfortable with Alex and Tom. Right at this moment, if Alex were a bird, she'd probably have hung upside down too.

She glanced at him. He looked her way. Very slightly their faces edged towards each other. But then Captain Beaky squawked. With a start, Alex straightened up and grabbed her notebook. 'Washing to do. See you tomorrow.'

'Everything okay?' Tom asked as she got to her feet. 'Is it something I've said?'

She shook her head and hurried towards the door, heart pounding as she ran down the stairs, entered her flat and locked the door behind her.

23

It was almost dawn and Alex had been awake since three in the morning, messaging Hope. Cambodian time was six hours ahead.

Crap. I ran out on Tom last night. We were discussing our novel, on the rooftop. One minute I was relaxing next to him, the next I was in your flat sobbing. This is why I can't talk to anyone else. I detest that hysterical menopausal woman trope and won't risk anyone writing me off as that. I just feel so unprofessional.

A reply pinged onto the screen.

Wait... Tom is writing a book with you? How? Why?

Alex typed back.

He's got a talent. Working together has solved my writer's block. And we were getting on so well...

Another ping.

Are you and he...?

Good grief, no. I just saw Captain Beaky hanging upside down and thought that's me and if I'm not careful...

It was hard to explain, but at least with Hope she could try. Had her and Tom had 'a moment'? If so, it was unintentional; her body had simply reacted, on automatic, to close human touch. Tom and her? Sure, he was good looking, with the youthful hair and laid-back attitude that not many middle-aged men wore. But he and her, they were too opposite. Despite life's challenges, he kept focused on the next destination, propelled by a whistle and carefree nature she'd never understand, working alongside employees he knew would soon say goodbye, baking his scones, laughing with Captain Beaky. When Mum had fallen ill, Alex's life had imploded; she'd given up work, she'd made life-changing decisions because of it. Whereas Tom had carried on and faced Norm's illness; it had even become part of his business, making money – unlike Alex who had lost all her savings trying to escape the reality of Mum's diagnosis.

Part of her admired Tom and his easy-going manner, that ability to deflect the hurt. Her phone pinged with another message from Hope.

Take a deep breath. Just be honest with Tom, Alex, tell him how you felt. Right. Must go. Our coach is arriving at Banteay Chhmar. We're going temple exploring. Our tour guide is a lovely bloke and is sitting in the seat across the aisle from me. He's a huge Man United fan and mimicked my Mancunian accent. Leah almost died of embarrassment but he and I couldn't stop laughing.

Alex sat up in bed and her fingers tapped furiously.

Sounds like someone's got an admirer. What does this tour guide look like?

He's got one head, two arms and two legs. H xx

I expect a full report later. Thanks for listening. Have a good day. A xx

Alex hugged her knees, like a schoolgirl up late at a sleepover, sharing innermost feelings. When was the last time she'd spoken like this, to another person?

* * *

Light rain fell outside as Alex washed her face and pulled on jeans, a shirt, and pinned on her name badge, all a far cry from the morning routine in her glass tower apartment where she'd get up early to co-ordinate her clothes, moisturise and conceal. She wolfed down a slice of toast. As she walked into the café, Val passed her carrying Fletch's guitar.

Alex smiled. 'Thanks for bringing that in again.'

'Thank *you*. My Fletch actually picked it up over the weekend. He hasn't done that for weeks. He played me a Beatles medley.' Val gulped and she stopped, gathered herself. 'It hurts that none of you see the Fletch I've grown old with,' she said. 'It hits me now and again, how he used to entertain the grandkids, when they were little, singing the alphabet backwards and recounting their times tables in silly voices. He could do cryptic crosswords, I've never mastered those, and Fletch could easily schmooze his way out of any problem, his interpersonal skills were second to none.' Val hugged the guitar. 'I love him to bits. He'll always be my Fletch and I'm grateful he's not aware of how much has already gone, but it's hard... *so* hard, knowing that new people we meet will never know the whole man.' She turned away and opened the staffroom door. Tom sat on the sofa, in front of his laptop, whistling as usual.

'I'll take it if you like,' said Alex and went to give her a hug.

Val passed the guitar, shook her head and stood back. She wiped her eyes. 'I'm okay, honestly, Alex, I just needed to get that out. Don't be too nice or I'll lose it completely, and that won't do. I've got bills to pay, care home fees to save for; tears won't protect our home from being sold to fund Fletch's future.'

Alex watched Val go back into the café, shoulders hunched, footsteps dragging, leaving behind an overwhelming sense of perspective that never came Alex's way when living on her own, in a glass tower, with only the problems of fictional characters to observe. She went into the staffroom and leant the guitar against the back wall, next to the mural of a window looking onto a garden. Tom shot her a broad smile.

'You must be the most interminably cheerful person I've ever met,' she said.

'Mum used to say I came out of the womb looking as if Man U had won the World Cup.' Tom closed his laptop. 'I'm glad you're here. I couldn't get to sleep last night, thinking about... Tell me...'

Simon used to keep pushing, asking her what was the matter, with the low moods, grilling her every time she snapped. Trouble was, she couldn't explain and this was another reason she stuck to younger men after she and Simon had split. She still enjoyed quality conversations but the content was less emotional, less intense, like a stone that had weight, but once jettisoned across a lake skimmed and bounced along, without hitting dark depths.

'...how about if Jack's café actually looks onto the beach?' he said. 'We can really bring the setting into the story then, and other characters like lifeguards, cold water swimmers, dog owners.'

'Oh... right...' Her shoulders relaxed and she dropped onto the sofa next to him. 'I've only focused on the beginning of our book, a defence, I guess, in case Miranda hates the whole concept.'

'But there are other agents. If you and I believe in this project we should write it anyway. I've researched and didn't know that not all publishers require you to have representation. If Miranda doesn't take it, let's submit it to other agencies, then if that fails we can submit to publishers ourselves or there's self-publishing and...'

A breathlessness, that felt good, grew in her chest. Miranda turning down this book had already loomed before her like a permanent ending to this career that had come out of nowhere. Yet Tom was saying rejection might be another beginning. He talked more about minor characters they could bring in, the café's staff, one server named Susie, his mum would have liked that. Tom chatted away like Captain Beaky when he was happy. Mum once pointed out that even though they were birds, emus didn't chirp – they didn't fly either. In recent years Alex could relate to this, that sense of not fitting in with other people, like the authors supporting each other on socials and attending writing retreats together.

'What do you think?' he asked, and shot her a shy look that made her feel odd, not in an unpleasant way.

'It all sounds great. Why don't we figure out the basic plot arc of the whole story for our session on Monday? Really polish a synopsis and show Miranda we mean business. Delay getting on with the actual opening chapters until the week after?'

He gave a thumbs up and stretched out his legs.

'Although I'm not sure how someone who wears odd socks will come up with a well-considered plan,' she added.

'I stopped wearing matching pairs when Dad first got ill. Now and then Norm accidentally put on odd socks. It was one of the first signs that something wasn't quite right.' Tom's voice wavered. 'Even though he laughed about it, I could tell it upset him. So I wore odd socks too.' He rubbed the top of his arm. 'Dad and I got chatting with Jade one night,' he said. 'She avoids social media, says it's a false world where everyone portrays themselves as perfect. I love her neck tattoo and had this idea of Dad and I getting our names inked, written wrongly to prove that mistakes don't matter, they don't change who we are deep down.' He pulled up the sleeve of his T-shirt. There, in black, was the word "Thomas", in capitals, but with the S written the wrong way around. 'Dad's got one in the same place, it's Norm with the R back to front. The three letters in Tom look the same, turned around, so I went for Thomas instead.' He gave a wry smile. 'Mum would have approved; she always did prefer my full name.'

Odd socks, badly written tattoos... whereas since signing her first publishing deal, Alex had done everything in her power to present a faultless image.

She got to her feet and wiped her palms on her jeans. 'Sorry about last night, Tom. You see...'

He stood up beside her. 'No explanation needed,' he said gently. 'You'll tell me when you're ready. If that's never, that's okay too. I shouldn't have mentioned that blog. It was thoughtless to remind you of the details of that review.'

'It was nothing to do with that. You meant well.' She gave him a curious look. 'How come you're so understanding?'

'I've been through rough times, like we all have, bad relationship break-ups, but nothing, nothing compares to the last few years... Losing Mum at such a young age hardened me, I felt so much sorrow, anger too, at everything she'd miss. As I got older, I told myself the worst had already happened to someone I loved, her death, Dad's broken heart. Turns out I was wrong... the way his diagnosis affected him... I wish I could forget his face when he first found out; the consultant was so matter of fact, couldn't get us out of the room quick enough,' said Tom in a voice that might still demand satisfaction and ask the consultant for a duel. 'We were left to fend for ourselves in terms of finding help. Thank God for the Alzheimer's Society.' He shrugged. 'Seeing how all this affected Dad... if I'm honest that's what really inspired my short story about someone hitting rock bottom and needing to escape into a safe place.'

Norm must have felt as if he was suffocating, must have longed for a place where he could come up for air.

'Who knew that simply picking up a pen was just as healing as picking up a biscuit or glass of Scotch?' he said, arms lifted in the air in a comical manner.

Of course Tom would end the conversation with a joke. She walked into the café. Reenie took a moment; her eyes dropped to Alex's name badge and then she waved. Alex went over to Kay to fetch the notebook, ready to write in it everything Reenie did today.

'What time do you call this?' asked Jade.

Alex's shoulders relaxed. A sense of home washed over her. Home wasn't a place where everything was happy and pleasant the whole time, it was a place where people understood you, flaws and all. Mum would despair of how a young Alex would drop dirty laundry on the floor and Simon always tutted at how she'd leave gadgets permanently on standby. Living alone, in her fancy apartment, with only herself for company, it was too easy for Alex to believe she was perfect.

Thinking nothing in the world smelt better than warmed croissants, Alex cleared a table while Reenie spoke to two female customers. They both ordered French toast and Reenie chatted about a trip to Paris in the eighties. She talked about how the

Parisians' style and glamorous hair salons had inspired her to go into hairdressing when she returned to England. One of the women was a nail artist, the other a personal dresser. The three of them agreed that pride in your own appearance could make all the difference. Reenie delivered porridge to the women's table, instead of the French toast. With big smiles they thanked her and one of them got up to put a tune on the jukebox. Fletch stood by Captain Beaky, and the two of them swayed to 'April in Paris'.

A businessman Alex had served clicked his fingers in time to the music. Fletch caught Alex's eye; he came over and gave a little bow and took her hands. Heat swept up her neck as he rocked her to and fro, but Val watched and joy filled her face, as if she was flicking through a well-loved photo album of her husband in the old days. Reenie and Kay side-stepped in time, arms around each other. Tom came out of the staffroom to Captain Beaky squawking louder than usual and when Fletch twirled Alex around, she found herself laughing. The nail artist held out a hand to the bemused businessman. A Dave Brubeck song came on. Alex recognised the style. Simon's dad used to listen to it.

'One of Captain Beaky's favourites,' announced Tom. 'What's the music called?' he called loudly, towards the cage.

Body grooving, Captain Beaky cocked his head and squawked, '"There's No Place Like Home".'

Alex took in Reenie, Jade and the art on the walls; she smelt bacon, heard chefs chopping in the kitchen and customers chatting... she'd missed the hustle and bustle of everyday life. She held Fletch's fingers tightly, as if afraid she might lose this moment where she didn't feel judged, didn't feel like a failure, didn't feel rejected. Across the room Tom held out his hand to Jade. She gave him a withering look that made him grin. So he danced on his own as if the only people watching were those who mattered, the people who got it, swinging his hips, eyes closed, arms slowly flapping up and down, not a worry in the world. As the tune came to an end, Fletch had a big smile on his face until he gazed through the front window to see a man in a checked trilby outside, glued to his phone. Fletch's jaw dropped.

'There's John!' he said and let go of Alex's hands. He went up to the window and pressed his nose against the glass.

Val went over to Fletch and gently pulled him away. Jade came out from behind the counter. Val rubbed Fletch's back. 'Love... John passed away a few years ago, remember? But I can see why you would think it was him. John did love a hat.'

Cheeks reddened, Fletch turned around and he jabbed his finger in the air. 'I know I get some things wrong, but I'm right about this. I wouldn't forget my best mate dying.'

Val went to the jukebox and put on another tune. 'One of your favourite songs, love; show Alex your moves,' she called and gave Alex a pointed look. Distraction. Good idea. Alex took his hands again while Val disappeared to the ladies' and Jade went back behind the counter and turned to the coffee machine. However, Fletch couldn't stop staring out of the window. She swayed his hands from side to side.

'He might still be there, might be waiting for me,' said Fletch and let go of Alex. He pulled open the door.

She hesitated. Well, it wouldn't harm him to take a look; the man would be gone, that would put an end to his fretting. As he walked out, Jade turned around to face the room. She hurried over. Val reappeared.

'Where's my Fletch?' asked Val.

'He just popped out but that man will be long gone.'

'Outside? On his own? Are you mad?' said Jade, an ugly shade of red sweeping across her face. She yanked open the door. Fletch was heading to the right, towards Lever Street.

'Fletch, love, don't upset yourself,' Val called out as she and

Jade hurried after him. Not knowing what to do, Alex hung in the doorway. Tom appeared and followed Jade and Val.

Above the chat of drinkers outside, at the benches in the square, Fletch's voice carried into the café, distant now, but excited. 'John, lad, hold up! It's me, Fletch... don't cross the road... wait... I'm coming.'

Car brakes screeched. A scream followed. Alex started running, to see Val and Jade crying, leaning over Fletch who was stretched out flat, on the road.

24

Tom and Alex sat in the packed waiting room at A&E in silence, numb under the fluorescent lighting, opposite a father and son, the boy in football kit, his arm in a sling. Tom and Alex had closed up the café and put Jade's bicycle in the staffroom as she and Val had travelled with Fletch in the ambulance. It was almost dark outside. The emergency department's reception phone kept ringing. The smell of disinfectant hung in every corner. Tom fetched a second coffee.

'Did you see that blood on Fletch's head?' Alex muttered and took her drink. 'They're taking so long. Yet that's a good sign, right?'

Tom exhaled, long and hard. 'Fletch is an intrinsic part of the Wrong Order Café, always the first to welcome customers and best pal to Captain Beaky. He'd spend all day standing by the cage if Jade let him. If anything happens to him...'

He pulled out his phone to check again, just as doors swung open. Val and Jade leant against the wall and Tom and Alex hurried over. Tom took Val into his arms and her shoulders heaved. The four of them walked to a more private spot, away from the doors. Val blew her nose, hair tousled and trouser suit creased, most unlike the smart, bookkeeper they were used to.

'He's been taken into surgery.' Val's eyes streamed once more.

'Granddad has broken his leg,' said Jade, voice sounding thick, as she linked arms with her gran. 'He's also got a concussion.'

'They'll know more when he comes around from the anaesthetic...' Val's voice broke. 'If he does.'

Alex cursed herself for the hundredth time for not stopping Fletch going outside. It reminded her of when Mum had fallen ill – Alex thought she should have made her go to the doctor sooner when she'd complained of back pain and went off her favourite dessert. In time she realised it wasn't her fault, but this was different – Val had specifically asked her to distract Fletch and she hadn't.

The opposite had happened when Simon left her; she never once blamed herself, not for any of it. An uncomfortable twinge pinched her chest. As for Simon's words about him leaving being the best for Alex... lately she'd considered he could have been diagnosed with an incurable disease. Did that explain his out-of-character health kick? Being away from the flat, away from her author environment, away from her fictional world that sucked her in and was reluctant to let go until each deadline passed had been like putting on a pair of glasses that widened her view. She'd been so wrapped up in how *she* felt, had Alex lost sight of the fact that something might have been seriously wrong with her ex-husband?

'You both go, now,' said Val in an uneven voice. 'You're real troupers for hanging round so long.'

Alex couldn't look her in the eye.

Tom placed his hands on Val's shoulders. 'We'll wait until he's out of surgery. I'm here for you, every step of the way.'

'Do you need anything fetching from home?' asked Alex in a voice stronger than she felt. Val dabbed her eyes with a scraggy tissue. Alex reached into her beige crossbody bag, or rather Hope's – it was more practical than her own rattan one. Tentatively, she passed Val a packet of tissues.

'I don't want to put you out. Our Jade can collect anything,' said Val in a flat tone.

'I'd rather stay with Gran, if that's okay?' All of Jade's edge, the bluster, had gone. Alex reached into the bag again; Hope had left a tube of mints.

'I'm sorry, Jade... Val... I should never have let Fletch leave,' said Alex in an unsteady voice. She offered Jade a mint.

'It's okay. I shouldn't have shouted. Granddad can be unpredictable.'

'He almost stepped into a scalding hot bath last week.' Val gulped. 'No one can protect him completely.'

Tom took out his phone. 'Right, fire away, Val,' he said in a bright voice. 'Let's have a list.'

'But Altrincham is a good half an hour away.'

'By the time we return I'm sure you'll have good news about Fletch to share with us,' said Alex brightly.

'Only if you're sure... thank you,' Val croaked. 'Fletch's pyjamas... there are fresh pairs in our bedroom drawers... Something familiar like that might ease his distress. His toothbrush is in our bathroom and by the front door are his slippers and...' The list went on. 'Jade's dad is travelling up from Bristol tonight; he'll be here tomorrow to help out.' She threw her hands in the air. 'If only that man hadn't walked past. Fletch missed John so much when he died. The two of them often went to the pub to play darts. He's stopped mentioning him so much these last months, but now this...'

'Don't upset yourself, Gran,' muttered Jade.

Alex followed Tom out to the car park. They drove without talking, Jazz FM playing quietly. Tom parked on the drive of the small semi-detached house they finally found in the maze of a leafy suburban estate. They let themselves in and Alex flicked on the hallway light. She spotted a table; the phone on it had really large buttons. Tom went upstairs to fetch the holdall from the spare room Val had mentioned. Alex collected a portable CD player from an armchair in the lounge. Val said Fletch had listened to it a lot since he'd found television programmes more difficult to follow. Tom hadn't come down and she went up to help. She found him in Val and Fletch's room, sitting on the bed, staring at a teddy bear that he clutched in his hands.

'Tom?'

He looked up. 'What have I been thinking, Alex? Running a café staffed by people with dementia? This is a warning. I need to close it before someone gets killed. Sooner or later a bad accident was sure to happen.'

Alex sat down next to him, not used to a Tom who was anything but optimistic.

'All I wanted was to make things better, in a way I can't now with Dad; it's too late for him.' Tears hung in the corners of his eyes. She shuffled on the bedcovers, waiting for an outburst of whistles or a joke, but neither arrived. He wiped his face and before she knew it her arms were briefly around his shoulders, his aftershave floral like his dress sense.

'But you have made things better,' she said and pulled away. 'Reenie and Fletch have got their lives back. It's not as if anything like this has happened before.'

'Reenie has scalded her hand in the kitchen and you saw those teenagers laughing at Fletch. Who do I think I am, putting some of my best friends in a position like that?' He gulped.

Alex couldn't stop staring at him.

Best friends, not simply staff? A demanding conscience? So the Wrong Order Café really was so much more to him than a means of making extra money? It was as if Tom were a book character, changing genre. Her perception of him was so different now to the one she'd had when they first met.

'It's been Fletch's choice to work there,' she said. 'Val and Jade will have helped him weigh up the risks and obviously approved.' Her breath caught and she covered her mouth with the back of her hand as the memory came back of Fletch flat out on the street. 'In any case, if anyone's to blame, it's me. Whatever Jade or Val might say, Val specifically put me in charge of keeping him distracted. But I let him outside...' Her voice cracked. 'I thought it would help. I've no choice, Tom. I'm leaving first thing tomorrow. I don't know enough about dementia. I'm a liability. I know it risks Hope's job but I'm sure she'd agree.'

Tom sat more upright. 'Nonsense,' he said. 'The notebook, the guitar... you bring more to the café than you might think.'

'But if I hadn't let go of his hands...' She gulped. She was a useless author. A useless café server.

'Fletch would have got angry. Forced his way out. Probably have run at top speed with even less awareness of where he was going. The outcome could have been a lot worse.'

She met his eye. 'And his life would be a lot worse without the café.'

'I don't know, Alex. Really, I don't. Maybe closing it down is drastic, but I need to seriously think about rebranding. The dementia element... I can't risk people's health and safety.'

'But mental health is important, isn't it? Reenie and Fletch would be lost without their shifts.'

'When we first met, you believed I ran this place more as a business, cold and clinical. Maybe you were right. Maybe I'm an awful person who's taken advantage of the kindest people.'

'Or maybe you're just feeling sorry for yourself, Tom Wilson,' she said, instantly feeling like a hypocrite.

Tom didn't reply but they sat holding hands, not breaking each other's gaze. It felt natural, easy and comforting. For the first time in a long time Alex felt truly connected to someone.

Truly... not lonely.

* * *

They packed Fletch's nightclothes and toiletries, stuffing the teddy bear in as well, and made their way back downstairs. They passed a small room at the end of the hallway; a big sign bore a drawing of a toilet and the door had been left ajar. Alex spotted the taps with laminated signs above them marking hot and cold. Light sensors ran along the hallway. Alex and Tom entered the kitchen; its door had a sign on it bearing a drawing of a glass and muffin. A clock lay on the windowsill with a large LCD display showing the day, date and time. All the cupboards were covered in Post-it notes with items written on them in capitals – food tins, snacks, honey, tea towels, cereal. The one under the sink had a padlock on it. She opened the cupboard marked snacks and took out the crisps and biscuits that Val mentioned were Fletch's favourite comfort food.

'This reminds me so much of living with Dad,' said Tom. 'My flat, at the top, used to be his – I lived where Hope is. When he began to get confused, left taps running, even the cooker on once, it scared the crap out of both of us. So I moved into his spare room. I labelled everything like Val has, I decluttered and spaced out all the furniture, highlighted tripping hazards. I had to be vigilant all the time. Selfishly, I expected it to be a relief when he went into the care home.'

'But you missed him? Missed feeling needed? Missed that approval and validation?'

He raised an eyebrow.

'Same here, when Mum went into a hospice. Towards the end, she used to tell me I was a good girl, like she did when I was little. Silly, but it meant so much. I was glad I had that time to look after her; she'd sacrificed so much to bring me up.'

'Same,' said Tom. 'After Mum died, Dad had to do the job of two parents.'

'Funny isn't it. Most people say that when their parents are... at the end, the roles reverse and you end up feeling like their mum or dad. But there was never any doubt in my mind, Mum was boss, she still shot me one of her glares if I fussed over her too much.'

Humour flickered across Tom's face. 'For sure. Norm can still keep me in line. He told me off for wearing "that bloody silly" pen behind my ear last week. It always did used to annoy him.'

A whiteboard in a bright yellow frame caught Alex's eye. It had 'Tuesday' written at the top and underneath 'Working at the Wrong Order Café, all day'.

Tom followed her gaze. 'Colour therapy is really important for people with dementia. Blue is calming and can actually lower blood pressure, hence the sky blue of the walls in the café. Yellow is cheerful, that's why I chose it for our tablecloths. Red stimulates, so is good for crockery, to increase appetite, and the bold murals are important too.'

'You've taken into account every detail, like the aviary for Captain Beaky, like keeping him safe in your flat. See? You're just the very person who *should* run a place like Wrong Order Café.'

'You think?'

Alex raised an eyebrow. 'Since when did I say anything I didn't mean? How old is he, now, the parrot?'

Tom explained that in captivity African grey parrots could live to be sixty, even older. George's brother said he'd had him for twenty years; he got him from a pet shop just after the Millennium New Year's Eve. Captain Beaky was terrified of hands and George reckoned he'd been abused. But with lots of patience and time, they soon became the best of friends. The rescue centre reckoned he was about thirty when he went to them, when George went into care.

'He's probably in his mid-thirties now,' said Tom. 'He must have been about ten when George bought him. African greys are incredible birds. They can recognise number sequences, shapes and colours, are monogamous, both parents bring up the young, they are highly social and live in large groups. That's probably why he loves the atmosphere of the café. Hopefully he'll be around for a lot longer yet.'

'How can you tell a bird is getting older?' Alex never got to see the ageing process with Mum, not really; despite her having just tipped sixty she was still vibrant, still active. Alex hadn't seen her father for years.

'Hard as it is to imagine, he'll probably become quieter, lose muscle if he's less active... he might get cataracts,' said Tom. 'His feathers will dull as he'll not groom so extensively... I might need to clip his talons as he won't file them down himself so much on the textured perches. So not that different to humans, in many ways. Dad was always so proud of his appearance, even in the earlier days of his illness, like Reenie and Fletch still are. So, when he resisted combing his hair and cleaning his teeth, I knew we were approaching a new stage.'

* * *

They drove back to the hospital, parked up and went to the reception desk, as midnight approached. After a couple of phone calls, Jade came out into the waiting room, crying. Alex opened her arms and Jade fell into them without hesitating. Alex held her tight until the sobs receded, her heart pumping loudly in her ears as it had every time she and Mum waited for the consultant to reveal the latest test results.

'He's... all right,' Jade said and stood back, chest hitching now and again. 'At least Granddad said Gran's name. The concussion may not be as bad as they originally thought and Gran is holding on to that thought. His fractured shin is in a cast and it will take a few months for it to recover fully, but it could have been so much worse. We're lucky the car wasn't travelling faster. Granddad just stepped out, there's nothing the driver could have done.' Jade took the holdall and thanked them both before hurrying back to her grandparents.

Alex and Tom went outside and stood in the cool evening air; car fumes from a queue of ambulances drifted their way. Tom bunched up his fist and pressed it hard against his chest.

'Gets you right there, doesn't it?' he said.

'What does?'

'Caring.'

She couldn't answer.

'I really should leave,' she said eventually. 'I don't trust myself not to mess up again,' she whispered.

'But I trust you.' He held out his hand. 'Hot chocolate? Your company might diffuse Captain Beaky's annoyance at being left alone.'

A brown feather swept their way and landed by Alex's feet on the pavement. She picked it up and spun it between her fingers, and looked at her co-worker with new eyes before taking a deep breath and slipping her hand into his.

25

Oh, Alex. Poor Fletch and what a shock for Val and Jade. Could you get me his address? I'll send a postcard. Please message me any updates. And of course Tom mustn't rebrand the café. He can't! It sheds a beacon of light on people who shouldn't hide away. The temples were great thanks. Covered in sprawling jungle. Sovann's a really knowledgeable tour guide and explained they were built in the late twelfth century. The coach party spent last night in Sisophon, a town sixty kilometres south. Leah wanted to video call her friends so I went down to the hotel bar and had a few beers with him.

Alex left her toast to burn.

He insisted on buying me one called Angkor that they all drink here. It's named after the temple we are travelling to today. H xx

Wait… Sovann? You're on first name terms? Out drinking together? Details immediately please. Oh, and yes, I'll find out Fletch's address. A xx

Alex stared at Messenger.

DETAILS??

She threw back a mouthful of coffee.

Was he a good kisser?

Finally, three moving dots indicated Hope was typing.

I'd almost forgotten what a libido was. H xx

The green circle on screen disappeared. Hope had gone offline. Alex grinned as if it was her enjoying a holiday fling, and not her friend.

Friend. Was that what Hope was? It felt like a long time since she'd had one of those.

'Coming Up For Air' and Tom's inspiration for the story came into her mind as the smell of burnt bread choked across the flat. She went onto Google. The first year after being diagnosed with dementia saw a 50 per cent increased risk of suicide. Tom had been brave to base his short story on something rooted in his dad's profound emotion. Alex had shared her hate towards Simon in her novels, yet that wasn't truly a feeling, hate always masked something deeper; in Alex's case it was loss, sadness, hurt, despair. Hate had simply been a coping mechanism on the surface.

When Alex arrived downstairs, the first customers were in. Yash must have agreed to cover Jade's shift and was taking orders. Unusually quiet, Reenie sat with Kay, reading her notebook. A couple came in; the woman had a shock of arctic white hair. They hovered in the doorway.

Reenie pointed to a page in the notebook. 'Fletch would have shown them where to sit.'

'Perhaps you should, instead,' suggested Kay.

'Isn't her hair beautiful?' said Alex. 'I bet it's 100 per cent natural.'

Reenie paused, then got up. She showed the couple to a table, chatting about how white hairs are new ones that grow without pigment, due to the ageing body producing less melanin.

'Thanks,' muttered Kay and she put down her cross-stitch. 'Reenie was so upset last night. As usual, she read out the day's notebook entry, over dinner, or at least what you'd written, up until Fletch ran outside. During dessert she flicked back a few days. She enjoys doing that, even though she can't recall the events you've recorded. But it was as if all she could see was Fletch's name and the parts you'd written about him and Reenie chatting or laughing together. For ages she stared at an illustration Jade did of him feeding Captain Beaky a grape, with his comb-over and glasses. The name Fletch felt even more familiar to her as she looked at it. An idea grew inside her head that something bad had happened to him. I told her that we didn't know yet how he was doing, but she said I was lying, protecting her... She hates it if she thinks I'm not telling the truth. Her suspicions are something new.' Kay sighed and talked about how, last week, Reenie accused Kay of stealing her favourite shoes. She'd also pointed a finger at Cliff several times lately for stealing money out of her purse, money that was never there in the first place. 'It's always so hard to know how best to react. Reenie's never been an angry person. Now and then she forgets our parents are dead. If she's really tired in the evening, very occasionally, she'll ask when they are coming home. I've got to get used to changes, it's how the disease progresses, but she's not at the stage yet where I can easily move the conversation on or skim over it by saying they won't be long. So it means she has to relive the grief.'

Reenie was still talking hair, and how the age you turn grey is hereditary. Alex disappeared into the staffroom, returning after a couple of minutes.

'Tom has agreed I can have my lunch break earlier today to coincide with the end of Reenie's shift,' she said to Kay. 'Pip is coming in, to help out, anyway, because Tom has an appointment with a marketing consultant this afternoon.' Alex had tried to talk Tom out of it, but he wanted a professional take on a makeover for the café. 'You see, I've had an idea.' Alex bent down and whispered in Kay's ear.

'I'm not sure about that,' said Kay. 'What if it doesn't turn out well?'

'After what's happened to Fletch, there are worse things that can happen, right?'

Kay stirred her cold latte and the corners of her mouth upturned. 'Okay. You're on. I could write it in the notebook, while it's happening. Reenie will get such pleasure reading it later.'

'Both of you meet me in staffroom when she's finished. Let's keep it a surprise.'

Alex mouthed sorry at Yash and set to, clearing tables and taking orders. She didn't take a mid-morning break. Jade had messaged Tom to say she'd be in tomorrow, but with no more news about Fletch, just saying her dad had arrived. When it was time for Reenie to leave, Alex winked at Kay. Pip had just turned up. Ten minutes later, the sisters joined Alex in the staffroom. Reenie stopped dead. A chair had been set up, on a sheet of plastic, next to the beech cabinet. Alex sat down in it, wearing a bin bag around her shoulders. She pulled out her hair bobble and the ponytail transformed into a mane of bourbon. Alex had removed a mirror from Hope's bedroom wall and propped it up on the cabinet, next to a comb and brush.

'I want you to cut my hair, Reenie,' said Alex.

Reenie folded her arms under her bosom. 'But... I don't do that any more.'

Alex faced herself in the mirror. Some women had a drastic haircut after a break-up, whereas Alex had grown hers longer since leaving Simon. It had teased her shoulders when married, but covered her breasts now. Long hair equalled youth. Long hair equalled not getting older. Long hair equalled relevant and sexy. *Well, to hell with all of that.* Alex hadn't got anything to prove, not any more.

She shuffled in her seat. *Where had that come from?* The last three years had been all about proving something to Simon, then to her agent, to her publisher, to her readers, even her one-night stands. Yet in this café, day by day, a sense had grown that, actually, she was enough, just by herself.

'What style would suit me?' Alex said, and nodded encouragingly at Reenie from the mirror.

Reenie took a step forwards. 'You trust me to do this?'

'One hundred per cent. And you'll be doing me a favour. The truth is, I'm an author, you see, and—'

'Are you?' said Reenie. 'Did I know that?'

'Yes, love,' said Kay gently. 'She writes racy romances.'

'I'm an author whose books...' Alex took a deep breath. 'They haven't sold well lately. Money's tight. I was hoping you'd cut my hair at a reduced rate.' Images of letters and emails from the bank popped into Alex's head. She couldn't sell up; her mortgage hadn't gone down one jot yet, and the apartment hadn't gone up in price, so she'd lose all that money she'd put in, every month, since her career began. That apartment represented hours of hard work. Yet it might be repossessed and she'd have to pay all sorts of fees; her credit scores would be damaged. Alex shuddered at the thought of being evicted.

Kay gave Reenie a thumbs up. 'Your scissors are in your bag, sis.'

Kay fetched the handbag from a cupboard at the back of the room. Reenie delved inside and brought out the scissors, pulling them out of the plastic sheath. She lifted up Alex's long hair and felt the texture. 'A bob just above the shoulders would really suit your oval face shape. And don't you be daft, I'm not going to charge a penny.'

A practical style. 'Go for it,' said Alex.

'What if... I make a mistake?'

Alex thought about Tom and Norm's tattoos. 'Chasing perfection has made me nothing but unhappy, so don't worry about that. I know I'm going to love whatever you do.' She leant forwards and opened the cabinet's doors. She took out one of the colouring books and tore out a page. On the back, with one of the felt tips she wrote, in capitals, 'CUT A BOB JUST ABOVE THE SHOULDERS'. She held up the piece of paper so that Reenie couldn't avoid seeing it, in case her mind drifted off and she felt uncomfortable having to ask what she was doing.

'Is this really my reality now?' muttered Reenie, as if the paper showed a photo of aliens landing in the Northern Quarter.

'You should see the notes I leave lying around when writing a book; my desk is littered with reminders,' said Alex.

'I'll take a photo of Alex first,' said Kay, 'then one afterwards, so you can see what you've achieved.' She took a shot and then passed Reenie the brush and comb. 'I'm sure one of your hairdressing friends can make any small adjustments if you aren't completely happy with what you've done.' Kay caught Alex's eye. 'They wanted Reenie to keep on working a while longer, asked her simply to drop a few hours. But Reenie didn't want to do anything but her best and was worried about failing her clients.'

Reenie's face lit up as she brushed through Alex's hair and then combed out knots. She picked up one of Hope's mist spray bottles that Alex had filled with clean water and generously sprayed the hair. Alex held her breath as, first of all, Reenie reduced the length so that she had less to work with. Ten-inch chunks landed with a thud on the plastic. Alex closed her eyes.

'Don't be scared,' whispered Reenie. 'My memory might not be the best, but knowing what suits a client comes naturally to me, always has. What a difference already. Getting rid of the length has lifted your face.'

Alex opened her eyes. It was already shorter than when she was married and took her back to a weekend in the mid-nineties; she'd been suffering from GCSE exam stress, so Mum had treated her to a trip into town. Alex had her long hair cut into a bob like her favourite singer, Whitney Houston. When she got back home, Dad did that thing of his, he laughed at her, called it a bowl cut, then said he was only joking, that she was too sensitive and shouldn't get upset, that she needed to grow a sense of humour – along with her hair. It wasn't long after that that Mum made the decision to one day leave him.

Reenie combed Alex's hair back and then pushed it forwards a little with her fingers to see where the natural parting line was. Alex's was in the middle. She divided the hair into sections, then cut at the back first, working on the neckline. Kay poured out three glasses of cordial and made Reenie take breaks. Alex held up the piece of paper from the colouring book, as Reenie gained confidence and moved onto the sides, cutting the hair slightly longer at the front, explaining that the angle would make the style even more flattering. Constantly, she asked Alex if the length was okay.

'Right, I'm done,' Reenie finally announced. Her movements had slowed, her eyes looked more hooded, but Reenie's smile had never looked brighter.

Alex faced her new look head on. Despite one edge that was a little uneven, the cut was so much sharper and bolder than her previous tumbling locks, yet less severe than when she tied it back, the style of that young girl in her GCSE year who continued to keep her hair cut in a bob; a girl who made it plain to her dad that she finally saw through his manipulative ways and they no longer had an effect.

'Oh. My. Word. I love it. It takes me back to the younger me who... who didn't define herself or her life by a man or a job. A person who simply... was.'

'That's how I feel, most of the time now,' muttered Reenie, 'unless I'm doing my shift here – like I'm just *being*.'

Alex curled an arm around Reenie's waist and pulled her close. 'I can't pretend I know how painful that is, but you should know, Reenie, you just being you is amazing, with your humour and generosity, your kind nature.'

Despite her short stature Reenie looked that bit taller.

Kay handed the biscuit tin around. 'We've all earned a couple of these.' She took a photo of Alex and on the sofa Reenie kept flicking between the before and after shots while Alex and Kay tidied up. The three of them went into the café.

Tom stopped to let them past and let out a low whistle. 'Someone's been busy. You deserve a takeaway panini, Reenie, and one for Kay.' He ran a hand through his fringe. 'Clearly I'm going to have to smarten up my act.'

Unable to stop herself from smiling, Alex cleared a table near Captain Beaky's cage. He gave a loud screech and flapped his wings.

Tom headed for the door with his laptop bag over one shoulder, off for his appointment.

Alex caught his arm. 'Let me know how it goes.'

A serious expression crossed his face. 'I've put some ideas together. Contacted the company that did the original sign outside and got a quote for a new one saying "Susie's". We'll need new menus and I'll have to advertise for staff.'

'You're really doing this?'

He rubbed his forehead. 'This marketing consultant holds the answer to that. I need to continue to bring in enough money to pay for Dad's care, so the café must find another way to stand out.'

'But, Tom... there's so much heart in the Wrong Order Café. No consultant can create that.'

Captain Beaky screeched again.

Tom hoicked up his laptop bag. 'It's okay. Parrots don't much like change – the same happened when Jade dyed hers blonde; it used to be red. He'll get used to your new style.'

Several times in the afternoon she pushed fruit through the bars, when she wasn't glancing at the door to see if Tom had come back, but the parrot just screeched again and moved his wings as if shooing her away.

Silly really. Why should she care? It wasn't as if she'd grown fond of the little bugger.

26

Tom and Alex sat in Tom's flat, in the midst of their second Monday brainstorming session, having both got up early. It poured down outside. Tom's feet were up on the coffee table, one sock striped, one spotted. Alex's were resting on top of his legs. Captain Beaky crouched on his lap. Miranda had emailed again yesterday, wanting a progress report. Alex replied vaguely, using words such as 'restructuring'. She hadn't told Miranda anything yet about the new co-authored project; her agent might reject the idea outright before even reading it. Alex told herself it would be different when they met in person. Tom scrolled his phone, reading the report that had just come through, from the marketing consultant. He'd not spoken much about the appointment, apart from to say the fees were reasonable and they knew the Northern Quarter demographics well. Alex poured them each another coffee. Browsed through her notes. Walked up and down. Sat down again.

'Tom! Enough now!' She took away her legs and his phone. She placed it on the table. 'You've hardly said anything about the rebranding since your appointment last week. What's going on? As an employee I have a right to know.'

'Dear oh dearie me, it would seem someone's become rather fond of this... What did you once call it? Compared to your supposed fictional high-end java bar, this was a much more *basic* coffee business.'

'The report. Has it confirmed your intentions?'

He folded his arms. 'One hundred per cent. Money well spent.'

'But you can't rebrand Wrong Order Café. It's utterly unique, just like the staff such as Reenie and Fletch who get written off as all the same with a diagnosis.'

'Couldn't agree more.'

'And what about all those tourists,' she continued. 'They... Wait. What?'

'I'm not rebranding. They didn't approve of the name change to Susie's, said it was old-fashioned. They talked about refurbishing in the style of boujee chic – I googled, it's really not me. Despite needing to stand out they believed the way forwards was to mimic other establishments that were already doing well. It felt false. Not true to my heart. The café is my life. I can't work 24-7 somewhere that's created out of nothing but facts and figures. And as time passes I can see Fletch's accident with more perspective. Nothing like that has ever happened before. We still need to be careful but I've decided what the café offers far outweighs the risks.'

'Oh, Tom. I'm so glad.'

'But I am going to get a bell fitted to the door, so that everyone can hear every time it opens and closes, letting people in and out.'

Captain Beaky squawked his approval.

'I reckon he's missed Fletch these last days,' said Tom. 'Pity he couldn't sign that card you've organised. I can't see that Fletch could come back for several months, if ever, not after what Jade told us. I'll have to watch out that this one doesn't pluck out feathers.'

Jade had been in work the last few days, said she needed a distraction. Yesterday she'd arrived with swollen eyes. Turned out the hospital stay had caused great confusion for Fletch; he'd been hallucinating, convinced nurses were hiding under the bed. Hospital delirium they called it. The head injury and general anaesthetic probably hadn't helped, not with his dementia and him being at a disadvantage to start with. Fletch had kept asking the staff where Val was, saying she didn't love him, insisting she hadn't visited.

'I'm going to speak to Jade and will ring Val,' said Tom. 'I'll make it clear there is always a place for Fletch at the Wrong Order Café, but in the meantime I have to take on someone else; we won't cope otherwise. It's a process that never gets easier. Fletch's predecessor was a lovely chap, Brian, so mild-mannered and gentle, you'd never have guessed he used to be a prison officer. It was very sad in the end.'

'What happened?'

Tom explained how Brian started suffering from panic attacks. Once, his wife had popped out to do a little shopping, like she often did, while he carried on working, but Brian suddenly had no idea where he was. He got muddled and decided he'd been locked up. The panic attacks became more frequent, even when she was there.

'The loss of Fletch provides an opportunity for someone else,' said Tom, looking as if he'd just committed the crime of the century.

'I'm going to miss him,' said Alex, surprised she meant it. 'Have you got anyone in mind?'

'It's a lady who lives on her own; she's managing by herself at the moment. Her children visit when they can and have helped her set up a system in her bungalow, with reminder notes where she needs them. She told me about all sorts of gadgets she's considering for the future, like a machine that dispenses medication on automatic, a talking watch, and a doorbell fitted with a camera that would let her family monitor the comings and goings in case she ever starts wandering. Apparently the neighbours are very helpful. She visited the café a few weeks ago. She's only just been diagnosed; she's very early into the disease.' He picked up his phone and scrolled through Contacts. 'Like Reenie, the worst thing for her has been giving up work. She wasn't planning to retire when she hit sixty-six, two years ago, but didn't feel like herself and she couldn't work out why. She assumed that's what getting older was like – a bit moody, tired, forgetting things. She used to work in the food hall at Marks at the bottom of Market Street, so knows the city well.' He stopped scrolling. 'Diane, that's it. She said she'd be grateful for any extra part-time income and the company, in a place where people understood her differences.'

Birds didn't retire, Alex thought, wondering if she ever would. Birds kept on migrating and nesting, until their life ended by a predator catching them, an accident or their heart packing in, not facing a long, drawn-out ending like Mum's. Yet Mum had said she'd rather have it that way, it gave her time to set her finances straight and say those things people didn't always share.

'I love you more than myself, dearest Lexie. More than birds. More than dreams. When I'm gone, carry on following your heart. I couldn't, not once I married your father, so do it for me. Do it for us. Make my ending a happy ever after.'

Alex flicked through her and Tom's joint sheaf of notes, trying to focus. The Wrong Order Café wasn't changing. 'Our main plot is grounded now. Two people meet in a Buddhist centre, in a room where people, themselves included, are unknowingly suffering from carbon monoxide poisoning due to a faulty boiler repair and broken ventilation system. That's why their tongues loosen and they share secrets.'

'I did a lot of research into that plot thread, the symptoms, recovery period, permanent damage.'

'Welcome to an author's biggest time suck – gathering reams of information for just a couple of paragraphs. But it's the only way to make sure you get the details right.' She read through the notes again and then, using red biro, made a few alterations to the synopsis. 'In the end, of course, Clara and Jack will get together. We just need a rough idea of how to present to Miranda.'

'Perhaps her young son will become part of the story, break the ice between them and their friendship evolves from there?'

'Agreed, he could be a great character,' said Alex. 'Okay. I'll put all of this together. Next, let's get on with our opening chapters for next Monday.'

'While this isn't a tragic story, I reckon aspects will resonate with people who've hit tough times, who are on their own like Clara and Jack,' said Tom, circling his feet. 'I've been lucky, always had Dad. He's listened to everything – bad break-ups, days in my younger years when I missed Mum so much, difficult shifts with difficult customers. He confided in me, or at least I thought so. I'll know, for sure, after we've talked to Jimmy.' He looked at this watch. 'Come on, it's almost eleven. He'll be downstairs in a minute. I'll make us all pancakes.'

'But what about now, Tom? What about the last few years, when you haven't had Norm to open up to?' she asked, a sense of concern for him washing over her. It took her by surprise.

'You'd be amazed how much crap this parrot has listened to.' Tom went to pick up Captain Beaky but he flapped his wings and... hopped onto Alex's lap. She managed to suppress a gasp, and slowly, very slowly, went to stroke his back. The bird shot her one of his beady looks and then settled down.

Tom stopped humming a tune and got up, shaking his head. 'He's over your new haircut, no doubt about it. I'll give you love-birds a few minutes while I prepare the pancake batter. Bring him down in his cage when you're ready.'

Oh. She'd been left alone. With a parrot. Alex had never owned a pet, what with Dad supposedly being allergic. Then Mum couldn't afford one after the divorce. Simon felt a pet would tie them down and it went without saying feathers or fur hadn't suited Alex's glamorous new lifestyle. Captain Beaky snuggled down; she didn't touch him again having noticed, over the weeks, that he didn't appreciate too much petting. Alex took a photo and sent it to Hope.

'Tom is like one of your perches,' she said to the parrot, 'he carries everyone, along with their problems... Norm, the young chefs, his staff, the flooded shop owner next door... All on his own.'

Alex and Simon had been through a lot, but side by side, supporting each other, career lows and highs, his mum's death, his heart scare, financial struggles at the beginning. Yet so easily she'd let go of him when the affair came to light.

'I didn't want this, Lex,' he'd said when he told her about Megan.

Anger had blinded her from believing what had happened could have in any way been out of his control, convinced that the only thing motivating his affair was his dick. But since she'd seen the doctor about her missed period, since she'd replayed arguments and emotions from the past, Alex understood that humans were often driven by invisible things, like hormones, hopeless-ness, unhappiness.

Captain Beaky ruffled his feathers and blew a raspberry. She giggled. He mimicked her noise. She laughed even louder. Mum told her once about a bird species called a kea, native to New Zealand, which produced a play call that unwittingly caused other keas to feel playful too, the first non-mammal species to demonstrate it could spread emotion, like a contagious laugh. No one used to make Alex laugh more than Simon. She sighed, wishing she could forget about him; it wasn't as if they were tied by children or assets or remaining romantic aspirations. But just of late, questions were growing.

'Come on, boy. Let's go meet this Jimmy.' She carried him over to the cage and he hopped onto the perch inside. When they got downstairs, loud voices greeted them. Jimmy stood by the hatch, drinking tea, while Tom stood in front of a frying pan. Alex put the cage on its stand and went over. She held out her hand. His chubby one gripped it. His diamond-checked golf T-shirt was stuffed into tight shorts.

'Pleasure to meet you, duck,' he said. 'Tom told me you are helping out while one of his employees is travelling and...' He squinted. 'Are you *Alex Butler*? The author? I've seen your photo on the back of my wife's books.'

'Yes. Great to meet you. How was your sister-in-law's birthday party?'

'Good thanks, but...' He put down his drink. 'My Iris is a huge fan of your novels; they are spread out on our coffee table. I've seen her pick up that *Glamour Puss* more times than I've teed off.'

'Really? That's very kind of her.'

What's happening here? Usually Alex would have passed him an autographed photo within the first few seconds of finding out his wife was a fan. Now and again she got recognised and it always left her feeling ten feet tall.

'Could I have a selfie? Iris won't believe me otherwise.'

With a bemused look in his eyes, Tom's lips twitched from behind the hatch. Alex did her best to ignore him. Jimmy fiddled with his camera app. Selfie taken, pancakes made, the three of them sat down away from the window, in case a passer-by thought the café was open. Jimmy swiftly cleared his plate, wiped his brow; the air was muggy now the rain had stopped. He burped and promptly apologised. The pancakes were the walnut and maple syrup ones Hope had talked about, light, fluffy, yet decadently flavoured.

'Norm always was one fine cook; he must have handed down his skills. Whereas my Charlie doesn't know a chocolate chip from a sultana.' Jimmy drained his cup. 'Right. This beautiful moon business. There's only one Japanese connection I've come up with.

'I know it's a tenuous link, to a Japanese phrase, but it's all we've got to work with,' said Tom.

'Well, I don't know if it's relevant. You know my parents moved to London just after our O-levels? It was the late sixties.' Tom nodded. 'Norm and I were as thick as thieves, back then, I didn't want to go. We'd planned to go to catering college together in Manchester. I kicked up a fuss.' He grimaced. 'Bit of a spoilt brat, looking back. Anyway, the only thing that eased the way was the chance of going to a top catering academy in Westminster. Mum and Dad loved Norm, he'd even come on holiday with us once; neither of us had brothers or sisters, so they said he was welcome to come too, stay rent-free at ours for the two years. Your grandparents agreed, Tom, and sent living costs, and Norm and I said we'd get part-time jobs.' His face broke into a smile. 'Imagine us, seventeen and heading to the Big Smoke, in the swinging sixties... what an adventure. We felt like film stars.'

'Dad talked about it once. The pubs you blagged your way into before you turned eighteen, the fights you nearly got caught up in on the Underground.'

Jimmy grinned. 'Yep. I worked weekends in a café, proper English cooking. Fry-ups for breakfast, mugs of tea as big as soup bowls. Norm was more adventurous and worked out back in a Japanese restaurant, one of the very first in London.'

'I'd forgotten that,' said Tom and he leant forwards. 'Dad hardly ever talked about it. He'd mention stocking sushi in the café a few times but once I quizzed him in depth, asking if sushi was much different these days, and he changed the subject.'

Jimmy rubbed his chin. 'Hmm... well, his stint there didn't end well. He got to know the owner's daughter, Aiko... now what was her surname? Furuta. That was it. She had a sister called Kyoko. I didn't see her often, but never forgot her name because it sounded like Kyoto.'

Tom ran a finger over his beaded bracelet. 'But they were only friends, right? Dad and Mum were still dating then, difficult as it was when he went away.'

'As far as I know, lad, and Aiko's parents were very traditional and wouldn't have approved of anything casual going on. I met them a few times. They treated Norm like a son. He often stayed for dinner. He and Aiko just clicked. As mates. But then Norm came back from dinner there one night – it was straight after we'd graduated and he'd gone to say goodbye as he'd landed a job back in Manchester. He loved London but had always missed the north-west – and there was Susie, your mum, of course. I could tell he'd been crying. He wouldn't talk about it and headed back north the next day. I went to see Aiko a few weeks later, the day before leaving on my first cruise ship job. Norm hadn't been in touch with me since leaving London and I was trying to get to the bottom of it. But the restaurant wasn't open; a sign was up saying something about a funeral. I told Norm in a phone call. He went really quiet and then changed the subject. When I came back from my trip, months later, the restaurant had closed down.'

27

Alex woke early on Tuesday, keen to get into the café. She wanted to get the latest news about Fletch, to talk hair with Reenie, to get sworn at by Captain Beaky, to taste the chefs' new vegan bacon; they'd worked on it for weeks, using thin slices of marinated carrot. She used to get up early in her luxury apartment, but that was to spend the day with people she'd created out of words, people she controlled. Yet not being in charge, rolling alongside others' real-life problems and spontaneous behaviour, made the world warmer, friendlier.

Her phone pinged. A Facebook message.

Great photo. Captain Beaky's clearly got a soft spot for you. He always used to butt away my hand if I went near. In Laos now, Leah wants to do a night safari, there'll be gibbons, tigers, black bears and cobras. Coffee is its biggest export so I'm quite at home with the drinks on offer. Before you ask, Sovann and I said our goodbyes. No regrets. He's awakened something in me. I'm not sure what, I just feel... more like the old Hope. I kissed a man and I liked it. H xx

That Katy Perry pop song playing in Alex's head, as if she were a teen, she typed back.

Watch out, a cobra could do more than nip. And same here, I'm... different. Oh and Reenie cut my hair. A xx

Alex sent Hope one of the photos from Kay. It was only half past eight. She had thirty minutes so she fetched her laptop and settled at the small kitchen table. She typed Aiko Furuta into Facebook's search bar. Alex couldn't explain it, but she just had a hunch they were on the right track with this line of enquiry, especially as Norm didn't like to talk about his time working at the Japanese restaurant. About ten profiles came up. When Simon had first mentioned Megan, Alex had hunted her down on every social platform, compelled to torture herself. Alex went into each of the Japanese profiles and skimmed through their feeds, pressing the word translate on posts about holidays or food. However, all the profile photos were far too young. She typed in Kyoko Furuta, the sister, instead. This time about thirty profiles came up. Slowly, she went through, eliminating them one by one, until she was left with only two – both women had grey hair; one lived in Osaka, the other America. On closer inspection, the American one was a memorial page; that particular Kyoko had died a couple of years earlier. She copied the page's link and sent it to Tom, hoping that if the sister of Norm's friend was on Facebook, it was the one that was still alive.

As Alex walked into the café, Jade was about to open the door, but Alex held her back gently and passed her a plastic bag. Jade pulled the handles apart.

'When I'm feeling really rubbish, losing myself in writing helps,' said Alex. 'I suspect working on artwork is the same for you. I ordered this stuff a couple of days ago. It's supposed to be really good for drawing manga. Obviously you'll know much more than me, but there are mechanical pencils for precision work, normal ones for softer touches, a selection of marker pens and a sketchbook made from high grammage paper. I... hope you don't mind.'

Jade lifted out a pack of pens as if they'd been crafted by Damien Hirst. 'I don't know what to say.'

'That's a first,' said Alex. She couldn't help smiling to herself as the morning progressed and she caught Jade sneaking excited looks at the contents of the bag.

When Alex took her first break, Tom sat with her at one of the tables. He'd been baking a batch of rocky roads and arranging for Diane to come in the next day for a chat.

'Why don't you have a sweet treat with your coffee, Alex?' asked Reenie.

'I have had my eye on one of those new pistachio fondant filled croissants.' Alex caught Reenie's arm before she went to write it down. 'Love my new hair. Thanks for cutting it.' Alex lifted up her phone and swiped between the before and after shots. Reenie's cheeks pinked up before she went to the counter.

Tom went on Facebook and studied the Kyoko profile Alex had found.

'I found two profiles. The other lady had passed, so fingers crossed this is the right Kyoko. Message her,' said Alex.

'What, now? What do I say?'

Alex took his phone. She typed for several minutes, edited and then read out the message, smiling at Reenie first as she delivered a pizza pastry to the table. '"Hello, my name is Tom Wilson. Apologies for contacting you out of the blue, but I'm looking for Aiko and Kyoko Furuta who knew my dad, Norman Wilson, in the late sixties. He helped out at their parents' restaurant in London. Dad was studying catering at a college in Westminster. Does his name sound familiar? He's not in the best of health. It's complicated and I'd be extremely grateful if we could have a chat. Thanks very much.'"

'Cheers, Alex. It would have taken me ages to put that together.'

She pressed send and gave back his phone. 'Have you mentioned this Diane to the rest of the staff? Did you ring Val?'

'Yep and yep.'

Despite the boyish, salted-caramel floppy fringe, the carefree freckles, in that moment Tom looked as if he'd been in his forties for decades. Alex cut the pizza pastry into four and passed him a quarter and for the first time, in a long time, felt the urge to cook someone dinner. He stuffed it into his mouth.

'Jade and Val understand,' he said. 'All three of us hope Fletch will come back. I just hope he's not on a fast train to being in Dad's position. Apparently, hospital delirium can speed the decline of someone with dementia, causing permanent damage in some cases.' He took another quarter of the pastry and explained how Val had got upset on the phone, Jade too this morning, as a couple of times Fletch had become muddled about who exactly they were. Both worried they'd lost the chance to say goodbye to Fletch while he was still, more or less, like his old self – the long goodbye they'd hoped for, telling him how much they loved him, reminiscing over the good times with photo albums, letting him know what a good husband and granddad he'd been. 'They don't believe they've done that enough. I can't imagine how hard that must be. At least Dad still knows who I am, even at this stage.'

Alex wanted to wrap Tom up in her arms and hold him tight, to squeeze comfort into him to make everything okay, the way Mum used to when she was little. In her arms, Alex used to feel there was no problem that couldn't be made better. Instead, she pulled away the pizza plate.

'Stealing my breakfast isn't going to help anyone, mister.'

'Knew I could rely on you for sympathy.'

'How did it go yesterday, with Jimmy? Did Norm recognise him?'

Tom's face lifted. To his amazement, when he and Jimmy had walked into the room, something flickered across his dad's face and he told Jimmy off for not visiting sooner. Jimmy sat down and Norm patted his fingers, then gripped them tighter. The two men sat, teasing each other, as if they were both back at primary school in the fifties.

'Next time, he's bringing a collection of photos he's got of the two of them, down in London. It went much better than Jimmy had hoped; he wasn't sure what to expect. Jimmy tried to talk to him about Aiko and the beautiful moon, and we thought we saw a flicker of something but it really didn't register.'

When Alex had first understood the concept of the Wrong Order Café, the prospect of unpredictability had scared her. The life she knew in Deansgate had become so orderly, revolving around a routine. Social birds who lived in flocks remembered their parents and siblings, like crows and jays, Canadian geese too, whereas others forgot them after the first year of life. Swamped with parental guilt after an especially sleepless night, shortly after her divorce, Alex's mum once asked her daughter if she wished she could forget her dad. Alex didn't. She owed him a lot, like her independence, her drive, her deep love for her mum, her ability to recognise men who had a *good* heart. Like Simon. He'd always treated her so well, until his affair.

'That's why this place is so important,' said Tom. 'This café shows customers that people with dementia are no different to anyone else, they just face different challenges, along with living their absolute truth. Jimmy talked about his wife and Norm pulled a disgusted face. We had to laugh, Norm did too. He'd never got on with her.'

Tom's phone pinged and Alex picked it up.

Hello Tom. What a surprise. I do remember Norm and would be happy to have a video phone call with you, if that was helpful. All the best, Kyoko.

28

The next day, at eight in the morning, late afternoon in Japan, Tom, Alex and Captain Beaky waited on the sofa, in the upstairs flat. The parrot nestled on Tom's lap and pecked at his leather watch strap.

'Sure you want me to be here?' asked Alex.

'Of course. It's because of you we might be able to put Dad's mind at ease.'

Or not. The video call might reveal that he'd cheated. That was the trouble with going back to the past, you didn't know what you might unearth. Yet Alex wouldn't want to fixate on something unresolved in the future. What if something she'd buried came back to haunt her? Legend had it ostriches buried their heads in the sand, a method of avoiding predators. Mum would scoff at this ridiculous theory. Ostriches were well capable of defending themselves, with a high running speed and legs that could give an almighty kick. What's more, if they buried their heads they'd suffocate. No, the most likely explanation of this myth was that you couldn't see their heads when they used their beaks to turn over their eggs that were laid in deep holes. Perhaps people from the past were like seeds, buried and forgotten, to emerge when least expected. Some were like beautiful flowers, a sweet reminder from happy times, like the old school friend who'd tracked Mum down; they had three good years together again before the end. But there were also seeds that gave rise to parasitic, all-engulfing weeds, memories and people you'd rather forget who, once dug up, wouldn't go away again.

Tom stroked Captain Beaky's back, all three of them jump-starting as a ringtone sounded from the laptop, on the coffee table. Tom accepted the call and a woman loomed into view, her hair tied up on top in a bun and wearing a grey-and-black-striped shirt that mirrored her hair's colour.

'*Konnichiwa*, hello, so lovely to see you,' she said, and bowed her head. She gasped. 'Tom, you look exactly like your father used to, with that long side fringe.'

'I take that as a compliment as I'm a good twenty years older than he was then.' Silence. 'Thank you so much for doing this. This is my friend Alex.'

Kyoko bowed her head again. 'I'm sad Norm is ill. My parents were very fond of him. Please, tell me how I can help.'

'Dad... he's got dementia.'

Her face fell. 'A merciless disease. Poor Norm.'

'He's fixated on... Perhaps Alex can explain better than me.'

Alex told Kyoko about Norm's beautiful moon fixation and about the animated series title Jade had mentioned. 'When we found out about his friendship with a Japanese family, we hoped that could hold the answer. It's tenuous, but we've run out of other possibilities. We know things between him and your sister ended in an upsetting way and wondered if that might hold the answer.'

Tom passed on everything Jimmy had said, and that they

knew about a funeral, the restaurant closing, Norm being upset about both those aspects and refusing to talk about it.

'The beautiful moon phrase is indeed a real thing,' said Kyoko. 'It would have been used by courting couples in the old days.'

Tom leant forward and Captain Beaky hopped onto Alex's lap.

'Norm and my sister, Aiko, became very close. The same age, the same dreams... she wanted, one day, to run her own restaurant and loved working in Mum and Dad's. Food never inspired me the way it did them. I'd find them debating whether you should cut sandwiches in half or diagonally, or whether white chocolate was really chocolate at all. She'd never been that way with a boy before and... I'm afraid, despite your mum...'

'Susie,' he said, hands clenched together.

'Yes, despite Susie, I found Aiko doodling both their names inside a love heart one day. Our parents would have been furious; strong principles were very important to them. She told me it wasn't serious and I just gave her a hug. I always felt protective of her – you see, as a young child she'd suffered from cancer.'

'I'm sorry to hear that,' said Tom, his voice a little detached.

'My sister had recovered from the cancer and Norm was one of the few people she talked to about those hard days. Not long before he graduated and was due to leave for Manchester, she began to suffer symptoms again.'

Perhaps that was why Norm had been crying.

'I don't know why, but this led to a big argument the last night he visited. I found her sobbing after he left.'

Tom frowned.

'I'm so sorry your sister passed at such a young age,' said Alex.

'Aiko? But she didn't.'

'The funeral sign?' said Tom.

'Ah, of course, I understand the confusion – that referred to our granddad. Aiko's symptoms, the headaches, tiredness, the aches and pains, turned out to be nothing but a virus. Understandably she'd panicked at first. The four of us travelled back to Osaka for the funeral. Those three returned, but I decided to stay with my grandma in Japan. On their return to England my parents discovered bigger premises had become available in a different part of London. They couldn't afford to own two restaurants but wanted to expand, and with a small inheritance from Granddad were able to buy the new place.'

'Aiko is still alive?' asked Tom. He and Alex looked at each other.

Kyoko bowed. 'Indeed. She still runs that very restaurant. I'm sorry I don't have all the answers and I'm not sure Aiko will want to revisit that part of her life. Years later, I mentioned Norm once and she clammed up. I will tell her about this call and pass on your contact details. Then it's up to her.'

29

Kyoko said goodbye and they both stood up. Alex put Captain Beaky in his cage.

'Well done, Alex. It's down to you that we've got a step further; you wouldn't give up. I'm grateful,' said Tom and he sighed. 'Even if it is all so unsettling. I can't believe Dad would have ever cheated on Mum. But thanks. Thanks for caring about Dad.' He held out his arms. After she moved in, they stood in a tight embrace. Simon always used to be the first to let go. So were the boyfriends she'd had since him. But Tom held on.

'Get a room,' squawked Captain Beaky.

Only then did Tom let his arms drop. 'Ah yes. I forgot. George trained to him to say that every time there's any funny business on the telly.'

'Funny business? You and me?' she said archly, turning away to stifle her laughter.

She carried the cage downstairs and put it on the stand. Reenie arrived and took off her summer anorak. Alex stood by the door, just outside, and breathed in the air's dampness that smelt so fresh despite the city's morning belch of exhaust fumes.

The shop owner next door appeared with her sandwich board. Today's bargains were cinnamon-scented candles to keep away spiders, and black tourmaline crystals to ward off bad luck.

She waved. 'Your boss is one in a million. I'll be buggered if I can turn off the water supply with my bloomin' arthritis. You know, he slept on my sofa one night last year when I thought I'd heard burglars.'

A man like Tom had never appeared in one of Alex's best-selling novels. In fact, she'd never written a male character women could truly warm to, not like Tom, Fletch, not like Norm... not like Simon before he'd been a cheat. Alex took out her phone and was about to go into Contacts, when a reminder text appeared, her regular Botox session was due in two weeks. Her finger hovered before she pressed delete. Squinting in the sunshine, she read another message.

Hi Alex, any more news on Fletch? Thanks for keeping me updated. Do you like this blouse? Handwoven silk is big in Lao. I couldn't resist it. Lately polyester, clothes' labels, all sorts of textures have become irritating. I get such itchy skin. I went into a menopause chat room online last night. It made me think more about HRT. One woman in there said the menopause was natural, there's no reason we shouldn't put up with it. But another said so is diabetes, Crohn's, lots of heart conditions, doesn't mean people should suffer, and I and everyone else agreed. H xx

Alex's eyes dropped to a photo of a tanned Hope in a multi-coloured blouse, hair windswept and eyes crinkling in the sun.

Fletch is much the same. I'll let you know as soon as there is more news. That Diane I told you about is coming in this afternoon, to see Tom. As for the skin sensitivity, sometimes I feel as if insects are crawling around inside my body. But HRT? Artificial hormones? Tablets every day? Yet last night I cried in bed. I don't know why. That's the worst thing. Not feeling in charge. The menopause is a story that hasn't been told, from generation to generation. I'm sad that the women, going back in my family, must have suffered without understanding why and had no way of accessing information. It's good that you and I are sharing our stories with each other. It's like Tom and his ambition with the café, trying to bring about change, to bust the myth that a dementia diagnosis means the end. I didn't even know that dementia isn't a normal part of ageing, Tom told me that. Relatives used to whisper about my great-uncle, say he'd gone doolally. Like with the menopause, the facts have been hushed up for far too long.

Through the window, Alex caught Jade's stern eye.

Better go or I'll be in trouble. Take care. Love the top. A xx

A customer arrived and Alex followed them in. The morning passed in a busy manner; Alex had a lot to write in Reenie's notebook due to a hen party of hairdressers coming in to line their stomachs before an afternoon of drinking. She could just imagine the manga hens Jade might draw, with spiky red combs and under-chin wattles. During her lunch break Alex began the first volume of *Attack on Titan*; Jade had hardly spoken all day and simply left the book on Alex's table. An hour before closing a lady with short white hair, in a smock dress and Doc Martens boots came in, a small black leather rucksack over her shoulder. Tom introduced her as Diane before the two of them disappeared into the staffroom.

Just after closing, as Jade cleaned the coffee machine and Alex wiped down the yellow tablecloths, ready for another day of spills and crumbs tomorrow, Diane and Tom came out of the staffroom.

'Jade, Alex... I've agreed with Diane that she can do Fletch's shifts.'

When he said 'Jade', Diane looked in her direction. 'We've also agreed that if Fletch comes back we can share the hours, and I'm happy to leave if he recovers enough to return full time.'

'Have you worked in hospitality before?' asked Jade in a polite voice.

'A while back, in the seventies, I was part of the catering team for the Genesis European tour.'

Jade put down her cloth. 'Really? That's amazing. My girl-friend's dad loves their music, says Phil Collins is the best drummer ever.'

'You'll have to get Tom to load the jukebox with rock music,' said Alex. 'His and Captain Beaky's taste could do with widening.'

Diane went over to the cage. 'Who's a pretty boy?' she asked.

'Fuck off,' he replied.

Diane gave a warm belly laugh. 'I'm going to enjoy working here.' She paused. 'I'm sorry about your... granddad, isn't it, Jade? I wish I was here under different circumstances.'

Back in Hope's flat, Alex ate dinner on her own, needing space and quiet. She'd taken out her laptop, to work on her first chapter for the writing session with Tom in a few days. Yet she still hadn't written a word by the time moonlight cut through the curtains and lit up her phone, making it wink at her. She approached the window. The moon hung above Stevenson Square. Today was the summer solstice, the longest day, the shortest night, a bountiful time for birds foraging for food. But the café hadn't changed its

hours; humans took less notice, these days, of sunsets and
sunrises that were equally beautiful, equally welcome. A poster
caught her eye, on a wall near to Lever Street, advertising a new
film starring Tom Cruise. She flexed her fingers, picked up her
phone and went into her list of contacts.

30

Simon responded just before Alex went downstairs to start her shift two days later, Friday morning. He'd been visiting Manchester, working remotely; his dad had taken a fall and got out of hospital a few days ago. He supposed they could meet for a quick drink before he went back to London this afternoon, if she really wanted. He suggested the Selfridges' coffee shop; it wasn't far from where he'd park in the Arndale. His response was abrupt, he didn't even sign off.

Out of breath, Alex arrived first, having speed-walked past Market Street buskers and conspiracy theorists. She hadn't had time to change her T-shirt, stained with food that had swerved past her apron. A group of young mums with toddlers had meant a manic morning.

She walked off the bottom of the escalator. Celebrity cosmetics, luxurious perfumes and designer sunglasses surrounded her, all so out of place in her life now. At the most, in Wrong Order Café, Alex applied a swipe of concealer and a quick brush of mascara. Today she'd grabbed a pair of Hope's sunglasses, scratched and plastic. In the coffee shop a face greeted her that lacked the warmth of Fletch's toothy welcome. The man directed Alex to a table for two, in the far corner. She sat down and ordered a latte with vanilla and whipped cream. As her lunch break was late, the midday rush here was also over. She photographed the room, with its grey and white marble tables and well-mannered customers. Breathing in the aroma of Parmesan cheese and tomato, she sent the shot to Hope.

Guess where I am? And yes it is good news about Fletch, the confusion is clearing a little. Early days, but Jade and Val are so relieved.
A xx

She took off Hope's beige crossbody bag and lay it on the floor. The coffee arrived and she took a large mouthful, while taking in the decadent surroundings. They reminded her of the extravagant purchases she used to make, like the luxury hotel rooms with *spectacular views* that all looked the same inside, or the countless restaurants she'd visited, to take photos of tiny portions of perfectly plated food, when all she really fancied was fish and chips out of newspaper. Working at the Wrong Order Café, the things that mattered couldn't be seen or posted on social media. Like the warmth that emanated off Reenie when a customer tipped her, the blush on customers' faces when Fletch treated them with such respect, the sense of wanting to dance when Captain Beaky squawked to a favourite jazz track, Jade's discreet air punch if she caught Alex taking a sneaky read of one of her graphic novels. As for Tom whooshing down the stairs, feet off the ground, hands sliding down the railings, it was something that had annoyed her in the beginning, when it had been so long since she'd found joy in small things, when so much of the behaviour she saw in people was done for effect.

'Lex?' said a wary tone.

Simon stood, hands deep in his trouser pockets, with the same long lashes she used to admire, the interminably hunched shoulders that made him always look cold, a frown he'd hardly ever directed at her for so many years. He hesitated and then sat down in the seat opposite and ordered a tea, keeping his summer jacket on, keeping it buttoned up.

'Like your hair; suits you,' he said in a polite voice.

'How's your dad?'

'Stubborn as ever. He's determined to carry on playing golf, even though the doctors have told him to rest his back. He was lucky considering he fell down the stairs backwards, narrowly missing slamming his head on the edge of the radiator.'

She twirled the teaspoon in between her fingers.

'How are things?'

She didn't reply.

'Your text was unexpected. How's the writing career going? A Facebook friend told me about one of your books being chosen for a fancy US book club.'

She went to reel off the top chart positions her first books had reached, to quote the best reviews, to mention fan emails, meals at The Ivy, to mention *her agent* in an important voice; she waited to feel euphoric that a mutual friend had passed on her achievements.

'Not the best, but I'm working on a new project, with a co-author. And you? Designed any interesting applications lately?'

'You really want me to talk about coding?'

She gave a small smile.

'London's overrated – too expensive, bad traffic, never-ending construction. What with Dad becoming more fragile, I'm tempted to move back up north. To be honest... I was running away.'

She stirred her latte as his tea arrived. 'Why did you have the affair? I've never let you explain, not fully.'

His face dropped like that of a prisoner who'd been told his parole had been cancelled. 'Lex. I'm not doing this. We'll only end up arguing. I messed up. Big time. End of.'

'Please. We had a good thing, didn't we? I want to know why it all went so wrong. Was it me?' She pushed away her drink. 'Was it my fault?'

He looked surprised.

'I've had time to think, okay?'

He rolled up his jacket sleeves. His new Fitbit had gone. 'Sleeping with another woman, I'll never forgive myself, Lex, for breaking my wedding vows. I was weak. But... it wasn't always easy to talk to you.' That wary tone again. 'The year or two before we broke up you were so angry about everything.' He lowered his voice. 'You went off sex, too. I felt like a failure. I couldn't make you happy and I didn't know why. I felt you could do better with someone else.'

'Go on,' she mumbled.

'One day, you pulled a face when I suggested we went to bed; we were in the garden. In fact, it happened more than once. I felt... worthless, unattractive and like the worst husband ever. I wanted to get close, but didn't know how to go about it. I suggested counselling, but—'

'I shouted you down.'

The frown lines on his brow eased. 'But it was about me too. That heart scare made me face my mortality. Then Mike followed his dream and moved to Greece. I felt like I was getting left behind, getting old, and being passed over for promotion at work confirmed all my fears. The gym helped with stress. I tried to get you to go with me in the beginning...'

She'd forgotten that. He'd wanted them to take up new hobbies together but at the time all her strength just went into getting through each day, fighting the self-doubts and anxieties that had stolen the person she used to be.

Alex took a deep breath. 'Recently I've learnt about the peri-menopause.' She told him about her doctor's appointment, about everything she'd found out online, about her new friend Hope.

'Oh, Lex. I had no idea.'

'Me neither.'

'Tell me more about it.'

He placed his hand on hers when she finished. 'I know Mum had a bad time in her late forties. Dad mentioned it once; she went to stay with her sister for a while. He never used the word "menopause" but I should have worked it out. If only I'd been more understanding with you.'

She turned her hand palm up and squeezed his fingers. 'How could you? Neither of us knew what was going on. And I should have thought more about the heart scare. I did my best to jolly you out of it, didn't I? I'd change the subject when you mentioned it, convinced it would do you no good to dwell. But one thing I've learnt, lately, is that it's fucking good to talk.'

'You used to tell me off for using the f-word.'

'I blame the new man in my life.'

Si raised an eyebrow. She quite liked the idea of having a captain for a boyfriend.

'What about Megan?'

'Christ, best forgotten. Someone else I hurt. Classic midlife crisis; makes me cringe now. I genuinely believed I cared about her. As for the N-Dubz on repeat, the constant box set bingeing, unappetising green juices for breakfast, clubbing mid-week when all I wanted to do was go to bed... But I guess you wouldn't know about any of that.'

'No, I can't imagine it,' said Alex in a demure tone. 'Is there anyone special now?'

Instantly, his face lit up. 'Thalia. I met her on my second trip to Greece. We keep in touch on socials. She's been over here twice. We'll see where it goes.'

Her coffee went cold as they chatted about family, mutual friends, his work, Greece, the Wrong Order Café, her new writing project, even his coding. As the end of her lunch hour approached, they got up to leave. He paused and held out his hand. Alex stepped forwards and gave him a quick kiss on the cheek.

'Thanks for meeting me, Simon.'

'Thanks for asking.' He tilted his head. 'Splitting up may have broken us apart, but I reckon it's helped each of us put ourselves back together.' He reached into his pocket and pulled out a feather. Half was grey, half was striped with a vibrant turquoise colour. 'I found this outside Dad's house this morning. Googled the markings. I reckon it belongs to a jay. I'm sorry your mum passed. Sorry you had to go through that on your own. She was a great lady.' He handed it over and left.

Alex stood outside, under the Mancunian sun, running a finger along the feather as a wannabe boy band, a few metres away, sang around a hat half filled with coins. Like parrots, jays were good mimickers and to put off predators had been known to imitate owls, sparrowhawks, cats, even police sirens. Her life as a glamorous author had been an imitation, she realised that now, but not to hide from predators, to hide from herself. Her phone pinged and she pulled it out of the crossbody bag. A text from Tom.

Hey Alex, I forgot to mention it with so much going on. The last Saturday of every month is open day in the Wrong Order Café. Tomorrow, people with loved ones who have dementia will come in for a drink and to chat to other carers, along with representatives from the

Alzheimer's Society and Citizens Advice. We open up the staffroom.
Norm comes in too, with other residents from his care home. I've
forgotten to pick up paper plates, they make the workload lighter.
Could you grab about a hundred, in bright colours, on your way back?
I'll be the one in the kitchen, baking until the early hours! Tom.

31

Alex yawned and stretched; the smell of aftershave filled her nostrils. Her eyes focused as a painful twinge shot through her back. She sat up and rubbed her neck, taking in her surroundings, an early-morning process that was not unfamiliar. At first she'd found casual encounters exciting, waking up in sheets that weren't Egyptian cotton, next to a body instead of a cold space, with the smell of sex proving someone had desired her. However, as time passed, her enthusiasm had waned. Her lovers had been considerate, careful... well, mostly. Apart from the development manager who rolled over as soon as he'd come, suggesting she finish herself off, or the trainee lawyer who said to keep her shoes on, he had to be in court early the next day. Even when the sex was good, it began to feel like a chore – laughing at jokes that weren't funny, waxing down below, faking orgasms that felt empty even if they did manage to build on their own.

She rubbed her eyes. Tom approached with a mug. She was on the sofa under a tartan blanket. Of course. She'd stayed up late, helping him bake cakes to feed the open day visitors. Well, she'd been a gopher really, weighing out ingredients, beating mixtures when he told her to. She hadn't baked since before her divorce and had lost her confidence more than skills. Then Tom had made cheese toasties that they'd eaten in the roof garden and talked about 'Coming Up For Air' in his flat until the early hours.

'I didn't have the heart to wake you,' he said. 'One minute I was making hot chocolate, the next you'd slumped sideways.'

Captain Beaky sat on his perch on the play stand and made a loud snoring noise.

'Guess where he's picked that up from?' asked Tom.

'What time do proceedings kick off?' she asked and headed over to the parrot. He hopped onto her shoulder.

'Ten o'clock. All the staff will be in. Reenie too, and Diane. You'll meet Kay's husband Cliff and Val's going to bring Fletch if he's up to it.'

She stroked Captain Beaky's chest, wondering if he missed Fletch. Sometimes you missed people without realising it. It hadn't struck Alex that while at the bank those heartfelt chats over coffee, or after-office wine, had emptied her of the kind of thoughts and feelings that, in recent years, had hardened her edges – edges now softened since she'd opened up to the staff at the café.

'The weather's due to be kind to us, so we'll put tables out front,' he said. 'Jade and Yash are getting in early, at eight.'

'What time is it now?' She yawned again.

'Seven o'clock.' He put a pistachio fondant filled croissant down on the kitchen table. 'Get this down your neck before you go back to yours.'

She performed a mock salute. It took her back to Mum who, even at the end, would tell her to make sure she was eating properly, tick her off about bedtimes if she couldn't stop yawning. Comments Alex wouldn't have missed as a teenager, comments that meant so much when she'd faced losing them. Mum's face had glowed with pride when Alex compared her to crows, birds that fiercely defended their young and even built decoy nests to fool predators.

* * *

After a shower, Alex pulled on a loose pair of cotton trousers and a T-shirt she'd bought from the Arndale, no longer prepared to spend her days in fashionably restrictive clothing. She locked up Hope's flat and thought about her meeting with Simon yesterday as she put her hands on the stair railings and slid downstairs, her feet off the ground. Apron fastened, she helped Jade move tables outside. Alex took a moment, under the sun, absorbing the warmth, before tidying up the pavement. She picked up discarded empty burger cartons and drink cups.

'Is your girlfriend coming?' she asked, straightening up.

'Nope,' said Jade. 'We've split up.'

'Oh... How are you doing?'

The two of them pulled up chairs and sat down. 'Things haven't been right between us for a while. She found me with that new sketchbook and laughed at one of my drawings. She's never supported my interest, not in the way I've been there for her football, turning up at Sunday matches if I'm rostered off work, even though I'm not interested.' Jade swiped a fly away. 'She isn't artistic in any way and moving in together proved how little common ground we had. I used to believe in opposites attracting but now I'm not so sure. Any words of wisdom to pass on? Aren't you authors supposed to be experts on human nature?'

'I'm divorced. Almost broke. Believed the menopause was a pregnancy. My most intimate relationship is with a parrot. What do you think?'

'That you're just as screwed up as the rest of us then,' said Jade, and she got up, kissed Alex on top of her head and left.

As if the sun had directed all its rays in her direction, heat radiated down Alex and she touched her head. She read the café's sign. Jade was right. Alex and her life were pretty screwed up. It felt good to admit it and take the mask off.

A man from the Alzheimer's Society arrived. He requested a table outside as it wasn't raining, and he had an information stand to set up with leaflets for passers-by to pick up. Alex's eyes skimmed over the facts. Dementia was the UK's biggest killer, with almost one million people currently diagnosed, 700,000 unpaid carers out there, like Val, and 120,000 sufferers lived on their own, like Diane. She turned up next, in cut-off jeans and her Doc Martens. Tom asked her to tidy up the staffroom. He'd moved extra chairs in there. Yash plated a selection of cakes for each table. Last night, Tom and Alex had baked scones, brownies and cookies, along with decorating a carrot cake he pulled out of the freezer. He also took out several batches of retro cakes he'd baked a couple of weeks previously – classic rock buns, a traditional Victoria sponge, shortbread fingers, school sprinkle sponge slabs and iced fairy cakes. Reenie helped herself to a rock bun as soon as she arrived and proceeded to give Cliff a tour of the café.

By lunchtime the room heaved, Reenie and Diane refilling guests' plates, while Jade and Yash handed out drinks and Alex and Pip kept tables clean and restocked and emptied the dishwasher several times. Tom mingled with the crowd, inviting newly diagnosed sufferers and their loved ones to speak to the woman from Citizens Advice for answers to questions about lasting power of attorney, wills, financial support, carer assessments and attendance allowance. Alex recognised a man in a black cap – he'd come in a while back and spoken to Fletch about his newly diagnosed dad who loved karaoke but now felt he had nothing to live for. His arm was around the shoulders of an older man and the two of them talked to a representative from the local dementia choir.

Norm arrived, along with two other residents and members of the care home team. Tom seated them in the corner, by Captain Beaky's cage, 'The Girl from Ipanema' playing in the background. Alex sat down and straightened Norm's glasses before lifting the cake plate to show him.

'Those sprinkle cakes smell delicious,' she said, and took a slice. She put one on a paper plate for him and talked about the weather, while they both ate.

'Those biscuits look damn good,' he said, after he'd finished, and pointed to the cookies, hand shaking a little.

She passed Norm one and he studied it before taking a bite, crumbs falling down and leaving the biscuit in the shape of a crescent.

'I should have told her the moon is beautiful,' he mumbled.

'Don't you go worrying about that, Norm,' cut in the care worker next to him. She patted his arm. 'This lovely cup of tea should have cooled a little; here you are, chickie.'

Alex caught Tom's eye as he took a breather. She went over. 'Still nothing from Aiko?'

'No, and fair enough. It all happened a long time ago. Maybe it's for the best and...' Alex followed his gaze to the window, as his voice petered out. A wheelchair had appeared outside. The two of them hurried out of the door that had been wedged open. Tom said hello to Val and knelt on the pavement. He took Fletch's hand. 'How are you, mate?'

'Bloody bored of this chair, for starters.' An elderly couple arrived. 'Welcome,' he said and bowed his head to them. 'Someone will be with you shortly.'

Tom spoke about how much everyone had missed him; he

and Alex asked about the hospital. Fletch recalled snippets. When the conversation stalled, Tom stood up and put an arm around Val. 'He's looking good.'

'He may not recover completely, and he'll need a lot of physio to build his strength up when his leg is finally healed. I don't know if he'll ever be able to come back to work, but the physical losses aren't so important. At least my Fletch, the man inside, is coming back to where he was before the accident.'

Alex took a photo of Fletch and Val, and sent it to Hope.

Early days, but he remembered the café. Enjoy your last week of travels. A xx

Today was Saturday, 24 June. Next Saturday was 1 Jul, Miranda's deadline, Hope's arrival back in England. Alex pressed send. *Last week.* For some reason those two words punched the pit of her stomach. Which didn't make sense. In a matter of days she'd be back in her luxurious flat, she wouldn't have to water plants, or fill a dishwasher, or jump every time Captain Beaky loudly squawked 'Legs'. She'd be able to get her nails done again, without the worry of them chipping. The break had done her good – she was moving forwards with a new project, she'd settled things with Simon, she'd learnt things about herself and found new perspective on everything that had happened in the last few years. She'd even made friends, or so she liked to think, real friends made out of flesh and blood.

All of this was positive.

So why did she feel as if Hope's return would burst a bubble that would drench everything in negativity?

What was she going back to? No concrete contract, a life she'd shed. Her author identity had filled the cracks of an incomplete life, it had plastered over the gaps left by Mum and Simon, and for the first time in days she felt an urge to slip into a smart pair of shoes and face of foundation. Glad of the distraction, Alex hurried over to a distressed woman and her husband, and led them to the disabled toilet out the back. Tom had stocked up on incontinence pads in case of accidents.

Sandwiches freshly made by the chefs, and cut into small manageable triangles, disappeared off plates, as did the leaflets outside and the Citizens Advice woman barely had time to eat. A journalist from the *Manchester Evening News* turned up. The staff, along with Norm, stood outside and had their photo taken. Then, at Tom's request, everyone went inside. He tapped a teaspoon against a cup.

'Cheers, everyone, for attending our open day, we'll have a lot of shots to add to our photo wall. It's thanks to my dad...' he nodded at Norm '...that any of this is happening. You're all welcome here, any time, for a chat, for information on finances and care, for a shoulder to lean on or a slice of something comforting. I know...' His voice faltered. 'None of us are on an easy journey. Before we set up the dementia element of this café, Dad and I, too, were struggling. Like sailors at sea with no direction, Dad's diagnosis left us both feeling alone and... helpless, desperate for some sort of compass that would show us the way. But now the café and its community feel like a well-run ship, each member of the team playing an important role, with Captain Beaky at the helm, steering us through in his own inimitable way.'

Captain Beaky ignored the plaudit, headbanging in the corner to Diane's phone quietly playing rock music.

'All of you, our guests, our customers, you too have become an intrinsic part of the café, making it come alive. That's what we're about here, living life to the full, whatever the circumstances, whatever anyone else might say you *can't* do.' Tom raised a mug. 'Here's to sticking together through choppy waters.'

Alex raised a cup as an unfamiliar sensation made it difficult for her to avert her gaze from him. Accompanied by clapping, he went over to Norm who was watching the parrot. Tom held his hand.

'Are you enjoying yourself, Dad? I don't know about you but I've eaten far too much.'

'I haven't been offered a bloody thing. Not much of a party, if you ask me. I could starve.' Norm looked around the room, his gaze falling on empty plates and mugs, chunks of cake on the floor, spilled coffee on tabletops, a few discarded leaflets –most had been pocketed – a pair of glasses left behind, no doubt someone would return tomorrow to retrieve them. However, as the door came into his line of view, a distressed noise erupted from deep in his chest. Eyes wide, Norm fixated on the doorway.

There, with a dyed-black pixie cut, stood a petite woman catching her breath, a rucksack on her back. Tom hadn't seen her before. In her early seventies by the looks of it, she stared at Norm with the same jet-black eyes as Kyoko's.

32

Alex settled Norm on the sofa in the staffroom. Tom brought in coffees as Aiko sat next to his dad, Alex in the chair opposite. Aiko took off her silk *sukajan* jacket, letting it fall on the cushions next to her.

'I had to come, as soon as my sister told me,' she explained, 'but apologies for turning up like this.' She shook her head. 'I can't quite believe I'm sitting here, next to your dad, after all this time.' Her voice became unsteady as she faced Tom. 'Our grandmother had dementia... When my sister told me that he's been upsetting himself over a stupid incident that was my fault... I should have got in touch with Norm over the years, but I was too embarrassed.'

Tom's expression softened and he settled into the armchair, next to Alex's. Norm fiddled with the fidget blanket Alex had put over his lap. Cautiously, Aiko took his hand.

'Norm. It's your friend, Aiko.'

No reaction.

'What fun we had, back in those days; you used to wear a tweed flat cap, and that tight jacket. Mum and Dad used to call you Norman Wisdom, not Wilson, even though your impression of him was terrible!'

His head tilted slightly as she spoke about their shopping trips to King's Road and how Norm wanted to grow his hair long, like the Beatles, but didn't dare because Aiko's dad had threatened to sack him on the spot how they couldn't believe their eyes when her parents bought their first hi-fi system from a shop on Tottenham Court Road, and how they loved travelling on the Underground with its cigarette smoke and buskers.

His eyebrows furrowed together. 'Aiko,' he asked, in a scratchy voice, 'did your parents ask me over for dinner tonight? If so, it's my turn to wash up.'

Her face broke into a smile. 'No. I've come up from London to visit you here in Manchester, where you live now.' She rummaged in her rucksack, before pulling out a black-and-white photo of her and Norm sitting behind a cake stacked with fruit, whipped cream and chocolate curls. 'Dad took this on my eighteenth birthday. You baked this, Norm. Dad ate so much he was up all night with indigestion.'

Hand shaking, he took the snap and held it so tightly it bent in the corner.

'What happened, back then?' asked Tom. He moved to the sofa and put his arm around his father.

'Your dad and I were very close, fond of each other,' said Aiko. 'I dreaded his return to Manchester and – I think my sister told you – was panicking that my cancer had returned.'

'That must have been frightening,' said Alex.

'Yes. But it was no excuse for my behaviour. I... had a big crush on him, you see, and confessed my love the last night he visited. Kyoko has always said I'm impulsive.' Her cheeks flushed. 'I didn't want Norm to leave. I'd never had a friend like him before, we could talk about anything.'

'He... had feelings for you too?' asked Tom, in a strained tone.

'No! Not at all. He was madly in love with your mum. It's cringeworthy now. I'd convinced myself he felt the same too.'

Tom exhaled quietly and held Norm tighter.

'One reason my parents liked Norm so much was that they considered him honourable. They accidentally overpaid him once, and he told them straight away. It's one reason I liked him too. He'd never have got together with me while dating your mother. My parents thought I was too young to have a boyfriend anyway. They trusted your dad.'

Norm stopped fidgeting and reached out, in her direction. Aiko took his hand with both of hers.

'I was a shy girl and loved the old traditions, didn't I, Norm?'

'Shy my foot, you were a talker,' he said, and his eyes twinkled.

A flush of pink filled her cheeks again. 'I'd explained the beautiful moon analogy to Norm previously, and said that phrase to him on that last night. But, Tom, your father, understandably, couldn't reply the way I wanted, couldn't say back that the moon is beautiful, in other words, that he loved me too. Your mum was everything to him.' She shook her head. 'Now I know he believed I'd died a few weeks later, when it was my granddad. No wonder he's felt guilty, even though he shouldn't have.' Gently, with one finger, she lifted Norm's chin so that his gaze met hers. 'Look at me, I'm still standing, fifty years later. I've had a good life, enjoyed my work, got married.' She pulled out her phone and showed Norm a photo of her and a man with a white beard. 'This is Reg, my husband. What a good thing you didn't say to me that the moon is beautiful, because you went on to marry Susie and had your caring son. I married Reg and we've had a great life, setting up a chain of Japanese restaurants.'

A single tear ran down Norm's face. 'It's okay, then?' he asked, in a whisper. 'I didn't do a bad thing?'

'Everything's fine,' she said, eyes glistening. 'You've had a good life. I have too.' The two of them took a moment, holding each other's gaze. 'Tom, why don't you take a photo of me and Norm together? Then if he still talks about the moon, you can show him the photo, tell him none of it matters now, tell him that we are still the best of friends.' Aiko slipped her arm around Norm.

'I do like a hug,' said Norm.

The two old friends sat together, in comfortable silence. Eventually, Aiko finished her drink, Tom asked about her restaurants, she quizzed him about the café and its unusual name. Norm's eyelids began to droop and Aiko consulted her watch.

'This is a flying visit; I wasn't sure how... I mean... I'm sorry that my past foolishness has caused so much upset. You've all been very gracious.'

'Don't apologise,' said Tom. 'We're all foolish in our youth.'

'Some of us still in our forties,' said Alex.

Aiko went to stand up but Norm gripped her arm, top lip trembling. 'Sorry I'm such a mess, gal.' The lucidity passed as soon as he said it.

Despite her stiff joints, Aiko knelt on the floor in front of him and looked up into his face, her hands cupping his cheeks. 'I've never had a better friend than you, Norm,' she whispered. 'I'm so glad we've found each other again. Our friendship may have appeared broken on the surface, but today proves it still runs deep. *Wabi-sabi.*' Aiko sat next to him again and kissed his cheek. He leant into her and they sat with nothing between them, not the decades apart, or his illness. Without realising it, Alex's hand had slipped into Tom's.

'I'd better get back to the kitchen otherwise your parents will have my guts for garters,' Norm said, gruffly, jolting them all back to the moment. Alex and Tom let go of each other. Mouths upturned, eyes laughing, Aiko and Norm's faces mirrored each other's.

'I'd like to visit again,' she said to Tom, 'if that's okay?'

'More than okay,' he replied.

'What's *wabi-sabi*, if you don't mind me asking?' said Alex.

'Not at all.' Aiko bowed her head. 'It's a Japanese way of thinking about the natural cycle of life and how it's imperfect, impermanent, incomplete. It encourages you to seek the beauty in imperfection, such as... the striking russet and orange swirls of rust on an ancient sheet of metal. It's about accepting the way things are and appreciating simplicity. Norm and I would use the word jokingly, if our cooking didn't turn out as expected. He made Japanese dumplings once, far too big. I couldn't stop laughing, nor could my parents. They were giants. Yet English customers loved them, said they looked like cute Cornish pasties.'

'*Wabi-sabi*,' muttered Norm.

'My grandmother got dementia...' said Aiko. 'It's an ugly illness. It's hard to find any beautiful aspects, yet her social reservations disappeared. She was more affectionate towards me and my family at the end, in a way she'd never been before. And her illness made us appreciate our present, made us realise joyous moments should be truly celebrated because nothing in life stays the same; we're in a constant state of flux. It also helped my family appreciate the smallest of moments with my grandmother... the delight on her face if she especially enjoyed a noodle dish, a twinkle in her eye when she made a joke, even if none of us understood it. It helped us move towards acceptance in terms of how she'd changed.'

A disagreeable sensation wouldn't allow Alex to sit still and she picked up Norm's fidget blanket. Her author life had been the opposite of *wabi-sabi*, with her only being satisfied with utter perfection, in terms of the image she projected and the ranks she achieved. Alex also longed for permanence in that she never accepted less than maintaining her number one positions – whatever the cost – and never losing her youthful looks. She worked hard to become a complete package, striking as a person, striking on bookshelves. She had never properly appreciated just what she'd achieved, the next goal was always on the horizon, shinier and seemingly more perfect than the ones before.

Aiko chatted some more and Norm nodded off. A car backfired and he woke up, Aiko taking this as her cue to leave, to catch her train back to London.

'See you soon, Norm,' said Aiko. She gave a small bow of her head. 'Next time I'll bring sushi.'

'None of that cucumber muck, make it fish for me,' he said and waved his hand in the air. 'And make sure your mum puts pickled ginger on top. She knows it's my favourite.'

33

Alex got up early and went to Market Street; another Monday, another day off. She was going to attempt to bake a cake, to surprise Tom with when she went around this evening, for another session working on their novel. It had been a long time since she'd wanted to surprise anyone. A flash of green caught her eye on the corner of Piccadilly Gardens. On closer inspection it was a plastic bag. Her mum had come back from the city centre once, unable to stop talking about the kingfisher she'd spotted. She'd explained how kingfishers had inspired the building of Japanese bullet trains. Not only because they flew low and straight, as if fired from a gun, but due to the shape of their beak that was one-third their height. Its sleekness meant it could cut through water without alerting prey. This concept was behind the design of the front of these trains, which used to cause a sonic boom when entering tunnels, but didn't once remodelled.

Alex's career had been like a high-speed train that had started off with a big boom, but then lost its way, slowing down, coming to a halt.

Her phone vibrated.

Hi Alex. We're back in Thailand to relax for the last few days. This afternoon we're going for an authentic Thai massage. I've felt so ashamed of my body these last years, the changes no Instagram filter could soften. Like the floppy underarms, thickening waist, dimples on my legs... Travelling around Asia has given me perspective. Our bodies are bloody miracles, keeping us alive, adapting to new environments, and it's up to us to help them where we can. I'm going to the GP as soon as I get back to discuss HRT. Can't wait for us to meet too, and chat – if you'd like? H xx

Alex reread the message.

Hi Hope. It's so good to hear you sounding positive. I'm going to the GP as well. Hormone replacement may not be the route for me but I owe it to my future to check out the options. I've got so much to tell you about. You won't believe what's happened with Norm. Yes, let's get together. A xx

Alex slipped her phone into her back pocket and carried on walking until she reached Waterstones in the Arndale, hoping to find a book about baking that would inspire her. She could have browsed through Hope's book collection; no doubt she'd have found something suitable. However, with the looming end to her time at the café, the prospect of returning to her apartment, to full-time writing, Alex couldn't resist taking a dip back in the world that used to mean everything. To test it out. The smell of books, an appealing mix of wood and vanilla, filled her nostrils as she walked in. On automatic, she headed for the women's fiction section, found her novels, and by force of habit, positioned them more prominently. Laughter caught her attention. On the other side of the room a table had been set up, with piles of books on top and a chair behind. Alex used to enjoy signings, they felt almost cleansing, talking to loyal readers, the one part of her new life that had felt genuine. The author had ironed blonde hair and wore a beige trouser suit with shoulder pads you could stack books on top of. Sporty and bright eyed, she looked across at Alex, puzzled, and then waved in a regal manner.

Oh no.

Mary Jane Smith, a fellow Mancunian, who wrote the same genre as Alex; both of their debuts came out in the same year, both topped the charts. Alex's got to number one and kept Mary's off that coveted spot. They'd met each other at a couple of book events in London, Alex happily dropping her foreign rights deals and continued great ranks into the conversation. She couldn't help it. Especially as Mary was younger and reminded her of Megan. Funny how, when you felt really down, for a second it helped to hurt others. It made the way you'd suffered feel less personal. Mary's career had taken longer to build than Alex's and took off at top speed at the point where Alex's had waned. Alex's last book hadn't even made the top thousand whereas Mary's stayed in the top ten for months.

Mary strode over. 'Alex? Is it really you?' She eyed her up and down, taking in the plain T-shirt, harem pants and well-used trainers – Alex and Hope were the same shoe size.

Alex felt like a bird with no sharp beak or claws, without the protection of her flawless author uniform, her climbing sales. 'New release?'

'Yes. I'm here early to sign several hundred copies before fans arrive. So exciting! What about you? You haven't got another book up for pre-order.'

'I'm... taking a break. Things haven't... panned out quite as I planned.'

'Doing what?'

'Working in a café.'

'You'll have to try harder than that to catch me out.' Mary grinned. 'What's really happening? Ghostwriting? Blogging? Podcasts? I know one ex-author who set up her own literary agency.'

Alex squirmed.

'Oh crap, apologies, you meant it?' said Mary. 'Wow. I mean... well done you, branching out into a different career. I hope it goes well.' Clearly embarrassed, she turned away, with sympathy, pity for Alex, all over her face.

Face burning, Alex left the shop, aware of perspiration under her arms as she almost ran back to the Northern Quarter. Grateful that the café was closed, she hurried up to Hope's flat. She went to the sink and downed a glass of cold water, feeling like a nobody. Alex Butler wasn't used to that and didn't like it much. She took a deep breath, recognising the ego that she'd scraped together after being dumped by Simon, the ego that had got out of control as an author. She picked up her phone and went onto Amazon; she hadn't done that since Hope left for Thailand. She'd barely looked at any of her social media platforms either. Mary Jane Smith's new release came up, already in the top twenty. Alex was about to check her own ranks, an act of self-harm, she knew that, when a loud knocking sounded on the door downstairs. She ignored it for several minutes but thought her name floated upwards. Alex went to the window before hurrying down into the café. She opened the door.

'Erin. What are you doing here?' Alex beckoned in Miranda's assistant.

Erin had been visiting an author in Salford, on Miranda's behalf, while she was in Italy. She'd never been to Manchester, loved the city. 'I went to your address and the doorman told me you weren't living there at the moment, but mentioned a café that got orders wrong. I googled it.'

'Yes, I fancied a change of scenery, to get the creative juices flowing. Coffee?' asked Alex.

'That would be great. Thanks. Black no sugar.'

Realising she had no idea how to work the coffee machine, Alex led Erin up to Hope's. Erin went straight over to the bookshelves and browsed through the titles before turning her attention to the plants.

'Love this place,' she said. 'And it's twice the size of my London flat.'

Alex brought their drinks over to the sofa. Erin had joined the agency two years ago, a couple of years out of university, ambitious, understated with her make-up free face and bland palette of work clothes. She'd very much impressed Miranda, always in early and the last to leave the office. She soon acquired a reputation for perspective, logic and a keen, no-nonsense business sense.

They chatted about the publishing business while Alex tried to recall the progress reports she'd emailed in about the chapters she was supposed to be rewriting.

'Lovely to see you, of course, Erin, but... what's this visit really all about?'

Erin took a gulp of coffee and then put down her mug, before questioning Alex about the changes she was making to her latest novel.

'Is this why Miranda sent you? To check up on me?'

'No. She's just concerned, that's all. Said the feedback from you about progress sounded vague. I was up here anyway, so it made sense to call in...'

'No one likes to dawdle if they've a long train journey back home. You came here for a reason. What couldn't wait until Miranda got back? It's only a few days now.'

'But the deadline is looming for that publisher. Miranda

might well be friends with the commissioning editor but there's no leeway on the submission window. She mentioned you'd been *restructuring*?'

'Yes... I thought... what with the Milan setting, a mafia element might spice things up.' Frantically, Alex thought back to preliminary notes she'd made on her original manuscript, before the idea of co-authoring with Tom had come along.

'*Might*? You've not incorporated it already?'

Alex fixed a smile on her face. 'It's all in hand. Don't worry, I'm used to meeting deadlines.'

Erin went to say something but changed her mind. 'Of course you are.' She drained her mug. 'And you're right about the trains, I don't want to miss mine. I'd better check it hasn't been cancelled. Rail services are a bit of a mess at the moment.' She took out her phone.

'I'll see you, no doubt, in the next month or two,' said Alex brightly as Erin stood up, still scrolling down.

'I look forward to it. Just watch out for the building works planned in Camden,' she said, in a distracted voice. 'They could make the office difficult to access for a few weeks, starting from September.'

'But the office is in Fulham.'

Erin looked up. 'Sorry, Alex, got lost in the train app, for a moment. You were saying?'

'Why would I travel to Camden to see Miranda?'

'Oh, um... no reason.' She headed to the door.

'Erin? What's going on?'

She turned around and moved from foot to foot. 'This puts me in an awkward position... no one knows yet... I could get into trouble...'

Alex went over. 'Remember when you first started and came to one of my launch parties, the caterer provided fish goujons and chips in cones? You accidentally squirted tomato ketchup down Miranda's white cashmere jacket, that she'd left on the back of a chair. She complained for days afterwards that even the dry cleaner couldn't get the stain out.'

A tide of red swept up her neck.

'I kept shtum. You can trust me. What's going on?'

Erin paused. 'Okay, but please, not a word to anyone else... Miranda's leaving the agency to set up on her own.'

'What?'

'I'm going with her. Along with several of her authors.'

Alex shivered. Miranda hadn't asked her. Despite the business nature of their relationship, Alex never really imagined a life in publishing without Miranda, hoping she'd really like the co-authored project. Erin talked about how Miranda setting up on her own meant that any commission would go directly to her, and that Miranda wouldn't have to worry about clashing with another agent's list when she wanted to take an author on. The status appealed to her too, being her own boss.

'To be blunt, Alex, if you don't land this deal she'll leave you with the agency and there are no guarantees another agent there will want to take you on, not with the way your career has slumped. The agency might let you go. I'm sorry, but seeing as you know now, I feel it's best to be honest. You know how much I admire your writing...'

Since arriving at the agency, crafting fan Erin had personally handmade every publication day card the agency sent to her.

'I want to keep working with you. This slump, I'm sure it's nothing but a blip. Just make sure the chapters you hand in to Miranda at the end of this week are your very best work. They need to dazzle.'

In a daze, Alex saw Erin out.

34

Late that afternoon, Tom got back from visiting Norm, feet plodding upstairs as if he wore boots like Diane's. Alex hadn't baked a cake. Instead, unable to fight the urge, she'd spent hours scrolling on Twitter, Facebook and Instagram. No one appeared to have missed her. A couple of readers had tagged her in tweets applauding her stories, a blogger on Instagram had posted a photo of their upcoming July reads; Alex's latest was among them. Alex still had 30,000 followers on Instagram, just under that number on Twitter. Fully submerged in the online world, she noted the huge number of likes and comments from readers on old posts. She'd forgotten how quickly social media sucked time and hadn't even eaten lunch, prioritising studying Miranda's platforms to see which of her authors she was promoting.

Miranda was going to ditch her. Like Simon had. Mum had left her. Dad had never really been there. Alex closed her eyes, barely able to breathe. She picked up her notebook. Pull yourself together. So what if she ended up without an agent? She no longer had anything to prove to Simon and had a co-author for bouncing around ideas with, for support.

Still. The pressure was higher than ever, now, for their joint project to really sparkle. She knocked on his door and smiled as she walked in, going straight up to the play stand and Captain Beaky.

'Legs!' he squawked.

'Hello, little chap. Sorry I couldn't keep you company today, I had a spot of shopping to do.'

'Silly bitch!'

That comment had irritated the old Alex. In the blink of an eye you can change and not even know it.

Tom pottered in the kitchen, minus his usual whistling. It can't have been easy leaving Norm behind after every visit, especially as the two of them used to live together. Alex had moved out of her mother's rented house as soon as possible after her death. Even though she'd been a diminutive figure, physically, especially at the end, the space left by her in the house was too big to bear. Alex missed the wildlife documentaries playing on the television, the CDs of birdsong, the vacuuming she'd insist on doing first thing in the morning, the oven aroma of lasagne and cottage pie, of apple crumbles.

'How was your dad?' she asked Tom and went into the kitchen. 'Let me make a brew.'

He sat down on the sofa.

'Did he mention Aiko?'

'No, the beautiful moon phrase instead,' said Tom and he brushed his fringe out of his face. 'But I showed him the old photo of them together, then the new ones we took on Saturday. His face relaxed as soon as he saw them. I reckon there's a good chance his fixation will fizzle out now.'

'It's amazing that he recognised her at all after such a long time.'

Tom didn't say anything for a moment. 'That's the thing with memories, they never disappear; dementia patients simply lose the ability to retrieve them, access to those far in the past being easier than more recent ones.'

Alex passed him a mug and sat down. Captain Beaky flew over and landed on Tom's lap. Tom reached into his pocket and fed him a nut. 'Birds have amazing brains and long-term memory,' he said, 'to lead them to food sources they've visited before or to remind them who the predators are. Some biologists believe crows are the most intelligent species second to humans, before apes, even.'

She ran a hand down one of Captain Beaky's feathers. The bird talk made her feel as if Mum was in the room. She and Tom would have got on well.

Alex opened her notebook. 'How have you found writing your opening chapters? I've thought more about the ending now, I can't help it. I'm looking forward to writing the part where they'll make tentative steps towards being friends.'

'Perhaps, in the final chapter, they'll end up at the Buddhist centre, book a meditation session together – they'll have come full circle.'

'We're still going to need so much more to grip the reader, twists and turns that are threaded in realistically, deep characterisation... We need to really wow Miranda, so let's get together every night this week; we can read each other's chapters, make them shine.'

Tom fed Captain Beaky another nut and chatted to him.

'You've got your second chapter at least planned out, right?' Alex asked.

'Yeah, but the first still needs a thorough rewrite. I was going to edit it tonight but, sorry, Alex, I'm not in the mood today. Can we do this another time?'

'Ha, ha.' She pushed his shoulder playfully. 'Miranda's back at the weekend. We've only got five days left.'

'Miranda can wait a bit, surely? I can't force it.'

Alex faced him directly. 'Wait, you're *serious*? That's like saying one of your customers could wait a few hours to receive their order. If you really want this, Tom...'

'We've got our prologue done, the synopsis, my first chapter will be ready, yours too.'

'That isn't enough to give her a true feel for our direction.' Alex frowned. 'You need to be fully on board, 100 per cent committed to pressing ahead. The time we have now is a good training ground for pushing through writer's block. Any deal will be my sole income once Hope returns. I can't afford to mess this up.'

'I can still give you a few shifts once she gets back. That way we can take our time.'

A few shifts here wouldn't pay the mortgage, let alone the arrears. 'There's no such thing as taking your time, not in the publishing industry.'

'Then I'm not sure I've got it in me. I'm not a robot.'

What? 'Just like that, you've gone off our co-authoring project?'

He put Captain Beaky back on his stand. 'It's a book, Alex. A story. Made up. I'm not a surgeon backing out of your operation, or a pilot leaving the cockpit halfway through your flight.'

Her eyes pricked and she got to her feet. 'You're saying that what I do doesn't have value? You've simply been humouring me, playing with my future?'

'What have you been doing these last weeks? Getting to grips with the job, like learning how to use the coffee machine? Or when it's quiet you've helped the chefs with their prep? No.

Instead you've focused on scoring brownie points in the popularity stakes by writing Reenie's journal and getting Fletch playing the guitar again.' He rolled his eyes. 'You're so entrenched in the culture of chasing likes and followers, it's tipped into your real life. Did you even bother asking Hope what her job entailed? How she'd cash up every night? How she'd taste any new dishes the chefs came up with so that she could recommend them to customers?' Tom threw his hands in the air. 'You accuse me of playing with someone's future? You almost left. Twice. Hope would have lost everything.'

'It wasn't like that... I didn't... Fine. Forget the whole thing. Maybe "Coming Up For Air" was a stupid idea.'

He had taken the pen out from behind his ear, holding it tightly between both hands, flexing it backwards and forwards as she spoke. Tom jumped as it snapped in half, as if jolted out of a trance. 'Look... let's both chill a bit and talk this through. I'll get cake and we'll talk.'

'Cake doesn't solve a single thing. All that sugar hit does is prevent people facing up to the truth, it's an escape and no different to me writing books.' Her words pinched his face. 'We both offer people a coping mechanism, a break, just for one moment, from the daily grind. Your café won't cure Reenie, Fletch and Diane, but you think you can simply wrap up their illness with sprinkles and hot chocolate, with humour derived from them getting orders wrong. My first impression was right,' she said and headed for the door. 'You're nothing but a businessman through and through. And I'm a businesswoman. Profits above all else, right?' The door closed just in time to block out the sight of her angry tears. *Crap, why did she say that?*

Several email notifications popped up. Miranda; why was she messaging? Alex felt like she was young again, sinking under the swimming pool's water with no one to catch her. Back in the flat, she went into the bedroom and lay on the bed, still with her shoes on. Erin might have reported back, told Miranda that Alex didn't seem to have made much progress with the rewrite. Crap, now the phone was ringing; why was Miranda ringing her from Italy? She accepted the call.

'About time, darling!'

'Hi, Miranda. How's Tuscany?'

'Forget Tuscany, girl. Listen to this...'

Miranda hadn't wanted to get her client's hopes up, but she'd submitted the opening chapters and synopsis of Alex's fracking book to three other publishers who'd agreed to look, even though the manuscript wasn't finished, convinced there wouldn't be a positive response. She'd often described Alex's stories as glamorous and romantic and that didn't fit with an ethical story grounded in fixing climate change. However, the last two had replied this afternoon and both were clamouring to sign her.

'They both love your characters, think the fracking setting is genius, that you've fused two genres meaning double the readers. More than one interested party means your book's going to auction.'

Alex's pulse built up speed.

'I reckon we're talking a mega advance, at the higher end. Both are saying it will be a major title for them, and have already put together extremely compelling marketing plans.'

It had to be a joke.

'You're back, baby, bigger than ever before. I fly home on Saturday morning. How about I come up north to you that evening?'

Miranda was *keen.*

'We'll meet at that bar in the Village we were due to see each other in last time,' she continued. 'I'll email you the time my train gets in. Say something!'

'But—'

'Hold that. The *tagliatelle al tartufo* has arrived. You can thank me at the weekend.' The line went dead.

35

Alex got up the next morning and pulled her case into Hope's bedroom. She stuffed in her clothes and toiletries and gave the plants one last water. Dehydrated herself, she downed a glassful before collapsing onto the sofa. It was only seven o'clock, early enough to avoid Tom and settle back into her Deansgate apartment, after picking up a bag of cannoli from Bernardo's for breakfast. A large advance and the promotions attached would soon wipe the smile off Mary Jane Smith's face. It would be a kick in the stomach for the publisher who'd let her go. It would place her firmly back in the heart of Miranda's agency, bringing back lunches at The Ivy, and it would stop those worrying emails from her mortgage provider. And it was the only option she had, now that Tom had ditched the idea of being a co-author.

Earning brownie points? Was Tom's opinion of her really so low? The question had circled around in her head, all night, like a vulture picking at the carcass of her life in the café. She'd wanted to help Reenie and Fletch, to think of people other than herself for a change. *That* had been her motivation. Should she have quizzed Hope more about her exact role in the café? Alex and Jade got on well now, didn't that mean she fitted in? Fitted into a life she'd never wanted, fitted into a life that stripped her of everything she'd considered important.

Alex put on her jacket and changed into a pair of her high-heel shoes. All this time Tom had thought the worst about her. She clutched the handle of her luggage and looked towards the door. However, her feet wouldn't budge and she let go of the handle and paced up and down. Instead of leaving straight away she'd rebook her Botox appointment. She'd need to get her usual stylist to even out her hair. Alex would ask for a colour too, grey roots had been coming through. First thing tonight she'd wax and then re-install Tinder. Older men were, altogether, way too complicated.

A niggling voice pricked her conscience.

It was Tuesday. Hope wouldn't be back until the weekend. How could she leave the café short staffed until then? That wouldn't be fair on Jade or Reenie, people she'd become fond of. Then there was Captain Beaky; she wanted to say a proper good-bye. She'd miss his unbothered attitude; if spirit animals existed he'd be her first choice. Plus she'd planned to help Diane, as much as she could, in the afternoon. Alex went to the window. Down in Stevenson Square people went about their daily business despite the clouds in the sky, despite the bags under their eyes, despite the uncomfortable suits and heels.

Alex would stick out the week. Keep to her side of the bargain. Then leave Saturday night, going straight to the Village to see Miranda. Alex fetched her laptop and sat at the kitchen table. She pulled up the first three chapters of the sexy fracking thriller. A heavy sensation returned again, as if the earth's gravitational pull had magnified. Birds defied gravity in several ways, she reminded herself, by flying and some waders fed upwards using droplets of water. She brought up her first chapter for 'Coming Up For Air' and instantly the heaviness lifted. Her fingers itched to get typing that manuscript instead.

She made toast before going downstairs at nine, having changed into Hope's trainers, taken off her jacket. Jade passed her a coffee as she walked in. She took a gulp before feeding Captain Beaky a couple of grapes. Then she served a group of executives. Alex had got used to the curious glances, new customers trying to work out whether she'd get the order right. Reenie stood by the jukebox, chatting to a young man with a fade haircut. Alex updated her notebook. A group of builders in hi-vis jackets came in. The morning saw a steady flow of customers.

'Any sign of Tom today?' asked Jade as Alex's break approached. 'He was going to cover for me. I've got a dentist's appointment at twelve; an old filling is coming loose.'

'No.'

'If he's not here in thirty minutes I'll have to cancel. Would you mind seeing if he's upstairs?'

Alex would have rather pulled out one of her own teeth. But she climbed the stairs and stood outside the door to his flat and knocked. No one answered.

When he still hadn't appeared by midday, a sense of discomfort gnawed at Alex's stomach. Tom never left the café without saying where he was going. Normally, he would have at least left a message or rung to let them know. By the time her lunch break arrived Alex had no appetite; it was half past two and Tom still hadn't come back. Diane was here and he'd definitely wanted to supervise her first shifts. Alex worked through and kept a close eye on Diane herself, then helped Jade cash up, promising to text her as soon as she had news. Alex locked up and went over to Captain Beaky.

'Where is Tom, little man, any idea?'

'You talkin' to me?' he squawked.

She stared out front, onto the square. Simon popped into her head and how her mind had so quickly turned him into a monster, despite their many happy years together. Yesterday afternoon, Tom had behaved totally out of character. No whistling. No jokes. Under any other circumstances she'd have felt grateful for a break from his infinite good cheer. Why hadn't she asked herself what was up? So what if he'd gone off the project? Writing wasn't for everyone; he'd given it a shot. She replayed their argument. How could she have accused him of exploiting his staff? Images dropped into her head of the night at the hospital, his arms around Val. Her phone pinged and almost fell to the floor as she yanked it out of her back pocket. Her hands fumbled as she lit up the screen. Oh.

Hi Alex. I meant to say – it's Tom's birthday Thursday. He doesn't like a fuss and the others might not remember. But for Fletch's last birthday he bought an air guitar album and put it on with coffee and cake in the staffroom after his shift, and we all played imaginary Fenders. I'd never seen Fletch so happy. For Reenie, he found a beautiful key ring with hairdresser charms including a silver hairdryer, a brush, comb and scissors. He gave me a beautiful gold bookmark and Jade got a funky tote bag from Afflecks. So on his birthday I try to get everyone to sign a card and contribute towards a present. Last year, I bought him a pair of bookends in the shape of parrots, you might have seen them. Maybe you could get him something. Sorry for the late notice.

By the way. That massage. I feel like a new woman – a woman who's taking charge of her life again! H xx

Could Tom's disappearance be related to his birthday? Another thought had struck her as the day had progressed.

Yesterday he'd visited Norm. What if it was bad news? Perhaps Norm had been rushed to hospital or had even passed and Tom was in denial or couldn't face talking about it. Alex found the care home's website, rang the number and talked to one of the care workers who'd come in for the open day. Apparently Norm was fine and Tom had been his usual jovial self yesterday afternoon, dropping off a batch of scones for the staff before he headed towards his dad's room.

Alex hurried up the stairs, Captain Beaky's cage swaying in her hand. She had the key to Tom's flat; he'd given her a spare so that if he was ever out Alex could keep the parrot company, if she fancied. She let Captain Beaky hop onto the play stand, put out fruit and nuts, and filled the water bowl. She walked into Tom's bedroom, curious to find the parrot bookends. The furniture was retro, teak, and the same colour as the laminated floor. She stepped onto a tasselled rug and her eyes ran over a shelf above a chest of drawers. The bookends stood opposite each other, forming a concertina of thrillers and women's fiction novels. The bookends were porcelain, smudged with shades of red and green, and far better behaved than Captain Beaky. A mosaic print lampshade hung from the ceiling, old-fashioned, from the seventies; perhaps it had belonged to his parents. In contrast, in the far corner, was an open storage box full of gaming consoles. The relaxing scent of joss sticks took her back to her student days. She turned to a print, above the bed, of the Manchester skyline, drawn in black against smudged pastels. Her gaze finally settled on a framed photo on his bedside table. It was Tom as a boy with his mother; she recognised them both from when Norm had gone through the family album. They sat on a beach by a sandcastle, his mum in a polka-dot bikini, Tom holding a bucket and spade. Sheets of paper by the side of the frame caught her eye. Tom's first chapter of 'Coming Up For Air'.

Alex picked up the frame and stared at the two figures, Tom and his mum sitting closely together, and in that instant she knew exactly where he'd gone.

36

Gasping, chest burning, Alex arrived in Turner Street and
stopped outside the red-brick building, its windows covered in
ornate metal, forged into a pattern of twisting leaves. She read the
illuminated white sign, before heading to the steps. As
commuters jostled past, she stopped dead and squinted through
the evening sunlight. There at the top, in front of the glass doors,
sat a man, head in hands, salted-caramel hair ruffled. He wore
yesterday's clothes. Slowly, she walked up the steps. Tom's head
lifted; he hadn't shaved. Loose change had been tossed on the
step in front of him.

'Hi,' she said softly and sat down beside him.

'Hi...'

'You okay?'

He didn't reply.

She moved close. Rubbed his back. 'How long have you been
here?'

'Since early afternoon,' he croaked, as if his voice hadn't been
used for decades, 'but the place had already closed. How did you
know?'

She ran a finger across his beaded bracelet. Mentioned the joss stick smell in his flat. 'And in our novel, Jack went up to the Buddhist centre to talk to his mum. In my experience, the most moving aspects of authors' stories come from a personal place. You said something, once, about Susie being interested in yoga and spiritualism.'

Tom didn't reply.

'Has coming here helped?'

The balls of his hands pressed against his eyes and she forced them away, holding his fingers tightly in hers. 'I'm sorry for what I said yesterday, I didn't mean it. You're a great boss. As for "Coming Up For Air", you've a perfect right to not want to continue. God knows I've considered giving up writing often enough. It's no excuse but I was extra stressed, worried my agent was going to drop me.'

A sob shuddered through his body.

Tom crying? The one who was always whistling, navigating his way through each day with a positive outlook, with an open, sunny nature, like a bird flying through life, feeding and singing, hiding the darkness of coping with bad weather or the constant threat of predators? Yet again he'd revealed a glimpse of the Tom underneath.

She slid her arms around his, each shake of his shoulders cutting through her. When the shaking subsided, Alex passed him a tissue and he blew his nose.

'Did Jade get to her dental appointment?' he asked in a tone she knew well, hard around the edges but prone to crumble; she'd called upon it often enough when life had to go on, regardless of the losses she'd suffered.

'No, but she was more worried about you.'

'How did Diane do?'

'Her face was a picture when one customer left a tip. She

loved being back at work and only got one order a bit muddled. Captain Beaky is fed and watered and back in his cage, in your flat.' She placed her hand on his. 'You must be starving.'

'I spent the morning wandering around the Arndale, visiting Dad's favourite haunts. He's always loved a bargain and couldn't go into Wilko without spending a tenner. Kenji was another shop he'd visit, not so much for its quirky products, but the fact not much in there costs more than a couple of quid. He could lose himself in that building for a whole day during sales periods, buying a tennis racket he'd never use or a discounted trendy shirt he'd never fit into.' He bent his knees and rested his head against them. 'After everything with Aiko, I reckoned Dad was doing okay,' he said in a muffled voice.

'What's happened?'

Dark shadows underneath his eyes hid the boyish, carefree freckles. 'When he recognised Aiko I felt on top of the world, as if I'd eaten a whole Victoria sponge and been hit with the biggest sugar rush. For a while I fooled myself that Dad's memories weren't slipping away quite as quickly. But then yesterday afternoon, when I walked into his room, he said...' Tom's face crumpled. '"Who are you?"'

Alex linked her arm with his.

'I said, "It's me, Tom, your son." Dad pulled a face and said, "Gawd, you aren't, are you?" We both laughed, but... I was crying inside.' Tom gulped. 'He didn't recognise me, Alex. He's looked confused about who I am before, and now and then I've suspected it's taken him a while to work out I'm his son, but he's never actually asked that question outright, out loud... I'm another step closer to losing him forever, aren't I?' Tears ran down his face again. 'It's always been me and Dad against the world but soon... we'll lose our bond.'

'Now you listen to me.' Alex sat up straight. 'Nothing could ever diminish your connection. You didn't know Norm was your dad when you were a baby, before you could speak or recognise faces, but that won't have stopped the two of you loving each other.' She wiped a tear from his cheek with her thumb. 'It's like that now. You and Norm have a special relationship that runs deeper than words on the surface. That sense of belonging, between you, is unbreakable, Tom.'

'I should have come into work today. I just couldn't face it.'

'The inspiration for your short story... you said it was the tough times the world is going through at the moment, how everyone must have secrets about how they are coping... I thought you were referencing Norm, and how he's dealt with his diagnosis. But is this story really about you, Tom, reaching your rock bottom?'

Tom blew his nose again. 'When we got the diagnosis, we both cried in the car park outside the hospital. He said Mum wouldn't want either of us to mope, we just had to get on with it, like we did when she left us. I saw that... steel centre of Dad again, that had got him through her death. Day by day it helped me carry on. But when Dad went into a care home I felt utterly hopeless. And so guilty.' Alex leant her head against his shoulder. 'That first night, on my own, in the flat, a huge sense of failure overwhelmed me, as if I'd let him down. I used the bathroom and, on the way out, caught sight of the paracetamol bottle.' He paused. 'It was a fleeting moment interrupted by Captain Beaky telling a game show host to fuck off. I'd never have done anything, I simply spent a few moments imagining oblivion, a place where I wouldn't have to witness the disease strip Dad of what makes him, him. *That*, in part, is what inspired the short story. The Buddhist centre in it provided a momentary escape.' He exhaled loudly. 'As time passed, I realised the care home was Dad's best option, all his needs are met with the staff's full attention and it took away a lot of my stress, so I'm the best I can be when Dad and I spend time together.'

They sat, silently, as the sun burned less fiercely and passing drivers shot them curious looks. When the traffic ended its dusk chorus, Alex stood up and brushed herself down. She extended her arm and pulled him up.

'I didn't mean what I said either,' he said, 'about you simply trying to earn brownie points, about not doing your job properly. You've been a real asset and I'll be sorry to see you leave at the weekend. About the co-authoring project, it's probably for the best. I need to focus more than ever on Dad now. Sorry to let you down.'

Voice full of fake excitement, she dismissed his concern and told him about Miranda's call. The last thing Tom needed, right now, was to sense her disappointment.

'You must be keen to get back to that smart apartment and working days that don't involve squawked obscenities and clothes that reek of coffee.'

Attempting a joke? This was good, even if it was about the fact that, once she'd moved back to Deansgate, their paths would rarely cross. A vacuum opened up inside of Alex. Wrong Order Café had come to feel like a cosy nest, feathered with pot plants and books and sugar treats, with music and jokes. She wasn't ready to be nudged out, not yet. It was a long time since she'd felt part of something. She'd enjoyed the bustle of colleagues and banter with customers, and the affection that had grown towards Reenie, Jade and Fletch, who'd still pop in now and again, as well as Norm and Captain Beaky. But most of all, she'd really miss... A shortage of breath engulfed Alex. *No. That couldn't be right.* An annoying cheerfulness, odd socks, those bloody open-toe sandals? None of those things belonged in her life, and yet...

Oh. My. God. She couldn't imagine life without them.

37

Alex avoided Tom the next day, talking *Attack on Titan* with Jade or menopausal hair with Reenie, and today, Thursday, in the morning, she helped the chefs prep fruit and veg whenever she had a spare minute. Back serving customers, later on, Alex checked her watch. It was almost time for Reenie to leave and Diane to arrive. Alex cleared a table next to Captain Beaky and on it placed a large knife. In her head she ran through a text exchange from the previous evening.

Hi Hope. Seeing as you told me about Sovann, I'm prepared to entrust you with some laughable information. I've developed a crush on Tom. Obviously the menopause is to blame. Hormones are unpredictable during puberty and that's the last time I had a crush – on Leonardo DiCaprio in the movie *Romeo + Juliet*. I never felt like this over Simon, ours was a proper, grown-up relationship, like the ones in my stories, a match of ambitions, a match of lifestyles. Whereas like with Leo, the last couple of weeks, I've thought constantly about Tom – the job, his dad, the parrot, our book, everything comes back to him. Yesterday, I found myself doodling his name next to a customer's order. I down-

loaded a jazz album and almost put on odd socks this morning. My
agent would pretend to vomit if I were a fictional character.
Forget the anxiety, flushes, sleeplessness, forget the lack of hope (no
pun intended), the worst symptom I can't control is the way this man
makes me feel. A xx

Alex smiled at two women who left a couple of pound coins
on their table, before gathering their bags and leaving.

Hi Alex. Now breathe. Don't do that – don't talk down your emotions.
Tom's a good person. I'm so excited for you! As for it being a crush,
you surprise me, aren't authors supposed to know about words? If
you look that one up you'll see this definition: 'an infatuation with
someone who's unattainable'.
Tom's straight. Single. Like you. How about this definition instead: 'an
intense feeling of affection'.
I leave you to find out what that's the definition for. H xx

Alex shook her head as she stacked crockery onto a tray. Hope
didn't know what she was talking about. *Alex* was the romance
author, the expert on *love*. In any case, the definition was irrele-
vant, Tom talked so lightly of her returning to Deansgate it was
clear he didn't feel the same. Even if he did, Hope had skipped
over an important part of the definition, the bit about love leaving
you open and vulnerable.

The door sounded and Diane walked in wearing a red leather
jacket today. Reenie insisted on trying it on. Jade winked at Alex
before disappearing out the back. Alex muttered something to
Reenie, Kay and Diane before the chefs appeared, along with
Jade dragging Tom. From behind the counter, Alex lifted up a
plate with... a circular sponge with a parrot iced on top. Its eyes
weren't straight, the beak had smudged and she'd run out of room

so couldn't give it talons. A sweet sickly smell rose into the air – she might have overdone the caramel essence. She'd never baked a cake for Simon. While she loved cooking, cake-making wasn't her forte and she'd always just bought him one from the supermarket. At her command, everyone sang 'Happy Birthday'; customers joined in and Captain Beaky grooved on his perch.

'Cheers, everyone. I don't know what to say.' Tom opened a card and a book voucher fell out. He did a little jig. No one would have guessed how devastated he'd been two nights previously. He and Alex had come back and eaten sandwiches in the roof garden; the two of them had flicked through Norm's old family photo albums. Before leaving, she'd slipped her arms around his neck, wanting nothing more but to see him happy again. It had felt like such a natural gesture. Slowly, the tension drained out of his body as his hands moved to her hips. She'd never been more grateful to Captain Beaky, because when she locked eyes with Tom, just at the moment when she might have let her guard down and done something stupid, the parrot had blown a loud raspberry and broken the spell.

'It's quite the best parrot anyone has ever iced for me,' said Tom with that mischief in his eye that she liked so much. She passed him the knife. Jade fetched a stack of plates. Alex held her breath as he cut in, glad to see the middle of the sponge had cooked.

'Not bad,' said Jade as she wiped crumbs from her mouth.

'High praise indeed, thank you,' said Alex as she watched Tom being Tom and handing out free slices to customers before he helped himself.

Reenie sidled up and slipped an arm around Alex's waist. 'Kay's reminded me, Saturday is your last day.' Random red blotches stained her cheeks.

'It won't be the same without you scribbling in the corner,' said Jade, 'or bunking off the really important stuff by chatting up the hot customers; don't think I haven't seen you.' Playfully, Jade punched Alex's arm before turning to Reenie. 'One way or another, between me, Yash and Tom, I'll make sure your notebook still gets filled.'

Reenie pulled on her light summer jacket and left. Alex tidied up the cake and put it behind the counter, then suddenly ran for the door, pulled it open and strode into Stevenson Square. Reenie had gone. Today was the last time they'd see each other. She'd miss her and Fletch's wisdom. Alex's shoulders drooped as she went inside.

Tom came over. 'What's the matter?'

'Reenie. I didn't get to say goodbye. I know she'll forget me in time but...'

'For someone who really didn't want to stay, you've done so well, Alex, sticking it out.' Tom gave her a thumbs up. 'Hope will be so grateful. Don't forget us, will you, when you're topping the charts again, or on the red carpet for the screening of a movie adaption?' He cut himself another slice of cake.

He didn't even suggest keeping in touch. But then why should he? Alex had made it clear, from the beginning, that this was only a temporary arrangement. Soon the Wrong Order Café would be nothing but a memory.

Ironic, really.

38

Five o'clock arrived on Saturday. Alex's last shift had ended. Yash and the chefs gave her a hug before they left. A Facebook message arrived and Alex clicked on it.

At the airport, about to board. June has gone by so fast. Come around on Monday, Alex, when it's nice and quiet. I'll cook us lunch. Maybe even an Asian dish. Say, twelve? You can tell me about you and Tom. All the deets as Leah would say! H xx

At least she'd be coming back one more time, even though the café would be closed.

Jade took off her apron and yawned. 'Gonna miss you, Alex. Working with you these last weeks has boosted my self-esteem no end. I must be pretty clever if I know the difference between a Frappuccino and a cappuccino but an award-winning author doesn't.'

Alex flipped Jade with her tea towel. 'At least you've helped me discover picture books for adults. I'll indulge in them whenever I take a break from creating my literary masterpieces.'

'And that left two,' said Tom as the door closed behind Jade.

'You aren't forgetting the main man, are you?' Alex asked. She'd hoped Jade would suggest meeting up; she made her laugh and Alex had actually grown to love graphic novels. However, Alex had lost her confidence in building friendships. She opened the parrot's cage, while Tom turned off the lights in the kitchen, and slid her arm in. Captain Beaky hopped onto her hand and gave it a little peck.

'Never thought I'd say this, but I'll miss you, boy, so much,' she whispered. 'You're so handsome, funny, with dance moves to die for. A real catch.'

He pooped on her fingers.

'You don't give a shit about anything, either. That's what I admire most. You live your life being your true authentic self, regardless of the consequences.' His head nodded to and fro. Despite the ear-splitting squawks, despite the potty mouth, customers and staff alike loved his idiosyncrasies. *Wabi-sabi.* Alex had tried so hard to fit the mould of a perfect, successful person, as simply being one of the crowd hadn't worked. It hadn't kept the interest of Simon. It hadn't saved Mum. She'd believed that becoming a kick-ass writer, who didn't take crap from anyone, who never showed emotion, would keep her safe. But all it had done was alienate people.

Maybe bad things happened whoever you were.

Perhaps money and possessions and collagen implants weren't effective armour.

As for toughening up on the outside... that only kept people out.

'Look after Tom, little man,' she said to Captain Beaky. 'He may be all whistles like you, but underneath he's hurting.'

Tom came back in and Alex closed the cage and went to wash her hands. She came back into the café and undid her apron. She passed it and her notepad over to Tom, wanting so much to cling on to them forever. Birds claimed territory by singing and nest-building, by making visual displays and, if pushed, chasing off intruders. But Alex was the intruder here, not the homebird.

'Right. I'd better change. I'm meeting Miranda in the Village at half past six.' She'd washed Hope's sheets before work, tidied and vacuumed.

He leant against the counter in his infuriatingly laid-back way. 'Canal Street is a great, vibrant part of the city,' he said. 'I've had drinks there with Jade. It's come a long way since the eighties when club raids still took place.'

Don't say it. Have a bit of dignity. 'Why not tag along? You and I could stay out when I'm finished.'

'It's a business meeting. Won't Miranda mind?'

'She'll probably be more curious than anything. I've never taken along a plus one. Not that you and I...'

'You must be excited and the money will pay off all those bills you were worrying about.'

'It's great and I can't wait to get writing,' she said, with the conviction of a taxman turning a blind eye. 'The issue of fracking is so current. I'm looking forward to getting stuck into the research.'

Captain Beaky flapped his wings and stared beadily her way.

'After slaving in a café all this time I'm ready to dive back into the glamour of my author life and that of my glossy new characters.'

Captain Beaky flapped again, even harder this time.

'What's up, laddo?' asked Tom.

Alex avoided the parrot's eye.

'Let me freshen up and settle this lad in my flat,' he said. 'Back here in twenty minutes?'

* * *

He returned downstairs first. Eventually, Alex appeared, having hesitated over which outfit to wear. The green leather jacket she'd arrived in, all those weeks ago, or her gold-buttoned blazer?

'You look nice,' Tom said and nodded with appreciation. He hoicked a black rucksack onto his back.

'I'm wearing exactly what I've worn all day – a baggy T-shirt, loose trousers and pumps.'

'But that's one humdinger of a smile.' He took her pull case and they went outside. Drops of rain landed on the pavement.

'What's in the rucksack?' she asked and pulled a telescopic umbrella out of her shoulder bag – or rather Hope's. She'd left her tiny designer rattan one in the flat; with any luck, Hope would consider it a fair swap. She went to open the umbrella but Tom still hadn't answered. Alex stopped walking. 'So, what's in it?'

'Wishes and dreams,' he muttered. 'Silly really. I should have left it behind.' He zipped it open and pulled out a sheaf of papers, written in long hand. 'My next few chapters. Obviously, they'd need tweaking if you wrote yours, and they aren't polished yet. After our argument on Monday I went to throw out my notes, but sat down instead and couldn't stop writing. It helps, you see, letting my emotions fall onto the page. If you were to change your mind...' He gave a sheepish look. 'Come on, let's go, before I spout any more rubbish.'

'Why didn't you tell me you were still working on our project?'

Rain trickled down his cheeks. 'I felt so bad after belittling your brilliant career. Books actually save people. When Dad first got diagnosed, I escaped into thrillers and murder mysteries;

reading stories where chaos was brought to order made me feel better and believe that, perhaps one day, my own mess would unravel. Women's fiction helped me process my own emotions, in a way I couldn't, at the time, with friends. When an experience is so... raw, you can't always talk out loud about it, but in my head I could talk to characters, sympathising with them as they went through tough times, inspired at how they faced challenges and kept going.' He pushed the sheaf of papers back into the rucksack and zipped it up. 'Ignore me. These scribbles are the fantasy of an idiot.'

Alex opened a plastic bag she was carrying and pointed at a folder. 'I brought everything we've done so far, the prologue, our first chapters, my second one too... Don't know why. Just couldn't let go.'

They stared at each other.

'You'd still be up for the co-authoring?' she said.

'Alex! You can't turn down a megabucks deal. It solves all your problems.'

'Does it? I was miserable before I came here. No friends. No mojo.'

'But—'

'I'll just have to sell my apartment if it comes to it.' There. She'd said it. A curt voicemail from the bank this morning had made her realise she couldn't put off the inevitable any longer. The Mancunian clouds might have been full, grey, threatening, with no sign of sunshine, but inside Alex, a long, rumbling storm finally broke and the darkness dissipated.

'That luxury apartment represents everything you've worked so hard for.'

She grabbed his hands, as wet hair stuck to both their faces. 'Up in that glass tower I've felt nothing but lonely, like Rapunzel, except in reverse, because when Reenie cut off my long hair it brought *back* the magic.' She wiped her wet forehead and put up the umbrella. 'Miranda doesn't like to be kept waiting and we need to keep her sweet if we're going to tell her to forget that auction.'

The Manchester Canal came into view with its narrowboats and ducks gliding side by side. Alex and Tom passed the rainbow oblong planter and headed in the direction of fairy lights and outside tables that were soaked. A handful of determined smokers sat under umbrellas. They followed the dance music inside and squeezed past bodies, both of them apologising for the unwieldy suitcase. Alex wanted to grab Tom's hands again and sway to the beat, but a tanned Miranda was already waiting on the black velvet couch, at the exact same table tear-stained Hope and Alex had chosen. Alex smoothed down her bob and gave a wave. Dressed in one of her usual trouser suits, Miranda stood up, nails sharper than Captain Beaky's talons. She air-kissed Alex and the three of them sat down.

'Good to see you, darling. Love the hair. Asymmetrical bobs never go out of fashion.' She eyed her up and down before turning briefly to Tom. 'Sensible idea to let the taxi driver bring your luggage in. Erin said the café you've been staying in had a lovely atmosphere, but I bet you can't wait to get back to your apartment.' Miranda clicked her fingers at the barman who looked tempted to throw his tray in her direction, like a Frisbee. 'A bottle of champagne and two glasses,' she said. 'We're celebrating.'

'Wait a minute,' said Alex, 'let me introduce my... friend, Tom.'

He held out his hand and shook Miranda's warmly. Hers remained limp.

'Great to meet you at last,' he said. 'Alex has told me all about how you picked her out of the slush pile. How rewarding that must have been for you when her books topped the charts.'

Miranda looked from one of them to the other. The champagne arrived and Alex asked for a third glass. Ignoring Tom again, Miranda talked non-stop about the auction, how she'd set the date, word had got around and now two additional publishers were interested.

She raised her glass to Alex. 'I always knew you'd hit the big time again.'

'Five weeks ago you had considerable doubts.'

'I'm a realist, darling; the odds were against you, but I've never doubted that at some point in the future, one way or another, you'd have got back in the charts.' She raised her glass in the air. 'It's always exciting when one of my authors is on the cusp of a new sub-genre. You wait, by this time next year there'll be announcements of high-powered, racy reads set at solar power stations and geothermal companies. And on that note.' She leant forwards. 'Big news. I'm leaving the agency. Setting up on my own.'

'Wow,' said Alex. 'Never saw that coming.'

'I'd love you to come over to me once your three-month notice period of leaving the agency has passed.'

Alex reached into her plastic bag and pulled out the folder.

Tom passed her his sheaf of papers. She pushed the lot across the table.

Miranda opened the folder and scanned the first page. '"Coming Up For Air" by Alex Butler and Tom Wilson? What's going on?'

Alex folded her arms. 'You're my agent. I pay you 15 per cent to represent my work. That includes this, so please, just read it. Then let's see about whether you still want to take me to Camden.'

But Miranda didn't seem to hear, already flicking through the paperwork.

Swiftly, Tom topped up their glasses. 'I'll get snacks,' he said, and came back with three packets of cheese and onion crisps. Without stopping reading, Miranda found one of the bags and pulled it open. The lot had gone by the time she'd read the prologue, the first two chapters, browsed Tom's extra work and was studying the synopsis. Unlike the words, her face was unreadable.

'An alternating love story. You writing Clara's chapters, Tom Jack's...'

Alex nodded.

'How long have you been writing, Tom?' Miranda tapped her fingers.

'I wrote a short story for a competition. Never sent it off in the end. The idea for this novel loosely came from that.' A sheepish look crossed his face. 'I've been writing for three months.'

'It shows,' she said and turned to Alex. 'As for Clara's chapter, her job as a property developer is reasonably high-powered, but where's the satin finish that your readers are used to? This is decidedly matt – everyday, ordinary.'

'You hate it,' said Alex, 'and that's okay. We're still going to finish it, right, Tom?'

'Try and stop me,' he said and beamed.

'I just can't finish the fracking project, Miranda. Apologies, but my heart's not in it any more.'

'You're really prepared to risk everything we've worked for so far?' asked Miranda.

'Alex Butler, glamorous, racy author. It's just not me, never was. I can see that now.'

'Big advance, Alex. You'd be the lead title.'

'Writing with Tom has reminded me of what's important.'

'I agree that—'

'Perhaps this co-authored project will land me a new agent and deal, perhaps it won't,' continued Alex, 'but I've got to see it through. I'm grateful for the career you helped me build, Miranda, you've worked so hard, and I'm sorry. I understand that you won't want me to move with you, I know this project isn't what—'

'Jesus, stop blathering on, woman!' said Miranda. 'If you'd allowed me to finish, I was going to say that I agree, heart... it's *everything*. That's what makes some authors stand out as story-tellers.' She picked up the folder and shook it. 'This, Alex Butler, contains something I've been waiting for, something not all authors find.' Alex and Tom leant forward. 'Your true voice. I caught brief glimpses of it in your first books. Tom's got his too. It takes some authors longer than others to tap into what they really want to say.'

Alex's voice disappeared for a moment. *Miranda* liked *it?*

'Voice is about authenticity, being original. Your writing has always felt as if you've read the genre widely and lifted other authors' styles. A reader wouldn't notice.'

'I've never copied!'

Miranda held up her hand. 'I'm not saying it's intentional. It happens more often than you'd think. Fans of the genre would never complain, they always want more of the same. But an author's true voice, their message and how it's written on the page, is utterly individual.' She pushed the folder and papers back over the table. 'There's no guarantees it'll sell; in some ways this is a fresh start. What about your solid Alex Butler branding, its loyal readers? I really think it would be a waste to lose that. Why not run both projects side by side?'

Alex glanced at Tom. 'I've thought about that but I just don't think I can.'

'But think of the earnings. And you've mapped out the whole of your cli-fi story. I'm sure you could come up with a sequel, so that means the characters and settings are already in place. Easy-peasy.'

'I don't know...'

'I'd negotiate a two-book deal, one a year, with realistic hand-in dates to make it feasible for you to finish your book with Tom on the side. Then, at the end of the cli-fi contract let's see where we are.' She ate the last crisp. 'I don't love every day of being an agent, acting as the go-between with clients and publishers. Sometimes I view it as a job that simply puts food on the table because I'm a single woman and I have to be practical. You're still relatively early in your career, Alex, despite the success; don't dismiss any options, not yet.'

She gave Alex one of her looks and Alex couldn't help smiling. 'Okay. I'll sleep on it.'

Miranda placed her palms, spread wide, on the table. 'These chapters have touched me with a... vulnerability. That's a bloody good sign and, in my opinion, you'll end up being able to write this new genre full time. This story could be not only relatable but incredibly moving.' Alex and Tom exchanged glances. 'Moving forwards, I'd very much like to represent both of you.' She reached out and shook Tom's hand again, properly this time.

She talked about deadlines, potential publishers, the challenge of co-authoring, and evening became night as the three of them bombarded ideas at each other about the story's plot arc, how Alex would have to use a pseudonym so that her two types of stories didn't get confused.

Midnight approached and Miranda left, despite the turned-up music and infectious dance movements of drinkers who gave the air a celebratory twist. Alex insisted Tom went back to the café, ahead of a busy Sunday tomorrow. She'd get a taxi back to Deansgate as she wanted to talk to someone before she left the Village. She and Tom hugged each other.

'This is unbelievable,' he said.

'I know. We've found our true voices, like Captain Beaky. Let's work out a schedule for writing.' Miranda did love a deadline and had given them until the end of the year to get the first draft to her. Alex couldn't wait to start working on 'Coming Up For Air' and had a feeling it wouldn't take that long.

'Thanks for the last five weeks, Alex. For stepping in for Hope. It's been good for us all.'

She'd wanted to thank him too. Despite their book project, this felt like goodbye. She stood for a moment, next to the empty space where he'd been standing. It didn't take long for it to fill with two women necking. She hauled her case to the bar and the manager she'd met five weeks earlier. Her greying dreadlocks were piled on top of her hair today. She caught Alex's eye and came over.

'Got your bank card this time?' she asked.

'You remembered?'

'Hardly surprising, all that crying.' She tilted her head. 'Cool haircut. Where's your friend?'

'Travelling back from Thailand. Long story. I wanted to ask, last time we were here, you were going to give us some advice, but a glass smashed at the crucial moment.'

The bar manager paused, then jerked her head and through clouds of vape smoke led Alex to a quiet corridor by the toilets.

'The menopause hits you right between the eyes sometimes.'

'Oh. How did you know?' asked Alex.

'Been there myself, cock. Ten years ago. For years I'd been lying to myself about who I really was and it all came to a head. I used to work in a bar in Spinningfields and got drunk in the cellar one night. I couldn't go home to face my husband, because I couldn't go on without telling him the truth...'

'That you'd had an affair?'

'No. That, really, I fancied women, something I'd been in denial about for many years. I eventually caught a taxi back and woke my husband up. Told him things couldn't continue as they were, that I was sorry, that I'd always love him but not in the way he deserved.'

'What happened?'

'I'll never forget the look on his face. I'd betrayed him and our whole marriage, had been in denial about that as well. I hope I never hurt someone like that again. He said some things he can never take back, same as my dad, and I haven't seen either of them since I got a job here. But I'm grateful for the menopause, despite the challenges, it was the best thing that ever happened to me... it was as if losing my hormones took away a filter that had warped the world's view of who I really was.'

'So, what was your advice?'

The bar manager leant forwards. 'It's called "the Change" for a reason.'

40

Monday morning, Alex woke up in her apartment, still not used to it despite moving back Saturday night, with the taupe and ivory colour scheme, the carefully placed furniture, feng shui replacing clutter. Her Egyptian cotton sheets and silk pyjamas didn't feel as comfortable as they used to. She missed the embroidered throw on Hope's bed and her plants, all so different yet peacefully living together. She also missed the fragrant row of herb pots in Hope's kitchen, their smell so much more invigorating than the pfft of artificial air freshener in her own place, that summed up everything about her life before working in the Wrong Order Café. A bath hadn't made her feel better, padding across the cold marble floor – carpet might be old-fashioned but everything about Hope's flat had shouted warmth and a welcome. A pigeon politely cooing outside her glass tower window only reminded her how much she'd miss Captain Beaky and his swearing.

Yesterday it felt strange not to be working in the café, under Jade's sharp eye and Tom's friendly supervision. She'd developed a real satisfaction at brightening a customer's day through five minutes of banter or by delivering a delicious slice of cake – and by cleaning a table until its bright yellow plastic cover shone its hello to the next person who sat there. The day had felt empty without the constant gurgle of the coffee machine, the aroma of toasted sourdough and bustling vibe from Stevenson Square sneaking in every time the door opened. She'd never noticed before how quiet her apartment was, surrounded by nothing but Mancunian air and the building's expensive soundproofing.

Alex stretched and got up. She grabbed a quick shower and cleaned her teeth, then ran a brush through her bob. At least today she was back in the café. Yesterday she'd spent writing and couldn't wait to pop in to see Tom, to discuss Jack and Clara – unless he was visiting Norm. But, most of all, today, she was keen to see Hope for lunch, the stranger who'd become a confidant, who'd inadvertently thrown Alex a life-saver and left her life in the café to travel the world. Hope had tasted romance and weird food, she'd achieved the impossible and this had inspired Alex to believe that she could turn things around, too. Alex browsed through her wardrobe for an outfit, missing the choice of Hope's comfortable clothes. Grabbing her loosest trousers and a jumper, Alex pulled on her leather jacket. She had something very important to do before going back to Stevenson Square, the result of lying awake most of the night. Who'd have thought working in a café, where they got the orders wrong, could have made her life feel right again? The bar manager's words rang in her head, as she waved goodbye to the doorman and set out on her mission.

* * *

Twelve o'clock sharp, Alex let herself into the café. She went upstairs and knocked on Hope's flat. She stood outside. The door swung open.

'Love your hair, Alex!'

'You're so brown!'

They paused awkwardly and gave each other a hug. 'You look amazing. Love those linen shorts. I hope the flat's okay. I laundered your sheets, tidied up...'

'My plants are still alive, that's the most important thing.' Hope pointed to the sofa. 'Make yourself comfortable, petal. I've just got to reply to a text.' She tapped on her phone and then fetched two bottles from the fridge and put them down on the coffee table, before sitting down herself. She lifted one up and held it in the air. 'Cheers, Alex. I've developed quite a taste for beer since travelling in the heat. Let's have these before I start cooking.'

Glass clinked. Alex took a swig. 'You're so... different, Hope. Happier. More confident. As if a weight's been lifted.'

'You seem so much more... relaxed.'

They clinked glasses again. 'Thanks for—' they both said at the same time.

'You first,' said Alex.

Hope put down her drink. 'Thanks for stepping in for me, for keeping this job open, it meant I didn't have to let down my daughter and gave me the chance to learn a lot about myself. You did railroad me into it but...'

Alex went to protest.

'Honestly,' said Hope. 'I'm grateful. I needed that push.' She talked about the temples, beaches and mountains she'd seen, the food, other travellers. Alex teased her about Sovann.

'So what exactly have you learnt about yourself?' asked Alex, as they both finished their beers. Hope looked as if she'd taken off a mask that used to suck out the happiness.

'That I'm a capable woman, not one big hot middle-aged mess. That I still know how to have fun. I can take control of my future.' Hope sat up straighter. 'Texting you, and working out why I've been so miserable, has empowered me. Thai women, on the whole, tend to have an easier menopause and that could be due to their healthier diet. I've lost weight over the last five weeks, I've eaten more fish and vegetables... The hot flushes have still been dire, but apart from that I've regained some of the energy that's sapped out of me in recent years. It's ace. First thing this morning I made an appointment with my GP.'

'I've got one too,' said Alex and she told Hope about talking things through with Simon. 'I'm grateful, too, that we bumped into each other that day in the Village, that you offered me this chance to get some perspective and work out exactly what's been happening to me.'

'And you met Tom.'

Alex went to reply, but a thud came from downstairs. 'Did you hear that?'

Hope strained to listen. 'Nope. Nothing.' She gave a long, satisfied sigh. 'It's not as depressing as it might be, coming back to England. The last month or so has shown me that you really don't know what's around the corner.'

'They do say Hope springs eternal.'

Swiftly, Hope picked up her phone. 'Here, let me bore you with some photos.'

Why was Hope directing the conversation in a different direction? Alex's eyes narrowed. Hope had just said the word 'ace', and... yes, she'd written it in a text once. *Springs eternal...* Alex thought back to the wording of the review that she'd blamed for her career's demise. Alex surveyed the flat and its books, books, books.

No. Alex was being ridiculous.

'And this temple was in...' Hope didn't stop talking, didn't look at her.

A shiver ran down's Alex's back and she jumped to her feet. 'The Eternal Springs blog. Is it *yours*?'

'What blog?' asked Hope, eyes still fixed on the screen.

'The one that said *Parisian Power Trip* wasn't as *ace* as my previous stories. Ace is a word that blogger uses; it's always jumped out at me as it's not very common these days.' Alex paced up and down. 'That review triggered a spate of criticism from other bloggers, then readers. My publisher took note. Fans lost interest. It was all down to you, Hope.' Alex rolled her eyes. 'It's obvious looking back. When you first found out who I was, in that bar, you knocked your drink over. And you knew what cli-fi was. I don't think your average reader would be quite so up on the newest trends.'

Hope met her gaze. Sat up straighter. 'The Hope back then didn't have the guts to tell you face to face.'

'You ruined my career!' she said and jabbed her finger at Hope.

'That's a bit dramatic,' she said, calmly.

Backbone. Hope had even more now.

Alex tried to look angry, eke it out for as long as she could, but Hope's indignation was the final straw and she burst out laughing. 'Sorry, I'm messing with you.'

'Alex!'

'Allow me that. Time away from the author world has opened my eyes.' She collapsed back onto the sofa and linked her arm with Hope's. 'Jeez. It's you. I can't believe it. All this time the phrase "hope springs eternal" has been staring me in the face. I've thought a lot about that blog lately after something Tom said. Your review was polite, constructive, written as a disappointed fan rather than someone simply trying to bring down a writer.'

'Remember the last thing I said to you, just before we parted, in Selfridges' coffee shop?'

Alex thought back. 'Not to give up on my writing.'

'Yes. I meant it. I can't wait to read your next story.'

'It was easy to blame you. I needed a scapegoat, but – no offence – I doubt every single one of the negative reviewers on Amazon had read yours.'

'I was genuinely sorry that review got a lot of attention but I have to be honest above all else, Alex. That could be why my blog is a success. You're really not mad?'

'No.' Even Alex sounded surprised. 'I've learnt that we should all speak our truth, and that includes people writing reviews. As long as they aren't as rude as Captain Beaky.'

Hope turned to face her. 'I set up the blog years ago, when I still had my bookshop. I'm still amazed at how it took off. I wanted to tell you who I was, in that bar, but we were both so emotional. It's one reason I went through with our deal and let you take my job for these five weeks – I felt like I owed you.'

'You've achieved so much; that blog is really respected.'

Hope explained how the trip had made her realise her job in the café wasn't the problem. She needed to change things on the inside, not the outside. So she was going to take her blog to a more professional level and spend more of her hours with books and the reading world, feeding her soul with a passion. She'd accept the offers from blog tour organisers to get involved, and the requests from the local and national newspapers who'd contacted her over the years to write reviews. She'd post sponsored content on Instagram; she'd always turned down the offers in the past but it would provide much-needed income.

'I'm going to ask Tom if I can run a book club in the staffroom, after hours. Who knows? Maybe at some point I'll be able to drop hours and work part-time at the café. There are lots of blogger events I can attend. Before, I preferred the anonymity, but now I'm ready to show my face to the world.'

'Please say this means changing that dreadful profile picture on Twitter.'

'It's cute.'

'It's a dog.'

'I almost forgot.' Hope fumbled with a chain around her neck. She took off the glittering four-leaf clover necklace and hesitated before holding it out in the air. 'Thanks for this. I reckon it kept me safe.'

Alex didn't need it. The necklace had been a reminder to get herself together, to not let anyone get close like Ryan had. However, the café had taught her that revealing the cracks in a perfect image didn't cause a leak of all the achievements. On the contrary, they only let in kindness and support. Healing would never happen if you pretended not to be broken.

'Keep it.'

Hope's eyes widened. 'But it must have cost so much. And it's so unique. You could sell it at the very least.'

'No need.' She told Hope about continuing to write as Alex Butler for two more books, alongside the new co-authored project. 'And I texted Tom yesterday and asked if I could work a couple of shifts a week.'

'Oh!'

'I'd miss everyone otherwise, and working in the café keeps me grounded. I need that. To be honest, I'll be glad to get out of my apartment and all of its fancy features.' The new advance would pay the mortgage payments she'd missed, get her back on track, but the apartment didn't feel like home. Hadn't ever really. Her voice caught. 'I'm going to miss this flat more than anything.'

Hope got to her feet and went to the window. She put the necklace on again and gazed down for a while, then, arms folded, stood in front of Alex.

'You could always move in here with me, if you got bored of the high life.'

Alex cocked her head.

Hope started laughing. 'I have a strong sense of déjà vu, like when I suggested you live here the first time around, in that bar. Alex. I'm joking. I'd love you to, of course, but it's hardly what you're used to. Although I'd be lying if I said it wouldn't help me, I'd only have to pay half the rent and could more easily follow my dream.'

'Are you serious?'

Hope stared. 'Are you? I mean... no... you can't be... but if you were, the spare bedroom is a decent size and Tom has a storage room upstairs. You could always take my offer as a stopgap, give yourself time to find somewhere you really want to live.'

She couldn't. She could. Fuck it, she would.

'I'd have to check with Tom, of course, but—' Hope's phone bleeped and she read a message. She strained her ears. 'Wait. Now I've heard something downstairs. We ought to investigate. Might be someone trying to get in, not realising the café is closed.'

They left the flat and descended the stairs very slowly. Alex wrinkled her nose. Savoury smells drifted upstairs along with a squawk and, in the background, the soft tone of Frank Sinatra crooned. Hope shot Alex a smug glance and gave her a push. Alex walked past the kitchen and into the café.

'Surprise!' shouted a chorus of familiar voices.

41

Fletch, Val, Reenie, Kay, Tom, Jade and Yash, Norm, Diane, the chefs... Balloons tied to chairs... Buffet food on the tables.

Hope gave Alex a side hug. 'It was Tom's idea to hold a goodbye party.'

'That's so thoughtful... but I'm not giving up work here, now.'

Tom gave a dramatic sigh and an exaggerated eye roll. 'Tell me about it. This party has been days in the making and then you text yesterday... But this is the Wrong Order Café – it's only right that our event doesn't go to plan.'

Alex smiled. 'Let's call it a welcome home party for Hope instead then.'

'And one to celebrate us writing a book together,' said Tom. 'I've been telling everyone about it.'

'We can also raise a glass to Granddad's health improving,' said Jade.

Alex crouched by Fletch's wheelchair. 'It's so good to see you. The café hasn't been the same since you left.'

'I'm working on coming back, aren't I, Val?' he said.

Val gave an affectionate tut. 'My husband is as stubborn as they come.'

Alex sat down next to Norm and helped him wipe mayonnaise from his chin. 'How are things?' she asked.

He patted her knee. 'You're a good girl,' he whispered. 'You did what I asked. Fish sushi. Pickled ginger. You're a good girl,' he repeated, until the rustle of a crisp packet removed his lucidity and he frowned. 'Some blasted party this is, I haven't had a single bite to eat.'

Kay had brought Reenie's notebook and was writing down everything happening at the party, like Reenie and Jade dancing to 'It's a Beautiful Day' by Michael Bublé, and Diane putting on her phone music and headbanging in the corner with a fascinated parrot.

'The café has missed Fletch's welcome,' Alex said to Val as both of them leant against the counter eating slabs of caramelised onion quiche.

'It would miss you too,' she said and nudged Alex with her elbow. 'You've become part of the fixtures, even though you weren't that keen at the beginning.' She put the quiche down on her plate. 'You found it hard, didn't you? Dealing with Fletch and Reenie – and yet you've turned into their cheerleader, defending Fletch against those rude teenagers, with Reenie's notebook and Fletch's guitar playing.'

'I...'

'It's okay. None of us are prepared for dementia,' she said in a soft tone. 'Not even if it's a loved one. There's nothing worse than the person you love losing their faculties, their skills, and then there's having to attend to their personal needs... I don't begrudge one moment of it, but it takes some getting used to, that's all. I've been to some very dark places.'

'I used to believe getting old, frail and ill was the worst thing that could happen,' said Alex. 'The prospect of getting older scared me. No one wants dementia, but seeing how Fletch and Reenie, Diane too, and Norm, are squeezing the last drop of fun out of their lives – a diagnosis doesn't have to be the end.'

'Of course, the scariest thing is not ageing at all.' Val shot her a smile before leaving to get a coffee.

Jade sidled over. 'I never foresaw this, you wanting to stay on. It's cool, I'm really glad. And this project of yours with Tom has inspired me.'

'How so?'

Her neck turned pink. Jade took out her phone and tapped on Gallery. She swiped through graphic art pictures.

'Wow. Yours?' asked Alex.

Shyly, Jade nodded. 'Knowing that you and Tom are going to follow your calling, regardless of not knowing how it will turn out... it's encouraged me to set up an Instagram page and maybe a website, see if I can get any orders. Last night Tom showed me Susie's drawings – she was brilliant. Getting to know you... maybe an artistic career of my own, or at least a part-time one, might be possible. I'm going to commit and invest in some manga drawing software, to see where that takes me.'

'Jade, that's brilliant, you've got such a natural talent.' One by one, Alex flicked through the pictures again while Jade talked about another graphic novel series she really should read. Jade rummaged in her apron pocket and passed Alex a sheet of paper before going back to the coffee machine. It was the storyboard from Jade's sketchbook. Like before she'd drawn Alex with long, jagged brown hair that defied gravity, and a rucksack on her back spilling books. This character held a sword made to look like a quill and went into a coffee shop, where there was the girl behind the till with spiky green hair holding out the poisoned mug of hot chocolate. Movement in the sketch showed how the one-eyed, magical giant parrot's talons were flexing...That was as far as the story got before. Eagerly Alex read on...

Alex's character lifted the mug to her lips and the giant parrot flapped its wings, to release a magic breeze that floated over and tilted the mug further upwards. As Alex was about to open her mouth, a couple burst into the coffee shop, both wearing chest armour, skirts and shin guards. One was a squashed-looking woman with ginger hair, the other was a man with one leg in plaster; he looked rather like a barn owl. They both wore fearsome expressions. The woman swiped her sword and duly bobbed Alex's hair. The couple stepped forwards as if to slay her next, however at the last moment the barn owl man cut the handle off the mug. It fell to the floor and hot chocolate spilt everywhere. The girl with the spiky green hair ran forwards but slipped in the puddle. The giant parrot tried to fly off but the woman with ginger hair locked the door. The four characters stared at each other then the story cut to Alex handing out the books from her rucksack. The last frame showed the four of them peacefully reading together. At home, in the café, happy in each other's company despite their differences.

Oh, Jade.

Tom appeared as she folded up the sheet of paper and put it carefully in her back trouser pocket. He took Alex's hand and electric tingles ran up her arm. Hope smiled at her across the room – the Hope who'd taken charge of her own destiny.

'Come with me, a minute, writing partner. I can't wait any longer.'

Alex found herself being led outside. A black feather lay on the ground and she picked it up. Its green and violet iridescence shone in the sun. In the 1890s, legend has it, that a group of Shakespeare enthusiasts wanted to introduce every bird mentioned in his poems to Central Park. That was how the

European starling ended up in North America, strangers in a foreign country they made their own – a little how Alex viewed her time in Stevenson Square.

'I've got this brilliant idea for a twist halfway through our story,' said Tom.

Alex shoved the feather into her trouser pocket, next to the drawing. 'Tom, that's exciting but this is a party. Writing is work, not your life.' Another important lesson she'd learnt these last weeks. 'In any case, I've got something far more important to say.' She stood up straighter. Alex could cope with rejection. It didn't change who she was, or whom she wanted to become.

'Would you like to go out to the cinema one night this week?'

'You mean… like a date?'

Heat flooded her face. 'Yes. I've wanted to ask for a while but you didn't seem bothered about me going back to Deansgate, before I turned down the auction, and I wasn't sure if I'd misread the signs.'

'Not bothered? Believe me, Captain Beaky has had to listen to a lot of self-pity over the last couple of weeks. I… I've felt it too… something between us?'

She nodded.

'But ever since that conversation where you knew about Drake and the Weeknd, due to younger boyfriends…' He ran a hand through his hair. 'Us men have insecurities too, even if their parrot tells them not to be a silly sod.'

A tickling sensation stirred in her stomach. 'Is that a yes, Tom Wilson? Or is it against the rules to date an employee?'

'This is the Wrong Order Café where rules are made for breaking,' he said, maintaining eye contact.

'What about if I move in with Hope?'

Tom looked as if their novel had landed a six-figure deal.

'Let's do this then – on one condition. Your cheerfulness, the whistling, on the days those things act as a mask, you'll show me the real Tom, you'll let me in.'

Heat shot up her arm as he took her hand in his and ran a thumb across her right palm. It touched the lower part of her arm and he glanced down.

'Ah yes. I almost forgot, my detour this morning.' Alex rolled up her sleeve to reveal cling film wrapped around her wrist. Carefully, she took it off and showed Tom the inside of her arm. The word '*wabi-sabi*' was tattooed there with tiny flowers entwined around each letter. She could have had the wabi-sabi symbol inked on, but the words spelled out reminded her of Norm and Tom's inspiring tattoos. Alex turned it left and right, admiring the tattoo artist's work.

'Chasing perfection is a road to unhappiness. Like your tattoo, and Norm's, this is to remind me that getting things wrong doesn't matter. The Wrong Order Café proves, in this filtered, airbrushed world, that the worst thing about someone isn't their mistakes, and the best isn't about always coming out on top, being picture-perfect. What's important is tolerance, kindness, living your truth and finding beauty in simplicity, and embracing change. There's always joy to be found if you search hard enough.'

Hand in hand, they went back into the café. Alex had considered getting the tattoo ever since meeting Aiko. The final push came from the bar manager in the Village, how despite all its downsides, its imperfections, the menopause had been the best thing to happen to her.

Tom squeezed her hand and his salted-caramel fringe flopped across his forehead. He gave her one of his mischievous looks, and even though Miranda would deplore such a hackneyed notion, Alex's heart skipped a beat. She kissed him on the cheek when she thought no one was looking, just close enough for her lips to brush his.

'Get a room!' squawked Captain Beaky and Hope winked at her across the café. Alex would never hear the end of it now.

A menu lay on the nearest table, a splash of coffee across it. Alex fetched a dishcloth and wiped its laminated front, the name of the café standing out as bold as ever.

Life was like a wrong order, you didn't always get what you'd expected, its story may not be the one you wrote in your five-year plans or fantasies. However it could still have moments of compassion, understanding, love, friendship, laughter, and just the right amount of ginger pickle.

ACKNOWLEDGMENTS

Twenty years ago I lost someone close to me. They had Alzheimer's disease. The ache of how they suffered never really goes away, but as time passes, happier memories mix in with the ones from that time. It was seventeen years before I felt able to create a story touching on dementia, and that was my 2020 Christmas novel *The Winter We Met*. Three years on from that, and I've felt ready to write a story that encompasses the condition more fully.

And it's been cathartic. Thanks to the research I've done and the characters I subsequently crafted, when I finally wrote 'The End' I felt more hopeful. It's my biggest wish that this is how *The Memory of You* leaves those readers feeling, whose lives have been touched by this dreadful condition.

The story was inspired by an article I read about a pop-up restaurant in Japan called The Restaurant of Mistaken Orders, with servers that live with dementia and a logo where one of the letters is placed in the wrong position. I was touched by its whole ethos and purpose, and felt it could inspire a story full of heart. This novel has been such a pleasure to write – from Alex with her airs and graces, to talkative Reenie and cheeky Captain Beaky.

A big thank you to my agent, Clare Wallace at the Darley Anderson agency, for her continued support and insightful comments. I'm grateful, too, for the enthusiasm from the get-go, with this project, of editor Tara Loder. Huge thanks to the whole hardworking team at Boldwood Books, including Nia Beynon,

Claire Fenby and Jenna Houston. Thanks also to Isobel Akenhead for her vision.

I can't ever write acknowledgements without showing enormous appreciation to all the bloggers who support my books, either with blog tours or reviews. I never take your generosity of time for granted. You are truly wonderful. Thanks also to The Friendly Book Community on Facebook, for your support and fun.

As for you, reader – I'm so grateful for your interest in what I have to say. I'd like to send a special hug to those of you navigating the menopause journey. Be kind to yourselves. It's a condition that has been dismissed for far too long but you have a right to feel better, a right to get help. A right to talk about it. It's a *pause* indeed. A time for reflection, to take stock, before moving forwards onto new opportunities...

The last word has to be about Martin, Immy and Jay, aka Team Tonge, who've always listened and cared. Love you.

And about the loved one I lost. Twenty years on I still think about you lots.

Look after yourselves, everyone.

Sam. x

MORE FROM SAMANTHA TONGE

We hope you enjoyed reading *The Memory of You*. If you did, please leave a review.

If you'd like to gift a copy, this book is also available as an ebook, large print, hardback, digital audio download and audiobook CD.

Sign up to Samantha Tonge's mailing list for news, competitions and updates on future books.

https://bit.ly/SamanthaTongeNews

Explore more warm, uplifting stories from Samantha Tonge...

ABOUT THE AUTHOR

Samantha Tonge is the bestselling and award-winning author of multi-generational women's fiction. She lives in Manchester with her family.

Visit Samantha's Website: http://samanthatonge.co.uk/

 twitter.com/SamTongeWriter

 facebook.com/SamanthaTongeAuthor

 instagram.com/samanthatongeauthor